DREAM ANGEL

HEAVEN WAITS

DREAM ANGEL

HEAVEN WAITS

PATRICIA GARBER

Copyright © 2011 Patricia Garber

Library of Congress Control Number : 2011922070
ISBN-13: 9780615446516 (Jungle Room Press)
ISBN: 0615446515

All rights reserved. No part of this book may be reproduced or transmitted in any form or by any means, electronic or mechanical, including photocopying, recording, or by any information storage and retrieval system, without permission in writing from the copyright owner.

This is a work of fiction. The characters are all either fictious or used in a fictious manner. Names, incidents and places are combined with the author's imagination for entertainment only.

This book is not authorized or endorsed by the Estate of Elvis Presley or by the estate of any other person.

Author's photo by MJ Photography.

This book was printed in the United States of America.

To order additional copies of this book, contact:
www.jungleroompress@gmail.com

DEDICATION

To all who love unconditionally.

ACKNOWLEDGEMENT

Dear reader,

Thank you for taking this journey with me. I realize it may not be the same spiritual awakening for you as it has been for me, but I hope that God reaches out to you while you read, uplifting you in a way that is meant especially for you.

When I started Eternal Flame, back in 2007, I was unaware that my story would take me down a road that would require I come face to face with a few demons of my own. I won't bore you with the details, but if one lives long enough events can happen that allow "hate" to fester. Therefore, I was completely caught off guard when Eternal Flame ended up being about "Forgiveness". Coincidence? I doubt it.

And like Eternal Flame, I began to write Dream Angel with no idea where I was going. When I got to the end, it became very clear that God had once again snuck in a surprise. Dream Angel is about obedience, of which I lack. It's about patience, of which I have very little. And to my surprise I even managed to skim over the always taunting sin of "Idol" worship. Even as I write this, I'm shaking my head, and disbelieving that I suffer from such a thing. I know who God is. I know who Elvis Presley is. Even Elvis knew who he was.

"Elvis you're the King!" One fan might say.
"No, honey, Jesus Christ is King." He always replied.

Simple, I say. Well maybe, and maybe not. I admit in writing these books I have put my work first. My attendance went down at church, and devotional time was few and far between. Though I may have been absent in mind, God was never far from my heart. He's a constant for me. I've felt him close by. Often, he's just over my shoulder. Some days he's cheering while others I imagine he can only shake his head. I'm not perfect. And, it wasn't until the end of Dream Angel that I even realized my purpose in writing this book.

What was God's point, you might ask. Mostly, that I needed to get out of my own way, and stop tripping over all of those self-placed obstacles. The truth behind this realization felt as if God had thumped me on the side of my head, a wake-up-tap so to speak. The Almighty had done it again. Again, I'd written about all those humanistic short comings that also applied to me! Again, "I" was learning lessons.

In telling you this, I can also honestly tell you I truly do love Elvis Presley, the man. No, I didn't know him. He didn't know me, at least not in this life. But I've spent thirty six years of my life adoring him. He was like a father figure to me when I was eight, and had none. He was my first crush at thirteen when I felt I was too tom-boyish to even qualify as cute. He was my first love, though I didn't know what love was. And now, he's my buddy and my friend. (All non fans may now roll their eyes. It's Ok. You have my permission.) Elvis might even be clapping in heaven right now—or possibly laughing—as I admit in public that I may have a "wee" bit of a problem. (I'm still shaking my head). But there are worse things I could be then an Elvis addict that probably won't benefit from a twelve step program. And even with all my quirks, God loves me, and that makes me smile.

I want to thank all my friends, home and abroad, that have supported me since Eternal Flame. I also want to thank my family—especially my mother and sister—for encouraging me when I wanted to throw in the towel and loving me no matter what. You are all such a blessing in my life. Many thanks to the three editors who helped me at some point during this project; I hope your glimpse into the Elvis-world didn't have you running for the hills. We are a crazy bunch but you could never meet a nicer, gentler, group of people.

To my very patient husband, Marc, who knows I love him with all my heart (Yes, he's read the book and yes, we're still married). You're always there by my side, and I'm always thankful. And to my God, who's been so patient with this crazy child stumbling around in the dark. I love you most.

Finally, and most sincerely, I want to thank Elvis fans around the world. When you're sure you're a little "different" from everyone else, it helps to look around in the asylum and see a friendly face. Thank you for being my friend. We are many and we are proud!

"Let's pretend he just didn't go," together.

God Bless.

PROLOGUE

Someone once said, "If you truly love someone, you should be willing to set him free." As far back as I can remember, I have never been good at letting go. No matter the object of my affection, if I loved it, it should be mine forever.

I can recall being six years old and tearfully refusing to climb into bed one cold, fall night. My night-time bear and protector from the prowling monsters that lived in my closet, Mr. Jigs, had gone missing. I cried for more than a month.

My parents searched for another button-nosed friend that would soothe me, but no substitute offered comfort. How could just any stuffed animal, plushy soft and fully intact possibly be seasoned enough to ward off whatever lurked in my room after the lights went out?

At the time, the loss to me felt as big a burden on my young soul as I could ever withstand. Of course, my age blissfully sheltered me from even suspecting that a much greater loss was on the horizon that would rock the very foundation on which I was raised.

One would think that after nearly thirty years of Godly upbringing, the daughter of a Baptist minister would have been prepared for the unavoidable moment when a loved one passes on. However, my faith was tested and, sadly, failed when my mother succumbed to a merciless cancer.

My strong will quickly turned to a wilted spirit, and an anger ignited in me so intensely that my soul was gradually engulfed with rising flames of bitterness. A wall of darkness surrounded me. I became an exaggerated version of that scared little girl. No childhood bear was strong enough to fight off the adult-sized demons that threatened me.

Over time, I crafted a wall around my heart. Each brick was strategically placed. The barrier had a purpose. Like an imaginary friend, it gave me comfort, and I grew accustomed to its lingering presence. I needed it. At least that was what I believed before God sent me a blue-eyed handsome angel who had a tender way with women.

Like an earthquake, this angel shook the stone walls around my heart. He reminded me that our ability to love someone else more than we love ourselves is what makes us unique in this sometimes disheartening world.

I was happy for the first time in two years. Like a flower enjoying the first warm rays of sun after long spring rains, I had opened up. To love so freely was pure bliss, and I thought that surely this love would never leave. After all it was not a love of the earthly kind, but of a heavenly nature. God would allow me this love that he himself gave. I held tight to my dream with clinched hands, refusing to consider that one day, just like my mother, my angel of love would have to leave.

Did not a poet say that love, once departed, may return? And, if he did, could he then be mine forever? I had to find out.

CHAPTER ONE

Even through the fog of deep sleep, I sensed his presence in my room. *He's here.* The thought did as much to warm me as did the comforter that covered me. Outside, a bitter midnight chill spread unmercifully across the South. Memphis was gripped by a prevailing winter storm. I imagined sparkling diamonds made of frost blanketing the landscape like a magnificent piece of art.

Though Memphis was far from my Atlanta home, I was nowhere near homesick. Even here in this strange hotel room, I lay as cozy as a baby, my heart fluttering with anticipation, and a smile across my face. "Good things come to patient little girls," an angel had once told me. Since then I had become good at counterfeit patience, hoping to score points for the effort alone.

Maybe tonight was my lucky night?

An aged wall heater hummed just below the window. The soft and temperate air ruffled around me. Strands of chestnut hair stirred gently over my face as a warm waft passed over me, teasingly carrying his sweet bouquet. Restlessness plagued my body. My mind drifted on a cloud of euphoria, interrupted only when a chair gently creaked.

Soft footsteps approached over the worn carpet igniting a shiver down my spine. I marveled how a man of his essence could have nearly imperceptible footsteps.

He reached my bedside in three short strides.

I held my breath. Butterflies lifted into wild flight patterns inside my stomach, and my heartbeat pulsed inside my ears. Though my thoughts were scattered, the minutes passed in torturous anticipation before the bed stirred as he sat down. Ignoring my sham of slumber, he moved closer, and familiar hands shifted under the covers to touch me. His warm silky fingers, caressing me from behind, triggered a firestorm across my skin. My breathing became erratic. I shuddered uncontrollably and melted against his sturdy frame. The warmth from his body was infinitely better than any crackling fire on a bitter winter's day.

"Faker." His soft Mississippi drawl tickled my ear as he nuzzled the nape of my neck.

Determined, he placed a kiss as light as a feather across my bare shoulder.

"You playin' shy now, honey?" He spoke in that butter-melts-in-your-mouth way that always escalated my desire.

Unable to withstand the teasing any longer, I rolled over into his waiting arms. The dark of night failed to hide his iconic features. His high cheek bones, flared nose, and square jaw were visual perfections, but of all his qualities it was his eyes that hypnotized me. Like deep mystic blue pools, they were set ablaze with a rousing fervor I had seen before. I never tired of getting lost in them.

I gathered myself closer and lay my head on his chest with a satisfied moan that mixed with his own exhalation, "I've missed you." I sighed, inhaling his deeply masculine scent deeper in to my lungs.

His spicy aroma tantalized my senses. He was as soothing to my spirit as a hot bubble bath, and I never felt happier than when lying in his arms, passing the time in slow, blissful moments of serenity.

Too soon, he tenderly pushed me away and looked into my eyes. I smiled in that bashful way that he enjoyed, and I was rewarded with that famous lopsided grin.

"There's my baby girl."

"Hi." I replied softly.

"Hi, yourself," he chuckled.

"How did you get in here?" I teased.

"I'm an angel, remember?" His palm rested against the side of my flushed face, and his thumb lightly fluttered across my mouth. My lips trembled.

He watched me closely, and I knew by his smirk that he was enjoying the eagerness in my eyes. Subconsciously, I parted my lips, and when I thought I could not take one moment longer, his lips were finally on mine.

Instantaneously, I was lost in lips of silk and a kiss as sweet as the richest cream. His mouth was measured and purposeful. He held me where he wanted, and his lips played about mine, a taste here, and a soft touch there. He stirred me slowly, so gently, his every move calculated perfection, and I melted in his arms. Then, when he knew our moment was at hand, he shifted his mouth over mine, sinking deeper and enriching our kiss. I opened to him fully. The salty-sweet taste of him fell to my tongue evoking my moans of pleasure.

A wave of ecstasy swelled. The white-capped waters teeter at the top and promising satisfaction. My whole body tensed, expecting a flood of delight, when his lips suddenly stilled. He pulled back ever so slightly, and the urge to pull him back raged, but I held firm. Through hooded eyes, his gaze smoldered. And, while I licked at his flavor left behind on my lips, his mouth curled in that heart-melting way as he gave me a slow, sly look.

In a single motion, he rolled us as one until I was on my back, and letting out a shriek that was quickly silenced by his mouth crushing down to my own. Where he once was patient he was now demanding. He tugged at me, his kiss varying from fervent to tender and then back again until I was like butter under him. The more I gave, the more he wanted. And, when his practiced hands moved smoothly down my torso to flirt with the soft skin of my inner thigh, I was already whimpering his name into the night.

He pulled his lips away.

"Say it again," he whispered a kiss away.

I blinked up in to his smoldering eyes, and even in the dim light I could see him smirking.

"Say it...just once." He raised one dark eyebrow.

I was still breathing heavily, and he kept his pillow-soft lips tantalizingly just above mine. The taste of him lingered on my tongue like a savored treat. My mouth parted for that first syllable of his delicious name, but the second syllable never followed. Without warning, the unwelcoming alarm I had set on my cell phone shrieked from across the room.

Over me, my lover's eyes widened, and, like shattered glass, his perfect features broke in to tiny particles.

I sat straight up in bed so fast that a muscle in my neck cramped with displeasure. I flung my arms outward in a desperate attempt to keep him from leaving, while shielding my eyes as a painfully intense light hit them. I turned to my left and then to my right before plopping backward into the bed with a heavy sigh. Like a ghost in the night, he was gone. The dreams were happening more frequently now, but that didn't mean waking from them was getting any easier.

The phone shifted from alarm to an actual ring. I leaned across the damp sheets to the bedside table.

"Hello!" I exclaimed breathlessly.

"Samantha?"

"Heather." I inhaled a slow soothing breath.

"Did I interrupt something? You sound breathless."

"No, no I was only... sleeping."

"It sounds as if I caught you doing something far more exciting then sleeping." She chuckled.

"You startled me from a dream, that's all." I yawned.

"Ah, one of *those* dreams." Heather giggled that all-knowing laugh that made me blush, especially when she was right.

"Was there a point to this call?"

"There was, but I've plum forgotten about it now. So, who was he?"

In a flash, I could see Elvis' face smirking over me.

"Nobody."

"Uh-huh. Would that nobody happen to be that famous angel of yours?"

I was silent.

"Sam, he isn't coming back." Heather's voice softened.

My thoughts drifted gently to that unforgettable last evening when my angel revealed that he was a man after all, weak in the flesh, tempted and wanting.

"Samantha Lynn Bennett, are you listening to me?"

I snapped back to attention.

"I know what I *should* be doing, but yet here I am."

"Exactly. Why *are* you in Memphis?"

"It's his birthday." I was beginning to regret having shared my destination on her voice mail before I left Atlanta yesterday morning.

"He doesn't celebrate birthdays anymore, Samantha. He's dead."

The shock value of "dead" slowly sunk in.

"I needed to be near him. Look...I have to go. I'm late to meet Steve." I hung up on her abruptly and wished I hadn't.

Heather knew nothing about Steve. In fact, I knew very little about him myself. The way we met was unexpected and could have been a scene straight out of a Nora Ephron movie. But, I was no Meg Ryan, and I wasn't looking for the likes of Tom Hanks. I wanted my angel, and I believed I knew where to find him.

My first stop when I arrived in Memphis was Graceland, to pay my respects. After all, the date was January 8, where else would I be? It was nighttime and unbelievably cold, too cold to be outside, but there we were the last two die-hard fans of the day to leave the estate. Even though we only spoke briefly through chattering teeth, something about him intrigued me. We shared a warming cup of coco that night, and without hesitation, I accepted his invitation to meet for morning coffee.

How does one attract an angel's attention? On one hand, I looked forward to a friendly face, someone who understood my love for a man I had never met. Or so Steve assumed. Another part of me, my much less confident side, hoped a certain angel would be watching.

Since his departure from my life, this question had been haunting every hour of my day. I could find no definitive answer. There were no written instructions for me to follow, and the Bible spoke sparingly of such things. I found myself relying on my own humanistic ideas which, of course, meant my plan was flawed from the start.

* * *

I had only thirty minutes before I was to meet Steve at the café across from Graceland. I jumped into the shower and raced to get ready. The legacy of my childhood upbringing to literally and unfailingly be at church on time was that as an adult, I could not tolerate lateness. As I rushed about the room like a madwoman, trying not to be haphazard and waste the little time I had, my cell phone insistently rang with the sound of "Treat Me Nice."

Heather was persistent, I'd give her that. I would have explained my plans to her, but she would only worry. I let the first, second and third calls all go to voice mail.

Racing the clock, I made a mental note to change my ring tone to something more reflective of my current mood. I considered "Hurt," and then just as quickly tossed that idea aside. "The Sound of Your Cry" popped in to my mind. Better? No, the song I had was upbeat, and I could use all the help I could get.

I loved my angel. Was that not an acceptable excuse for chasing after him? After all, it was he who so abruptly left me, confused and literally alone in a bed smelling of his savory cologne. And, I wasn't the type of woman who took men to her bed, even if they were Elvis Presley. I prided myself in being a good girl. Now, who was I? If God would only tell me how this was all supposed to work, this loving of angels, my life would be much easier.

But so far, God wasn't speaking. Or maybe it was I that was not listening? Nothing was clear.

What if God was silent for a reason? My mind spun like a caged hamster on its wheel. Did he expect me to let Elvis go after all we've been through? The words "letting go" felt as thick on my tongue as a mouthful of cotton. I defiantly shook my head at nobody in particular. It wasn't time to let go. Not yet.

In two fluid and familiar movements, I unpinned my long chestnut hair and quickly tied it back into the default time-saver: a ponytail. I paused to look at my reflection in the mirror. My oval features and defined cheek bones were hauntingly familiar, a walking reflection of my mother. And upon looking closer, my blue eyes sparkled with a new look, one of death-defying determination. This woman before me, throwing caution to the wind, was such a stranger to me the mere sight of her stopped me in my own tracks.

I reached for my purse, wondering if it was a sin to want what God himself had given me. I nibbled nervously on my bottom lip. No, I won't think of it today. Happily, I decided to side with Scarlett O'Hara.

CHAPTER TWO

A sharp cold wind blew even for winter. Standing outside my motel, I pulled my jacket to my face and marveled at the steely sky churning over head. Gauzy thin clouds sped by, tearing apart, bumping into other clouds, and forming new shapes in a poorly choreographed dance. I imagined them to be as restless as my spirit.

I tried to warm up by pacing as I waited for the cab. The rhythmic pattern of five steps up, five steps back made it easy for me to fall into deep thought. Once colorful leaves blew dead and broken around my feet, but I did not see them. I was again becoming entrenched in this all-absorbing dilemma and allowing it to take me over. The remembering was always the same.

My trip to Boston last spring had been beyond life-changing and still consumed me. Though it had been months since the devastating car accident marred the trip, and also brought my angel to me, it continued to mystify me. By nothing short of a divine plan, Heather had been driving when we had our misfortune on the freeway, and only I had been terribly injured. As was always the human condition, one could not help but wonder why.

Looking down at my watch, I grumbled under my breath as I realized I had just five minutes before I was expected.

"Miss! Miss!" A voice cut through the wind.

I turned to see a friendly bellhop peeking out from the doors of the warm hotel lobby.

"No need to stand outside, ma'am. The taxi will be a few minutes late."

"Thank you, but I don't mind waiting." Turning, I shoved my hands further into my pockets.

Must everyone tell me what to do, I fumed, my defiance surging while the cold helped to clear my head. My teeth had just begun to chatter when my phone vibrated violently in my pocket. Despite the fact I had my hand curled around it, the idiotic thing still made me jump. I did not have to look to know who was calling.

"Yes." I grimaced.

"So, tell me about this Steve." Heather's tone sounded tense, and for a moment I imagined I was having this conversation with my father.

"He's a gentleman I met last night while visiting Elvis' grave." My breath expelled like steam out in to a cold Memphis morning.

The line went silent. I wondered if I had lost her in some infuriating cell phone vortex, but her measured breathing gave her away.

"This doesn't sound too safe to be, you know, meeting with strangers." Heather finally said, sounding with what I noted was an extra measure of unease.

"He's a fellow fan, not a stranger."

"I'm coming to Memphis." She blurted out.

"What? Why?"

"Because you're acting irrationally!"

"I'm a grown woman."

"I'm still coming."

"Fine." I closed my phone with a snap.

By my figuring, I had roughly three hours before the next plane landed. I knew she'd be onboard. Heather and I were more familiar than most with the flight schedules in and out of Memphis. We had both worked them many times in our years as in-flight service clerks—flight attendants to the rest of the world.

I understood Heather's need to find me. Our camaraderie was full of expectant, and often dreaded escapades. Like fire and ice, we were very different. I was Audrey Hepburn to Heather's May West. Such extremes should have prevented us from ever becoming such fast friends, but somehow we made it work. We have co-existing down to a science, telling each other everything and never judging what the other is sharing. It is a friendship based on love and as irritated as I was by her reaction, I also knew if the tables were turned, I would do no different.

My reverie was cut short by the sharp squeal of tires nearby as my yellow-checkered ride all but bounced into the hotel parking lot, a steamy white trail of exhaust behind him. I waived eagerly.

"To Graceland, please." I said before the door was even closed behind me.

As we peeled away, I could see the bellhop, still shaking his head from inside his warm sanctuary.

"I don't understand me, either." I huffed, and blushed when I noticed my driver's quizzical look peering at me from the rear-view mirror.

I smiled, silently praying the driver's drop-offs were less flashy than his curb-jumping pick-ups.

* * *

The cabbie skillfully worked his way through the congestion on Elvis Presley Boulevard and pulled into the tourist viewing lane next to the mansion. My eyes never left the majestic white house above us as I handed the driver his fare. An ageless beauty, the mansion's presence commanded attention. With flanking grand Corinthian pillars, and Tennessee limestone brickwork, it symbolizes today the affluence it reflected when it was created. The large gated windows, framed by emerald-green shutters, looked down knowingly from the home's perch on the hill. I threw one final thanks over my shoulder to the cabbie and reluctantly turned my back to Graceland. Across the street sat the cozy café where Steve was waiting for me. I steadied myself with a deep breath and tried to pretend I didn't feel the eyes on the hill behind me, still watching as I walked away.

The wait at the crosswalk seemed interminable. Not only were my teeth beginning to chatter in rhythm with the blinking red hand, but my resolve to keep this date with a man I barely knew was starting to waiver. My conscious tugged at me and made my indecision worse. Was I genuinely interested in getting to know Steve, or was meeting him across from Graceland a sophomoric attempt to make my angel jealous? I flashed back to the night we met, remembering the oozing of Southern belle charm, and had my answer.

Elvis' powerful tenor softly echoed in the breeze. I crossed the street and shuffled along in a plaza that surprisingly held few visitors. I strolled around unoccupied tables and chairs without really seeing them. I was focused on every rich, breathlessly sung note. Even under stress, his singing could still make me smile.

Too soon, I reached the windowed door of the café. My hand hovered over the worn brass handle. My hazy likeness gazed back at me. I laughed, embarrassed. I was not normally a woman who acted first and thought about it later. Where had the level headed girl my mama raised gone, I wondered, and inhaled deeply before giving the door a quick jerk.

A bell jingled merrily as I entered the diner. The 1950's décor, complete with teal vinyl booths and a fire-red jukebox in the corner had the feel of a gentler time in history. As I stood there wishing I could beam myself back, a few lone visitors peered up at me briefly from their steaming morning brew. Scanning the room, I paused at every photo with Elvis' piercing baby blues and that same smile. The mere sight of him stirred up a quivering in the pit of my stomach.

Who knows how long I stood in that one spot studying each photo before I realized the last one was directly over Steve's blonde head. A morning paper opened before him to the sports section, he was looking at me, eyebrows raised.

"Good morning. Sorry I'm late." I slid in across the booth from him.

"Hello, luv. I was beginning to wonder if you were coming." His emerald-green eyes sparkled brighter than his smile as he folded his morning read.

Steve's accent charmed me. I didn't know enough about England to guess which region he came from, but it didn't matter. He was like a breath of fresh air. I believe I could have listened to him run on about nothing at all, and been quite happily entertained.

"I had trouble sleeping, and then I woke up late." I said, taking off my jacket.

"Can I fetch you some coffee, then?" He stepped out of the booth.

My mouth was poised with my request but he was too fast for me, and gone before I could share it. Peculiar, I thought, but who was I to judge. I had oddities of my own. Like the fact that I was in Memphis chasing angels, for one. Besides, he was a gentile looking man, tall

DREAM ANGEL

with wavy hair, and a lean but sturdy build. Harmless, I considered, watching him steadily before realizing I was staring. I peeled my eyes away only to meet Elvis' baby blues gazing down at me. Until that moment I had missed seeing the life-size portrait on the wall immediately beside me. Elvis' eyes were as soft as the clouds and even bluer up close than any photo could ever convey. For a moment I became lost in his idle gaze. As always, he was my personal composer, playing the strings of my heart.

"Here you go... one coffee." Steve announced.

"Thank you." I drew back, pulling my eyes away from Elvis.

"You scurried off so quickly last night I was beginning to wonder if I'd see you this morning." Steve chuckled while taking his seat in a slow motion.

"My manners are usually better than that. Can you forgive me?" I cradled the hot cup in my hands and squinted against the steam drifting up from the velvety beverage.

How did he know I took cream?

"I thought maybe you had another engagement." He sipped his beverage, studying me over the rim of his mug.

"Yes... well, I was hoping to meet with a friend, but he never showed." I smile lightly and took a cautious sip.

"He, you say?" He asked suspiciously as he scanned my face for the truth. "What foolish chap would leave your side allowing a bloke like myself to step in so easily?"

My cheeks burned. I loved a compliment as much as the next woman, but my shy nature always had me feeling like a teenager left in the company of men. A simple "thank you" never seemed good enough. And, as I was stammering about, momentarily knocked off balance, my attention shifted to a red jukebox against the wall behind Steve. The machine turned on with a click.

"You blush beautifully, by the way." Steve was still strategizing while the red and orange lights of the music box flashed

I ignored his intense stare, mystified as it shuffled 45's like a deck of cards.

"Did you see anyone put money into that music box?" I touched Steve's hand, politely interrupting, while eagerly reaching out to a passing waitress with my other. "Excuse me, miss, does this jukebox have a timer on it?"

"No ma'am, that machine is plum crazy, that's what it is," the grey-haired waitress said, as she hustled by, loaded precariously with full trays.

I grinned, looking down to hide my smile. I preoccupied myself with removing imaginary lint from the jacket in my lap.

"This cold must be affecting my brain." I gave a quiet laugh as an oldie-but-a-goodie softly began to play.

Elvis' voice floated in to the room.

"Sam, where is your gent now?" Steve gently asked.

My attention flickered from the bright and shining machine, then back to the man at my table. What was this song? Distracted, I felt myself cock my head like

DREAM ANGEL

the family dog, and a whole minute must have passed before Steve's question even registered.

"I'm afraid my gentleman's location is a mystery even to me." The truth was out of the question and a lie just felt wrong.

"Well, if he's smart, he'll get back to you before I steal you away." Steve's eyes flashed about my face in a scrutiny that flushed me, and not in a good way.

I pushed out a laugh.

"May I ask the man's name?" He asked, a little too casually I thought. "It's always good to know one's competition."

Having just met Steve, his hard pressed flirting had me fidgeting while warning bells of a turn in an uncomfortable direction rang inside my head.

"Well, it's... complex." I half-smiled only vaguely aware the chipper song, I couldn't quite place, had stopped.

"I'm a good listener."

My regret soared. He was misunderstanding and who could blame him. Out of desperation I had become, virtually overnight, someone even I disliked, an abuser of other people's emotions. How did I get here? I couldn't say, as it had all happened so fast. I considered my declining words carefully, but before I could open my mouth to speak the first few velvety bars of "He'll have to go" filled the room like a handmade quilt.

"Put your sweet lips", Elvis purred, and that voice instantly took me back to the late hours of our last night

when his whispered words of romance were just for me. My pulse skipped.

"If I'm prying, I apologize." Steve slid his hand across the counter and placed it over mine.

Words tumbled around in my head but nothing acceptable seemed to present itself. Suddenly, the song blared and we both jumped as Elvis' voice bellowed through the diner. Two employees raced past our table headed to tend to the "noise" that nobody was complaining about. I watched as they jerked out the wall plug, and still the music continued. My eyes widened. I was monitoring them, as they raced to the back, while also trying to read Steve's mouth that still moved. I leaned in closer, but his words were drowned out by Elvis growling the last sung lyric. His demand all but screamed in to my ear, slamming against my heart.

My friend had to go, I considered, and as if answering the lights to the juke box flickered once and then twice before falling dark.

"I-I don't know why I came it's…it's not right." I began to collect my coat.

"Samantha." He smiled at me but would not meet my eyes.

"I'm sorry, this isn't me," I said, now talking to both Steve and Elvis, as I believed he was listening.

"Please stay, Samantha. You haven't finished your coffee." He jumped up and caught me by the arm. His grip was tight and I winced from the sting.

"I can't stay. Please forgive me." I could barely hear what must have been my own voice over the pounding in my ears.

Steve's unbelievable reaction to me leaving him, for what was the second time, was as mind-boggling as his insistent behavior was scary. He was either the loneliest man in the world, or the craziest. Either way, I felt lower than the silt at the bottom of the murky Mississippi.

I tried my best to give one last humble apology and followed it with a firm goodbye as I put my coat on. The house on the hill that taunted me was pulling me in, and I was powerless, even if it meant Steve got left behind.

CHAPTER THREE

The wind blew against me as though Mother Nature herself knew my destination. I pulled my coat tighter around me and raced across the plaza's wet sidewalks. My resolve was stronger than the oncoming wind. Running to the front door, I pulled the door open too hard and practically jumped over the threshold into the still lobby. A warm waft washed over my face, and Elvis' soothing voice floated melodically throughout the room. With little pause, I sped through the red velvet ropes like a mouse in a maze determined to receive my reward.

"Hello. I'd like a ticket for the next bus," I practically demanded of the agent. I glanced back in the direction I had left Steve.

"Would you like the platinum tour?" The woman behind glass asked by rote and without looking up.

"Just the house tour would be fine, thanks."

As she processed the ticket, I looked quickly around the room. The crowd inside was similar to the one outside:

sparse and quiet. The hectic crowds of summer had long ago gone. All was tranquil.

A three-cord tune played in the background. As the attendant took my credit card, I fantasized about our reunion. I imagined urgent hungry kisses, and felt my cheeks flush hot as my longing to be whisked away in my angel's arms swelled. I was so enthused, my knees were shaking. In order to steady myself, I refocused on an elegant woman browsing a souvenir rack. Her blonde hair hung softly across her face as she leaned over a display of merchandise. Sensing my gaze, she looked up and I smiled softly.

"Here you go, ma'am. The bus will be here shortly." The attendant handed me a pass, still without looking up.

"Thank you very much." I tucked my ticket securely away as if it were gold.

Turning on my heels, I headed for the souvenirs.

"Isn't he beautiful?" The blonde woman exclaimed to nobody in particular as she admired a shirt.

I couldn't help but look over her shoulder at the vibrant screen print of Elvis in full motion, commanding a stage the way only he could.

"Yes, yes, he is." I choked back further words of acclaim for fear my high emotion may spark the tears.

The lovely woman was back to shopping when the ticket agent cued a grainy speaker and announced the next numbered tour to load – I was just in time.

A burly man who was well in to his sixties greeted me as I stepped onto the tour bus. He welcomed everyone aboard cheerfully, one by one. Once we all were seated, he cued the microphone on his headset and calmly waited for the buzz of conversation to die down before beginning his friendly banter.

"How many people are here today for their first time?"

Not a single hand went up as the bus eased across Elvis Presley Boulevard.

"How many have been here at least once before?"

A hand shot up from the front row. I craned my head around the plush headrest to see the passenger.

"Welcome back, ma'am," said the driver happily. "Now, who has been here more than two times?"

We passed through the famous gates of Graceland, and I mindlessly raised my hand with a few other visitors.

"Folks are returnin' today," I heard him say as I spun in my seat and stared back at the musical iron gates we had just passed through.

Our driver skillfully drove the bus along the route he knew so well. Blue Christmas lights left from the holidays lined the driveway and gave the look of a landing strip in the early morning hours. I watched out the window, feeling a little sad, as Graceland's grounds keepers carefully took down the Christmas decorations. This was Elvis' favorite time of year, and the festivities continued in his household until well past the New Year's Day, lasting until the day after his birthday. That the yearly tradition has continued to be maintained is just one of the many ways that his fans, not just visitors, who seek some nuance of Elvis find it.

"Here we are, folks!" The driver cheerily called out as we rolled to a stop.

While waiting to file off the bus, I peeked around shoulders and bobbed around heads to view the stately home. The commanding white stone lions sat vigilant on either side of perfectly placed stone steps. Their focus seemed to scrutinize each visitor as they dared to approach the castle they protected. I was riveted to my seat, imagining they had expected me.

"Watch your step, and y'all have a great tour."

Taking my time, I stepped off last. The others continued to the front door, where a tour guide emerged to welcome them. Hanging back, I was oblivious to her speech. My mind was elsewhere. For a time, my attention was glued to the custom-made stained glass "P" above the entrance. And then, above me and closest to my right was the bedroom window that I knew was his. The curtains remained closed, and no shadows moved behind them, yet intuitively I knew he was here.

"Ma'am," called the tour guide as she held open the front door.

"Oh, thank you," I took a deep breath and stepped into Elvis' world.

Even though I knew this house better than even my own, I was captivated anew by the custom staircase just inside the foyer. It was just noticeably wider than standard and lavishly covered in plush white carpet. I felt like a special guest finally arriving for a long-awaited visit. Stopping, I closed my eyes, and I inhaled deeply feeling the love that had made this house a home.

The luxurious stairway, decorated in red poinsettias from the recent holiday season, drew me closer to Elvis' private sanctuary. I moved without conscious thought. Like Eve drawn by her desire to have the forbidden fruit, I was mesmerized and more than half-way across the foyer before I again paused and closed my eyes. This time, I strained to listen – had I just heard my name whispered from the top of the stairs? Either I wanted it so badly that my mind was playing tricks, or it was really happening, and I was about to see my angel.

My eyes popped open and I quickly moved to take another step toward the staircase, but as I brought my gaze back down to eye level, I froze. In that nanosecond, some corner of my brain disengaged from my reverie long enough to register a figure in my peripheral vision. Although I hadn't seen the specific form, I knew with absolute certainty that the figure in white was Elvis. Nobody else would be standing so still, teasingly waiting for me to discover him. He always made me work so hard!

Now under the chandelier, and with an unobstructed view, I parted my lips to let out a fittingly smart remark, but as I looked up it died on my tongue. My smile faded. My heart sank deep into my chest, and it wouldn't have taken much at that moment to make me cry. I had, indeed, wanted the fantasy to be true so badly that I had tricked myself. The figure was definitely there, but it was only a life-size headless replica, smartly dressed in Elvis' signature style.

"Phantom Illusion Startles Fan to Death," the morning headlines should read, I thought with sad sigh.

Brought abruptly back to reality, I decided to not risk being singled out as straying from the herd. I turned back to the tour group, now in deep conversation near Graceland's formal living room.

"Did you see that?" Murmured the genteel-looking woman I had met earlier in the plaza.

"He's here, all right, Sue," her friend confirmed with an excited nod.

The two women huddled together, whispering words of awe and wonder. Their faces brightened like giddy school girls with a secret. They were clearly good friends, and I couldn't help but overlay an image of Heather and I twenty years into the future. I wondered if they, too, had entirely different backgrounds that were bridged by a common interest. For Heather and I, the love of flying had brought us together. For these two lovely ladies, it was obviously Elvis. From the time of his earliest concerts to all of these years later after his passing, one of the biggest marvels about Elvis has been how his fans accept one another unconditionally. A fan welcomes a fellow fan regardless of social or economic differences.

The two women's excitement had escalated, and I noticed they were gesturing toward the room beside us. Having already been fooled once, I nonchalantly glanced into the living room.

My heart took a wild leap inside my chest.

"Oh, God!" I slapped my hand to my mouth.

A room full of startled eyes turned my way.

"Are you okay?" Sue rested her hand on my shoulder.

Still stifling a shriek, I glanced at Sue and then back to the image before us. She followed my gaze.

Like a sleek jungle cat, Elvis lounged on the sofa with his long legs stretched out before him. He gave a slow, knowing nod with an easy smile.

"Sure, I'm okay." I squinted at Elvis while patting Sue's hand as it rested on my shoulder.

My understanding grew by the minute, and like a raging river the urge to run to him rushed over me, but I did not move. Instead, I distracted myself by admiring his well-tailored white slacks. As tall as he was, Elvis still didn't take up the entire wall-length couch. The effect of his slacks against the white fabric of the sofa gave him a definite Cheshire-cat effect.

He was knee-weakening gorgeous. His exotic features, flattered by a red shirt that only a supremely confident man could successfully wear, aroused every cell in my body. Motionless, I stared questioningly at his intense expression and felt my face flush with suffused heat.

"Do you need to sit down?" Sue asked.

"No, thank you. I... I was startled by... uh...." I scanned the room, looking for something to blame for my hesitancy. "...that!" I pointed to yet another headless statue near the fireplace. This time dressed in black, the lifeless Elvis seemed to be laughing at me through his absent lips.

"You see it too, don't you?" Sue asked as she narrowed her eyes and leaned toward me.

In wide-eyed surprise, I considered the thought of someone else participating in this lunacy. Is she seeing what I am seeing? I glanced back at Elvis, who smirked devilishly at me, his blue-black hair glistening with as much shine as his boots. His feet were crossed at the ankles and kept time with his inner drumbeat. I turned back to Sue.

"I..." My mouth hung open from an undecided thought.

"Careful now, honey," said Elvis.

Smirking, I sighed deeply.

"She's a-waitin." Elvis urged me on.

I cleared my throat, and tried to play it cool.

"You look as if you've seen a ghost!" Sue patted me on the back.

Elvis nodded in agreement and rose from the couch. He temptingly ran his hands down his trousers, aligning their sharp creases. Circling an enormous glass tabletop between the couch and where I stood, he sauntered my way like poetry in motion, pausing to acknowledge the headless Elvis loitering near the fireplace.

"Bad day, buddy?" Elvis asked with a light chuckle, and a nervous laugh escaped my lips as I avoided eye contact with Sue.

He continued toward me, and my gaze melted into his magnetic blue eyes. His movement displaced the air, propelling the smell of his cologne into my nostrils and I involuntarily inhaled.

"I'm sorry." I cleared my throat, looked back to Sue and forced a smile. "What were you saying?"

Elvis leaned casually against the arched doorway of the living room, his arms folded across his chest. Though he gave the appearance of listening attentively, his eyes traveled up and down my body in a smoldering appraisal that I tried to ignore.

"The way you started, I thought maybe you noticed it, too." Said sue, pointing back to the couch.

Elvis and I followed her direction. There on the immaculate surface of the cushion was the distinct impression of his perfectly formed behind. I glanced at Elvis for an explanation, but he only shrugged.

"You see it, too!" I turned back to Sue and feigned shock.

"Don't overdo it, Sam," Elvis warned.

Had he been close enough, I would have given serious thought to shoving a swift elbow into his side, if that was even possible.

"Oh, we see this all the time." Sue waved her hand dismissively.

"Sure, all the time," her friend spoke up.

"But he's only here when the crowds are small," Sue clarified.

I must have looked like a bobble-head as I looked back and forth between the two women.

"He?" I wanted verification from Sue.

"Me," Elvis said.

"Elvis," said Sue.

My thoughts were whirling with the madness.

"I'm glad you told me, or I might have thought I was going mad." I held my hands tightly to hide my nervousness.

"Oh no, he's here often." Sue said cheerfully as the four of us stared at the large couch with its mysterious indentation.

I loosened my clutched hands, feeling comforted that my secret was so far safe.

"I think he enjoys this little game of ghost." Her friend added.

"That does sound like him, yes," I smiled at Elvis' silly expression and his pointed finger moving in small circles close to his temple. *I recall it was you who was nicknamed crazy!*

"Oh, we have a few other secrets, too." Sue's tone of voice was coy, and her eyes twinkled.

"Really?" said Elvis, his eyebrows rising as he stepped away from the wall.

I moved into his line of vision and blocked him from our banter. I could hear him chuckling from behind me.

"What would that be, if you don't mind my asking?" I continued.

"Well, take the ceiling in the foyer for instance." Sue's eyes widened with excitement.

As she turned her back to the living room and returned to the foyer of Graceland, the four of us followed, staring upward to the ceiling.

"I don't see it," I confessed.

"In the left upper corner, see that patch?" Sue pointed.

I had to strain to see the small cracks of plaster that were partially repaired.

"What caused the hole?"

"Elvis' temper caused it." Sue laughed.

"He shot out the toilet upstairs." Her friend giggled.

My mouth hung open. That Elvis had a temper was well known, but the bullet-damaged wall truly brought home for me just how hot he could burn.

The front door of Graceland swung open, and a new group of tourists walked through, giving us nothing more than a glance as they passed by. I couldn't help but notice the look of I-cannot-believe-we-are-here wonderment on each face. And when I turned back, I was surprised to find we were all alone. Sue and her friend had melted into the passing crowd. It was just Elvis and I, but he was busy inspecting his handiwork.

"Why would anyone shoot a toilet?" I whispered.

"Aw, it never worked right, anyhow." He rubbed his chin pensively.

"And...?"

"It was running all the time, keepin' me awake." He threw me an impish look.

I waited, thinking maybe there was more. His lips twitched with amusement as he attempted to stifle one of his great laughs. Growing more tickled with himself with each moment, soon the sound of his chuckles spilled out into the foyer. I imagined the house swelling with happiness. His humor was always contagious, and I too, began to laugh openly. Our hysterics grew until a tour guide stepped back into the room with a look of befuddlement.

"Ma'am, I'm going to have to ask you to keep moving along. We don't want to hold up the line." The young man was polite but firm.

Elvis and I looked around at the empty room and fell into another round of laughter. I held my hand up to hide my smile and tried to pull together a serious response.

"I understand. Sorry, I'll move along."

I began to make my way down the hall, toward the bedroom used by Elvis' mother, but stopped when I heard Elvis growling from behind.

"Listen, son."

I turned back to find Elvis, swiping at tears of laughter that were quickly drying with his change of expression.

"This is my house. She'll do as *I* say!" His words were heated, and the crystal chandelier rattled over head.

The next scene played out before me like an Abbott and Costello meets the mummy skit. Elvis looked up and quickly stepped out of danger's way, as though anything could harm him. The tour guide slowly turned his eyes upward as what little color he had drained from his face. I again started to laugh. The young man cracked and galloped right by Elvis as he rushed for the exit.

"Boo!" Elvis exclaimed and I swore I saw the usher flinch.

CHAPTER FOUR

They say every King needs a castle, and at the age of twenty- two Elvis had found his in Graceland. With its sharp color pallet, and flamboyant furniture, Graceland is as unique as its owner. Every room has a theme, and every fan has their favorite. And, I was no different. While Elvis' chuckles fell silent, I collected my own humor and continued down the corridor to his mother's room, my favorite room at Graceland. A thick chain strung across the doorway to prevent visitors from actually entering. I practically laid my body against it as I leaned in to admire the rich colors.

The room's lavish setting was a long way from Mrs. Presley's humble beginnings in Tupelo. The bed was draped in rich amethyst silk. A white Christmas tree still decorated with purple ornaments emphasized a regal feeling to the décor that would have made a queen feel at home. I marveled at the floor-to-ceiling violet curtains and matching bedspread.

What grace, I thought. Was her son's sudden wealth overwhelming?

"Yes, it was." Elvis' velvet voice broke into my thoughts.

I turned to find him leaning against the snow-white banister that led up to his private quarters. His gaze burned between us and added to his distinctive rebel-with-out-a-cause posture.

You left without a goodbye, I internally sulked.

"That's because it wasn't," he said in a rather flippant tone.

I could feel myself pouting, but stopped when Elvis jetted out his own lips in an exaggerated mope. For a time, I had wondered if angels could listen to our thoughts. Elvis had proven in the past that he could do just that, yet I had never directly asked.

"Do you listen to *all* my private thoughts?" I said, hoping to sound confident, and in charge of my escalating emotions.

His eyes sparkled. "Not all."

"Oh?" I walked towards him with all the poise I could muster.

He stood up straighter and pushed out his chest but did not stop my approach. As I drew near, any frustration I may have previously felt melted over the sight of him taking in the view. His attention lingered in all the right places starting with my eyes and progressing south. I yearned to feel his arms around me and taste his lips, but when I saw him smirking, I stopped just beyond his reach.

You're listening now, aren't you? I taunted, and a half grin slid across his face as if someone had just whispered a secret in his ear.

My insides quivered from the thrill. I felt alive in his presence, whole, as if he were the missing piece to my personal puzzle. I wasn't sure if it was being close to an angel, to the man himself, or to God that had brought me that feeling but I liked it.

"Your thoughts are safe with me, honey. Cross my heart and hope to die." He drew a finger across his chest.

"A little late for *that* isn't it?" I stepped in closer, and enjoyed that smile of his widening to expose those pearly white teeth and deep dimples.

He was as stunning as a chiseled Greek god.

"I only peek when you do this." He mimicked my sullen expression, while pushing the outer edges of my lips into a smile.

I slapped at his fingers. *Stop, now, someone will see.*

"Ok, honey," he whispered in a deep husky voice that mesmerized me.

I refocused as Elvis' long slim fingers wrapped around my hand and he turned to led me away from his mother's room. His grip was light but solid, and I briefly wondered how nobody else seemed able to see him and yet I was holding his hand. Glancing around, I was relieved to find we were still alone and could hardly wait to properly say hello.

As giddy as a school girl, I withheld my need to skip in step, and watched with curiosity as he lifted a leg over the privacy ropes at the bottom of the oversized staircase that led upstairs. He paused to scoot an arrangement of poinsettias with the tip of his black boot as he positioned his feet carefully on the first step.

"Where are we going?" I asked over my pounding heart.

"We need to talk," he said matter-of-fact.

I swallowed hard. "You want to talk? Up there?"

We both looked upward toward the white door at the top.

"What's wrong with up there?" He let go of my hand, and looked down at me with a disquieting expression.

Suddenly, I was like a runaway car headed down the freeway in the wrong direction. "I-I just thought maybe you'd have found a different place to...uh... conduct business?" I threw out my first thought wishing life had a rewind button.

"Well now, honey, it's suited my, what'd you call it, "business" in the past, why should I change now?"

A twinge of misery pierced my heart. This was not the reunion I had hoped for, searched for. I had imagined long hours spent in one another's arms, angels singing and the sky parting over us. The controlled down-to-business man standing before me was a far cry from the hungry lover that had once held me. How could I have been so wrong? I silently scolded myself, my pride thrashing about and drowning in a self-made pool of expectation. My tears began to pool.

The front door to Graceland was directly behind me, and I cursed myself for wanting to run. Pressing a finger to my temple, I lowered my head and headed for the formal diner room. A glass-topped dining table and high-backed chairs overpowered the tiny room. I stopped near the tour ropes to draw a calming breath before glancing nervously around me. He was nowhere to be seen, but I knew he was near. I stood up straight when I heard footsteps.

"Baby girl, what's going on here, really?" He asked gently while turning me to face him.

The sound of my childhood nickname spoken from his lips made the tiny hairs along my arms stand up. I looked away, unwilling to meet his piercing stare.

"Your family would disapprove," I pleaded principles.

Convincing him my defiance was forged out of respect seemed more believable and less embarrassing than admitting my girlish fantasies were crumbling around me. Besides, if we had this "talk," what then, I feared the worst.

A new round of visitors filed alongside us, headed for the kitchen. I fidgeted uncomfortably while waiting for the group to pass. Elvis studied me, and his gaze felt heavy. Tense seconds passed into minutes as I waited.

"Alright honey, we'll do it your way," Elvis stepped closer to my side and pointedly added, "this time."

He leaned into my view to force me to look at him. Daring to glance up, I only briefly saw the grin that lingered around the edges of those sweet lips. He gathered my hands with his two, and gave me a tender squeeze.

"Meet me in front of Graceland, tonight at midnight?"

Despite my humiliation, I nodded my agreement.

"Good girl," Elvis lifted my hands to his lips for a tender kiss and paused. "Come alone."

His deep blue eyes held mine, but this time it was I who studied him. Exactly whom was he referring to, I wondered, and then before I could stop it Steve's features flashed. I cringed, quickly pushing the vision away, but it was too late. A tiny smile flickered across Elvis' lips. He kissed my hand, and then left the kitchen. My skin felt hot where his lips had only briefly touched.

"What should I do now?" I spoke aloud in the emptiness.

"You know the way out."

Elvis crossed the dining room and stopped to look about. He smiled, still moved by the grace in Graceland.

"You won't finish the tour with me?"

"I've seen it." He chuckled and continued out into the foyer.

Not wanting to let him go, I followed close on his heels. I stumbled inside his gate. He lifted one long leg at a time over the privacy ropes, landing once again on that first stair tread leading up the main white staircase.

"You sure you won't change your mind now, honey?" He joked, pointing a finger upward. My silence was his answer.

Smiling boyishly, he shrugged and continued up the stairs.

"Elvis." I called out to him anxiously.

"I'll be there, Samantha." He said sternly, without even a glance back.

He turned at the first landing and continued the climb. The front doors of Graceland opened behind me, and a new crowd of visitors entered. I watched the smiling faces of fans entering their idol's home. In the space of a heartbeat, I turned back to the king of this castle, but he had vanished.

CHAPTER FIVE

The cold stung my face as I walked against a northern gust down Elvis Presley Boulevard. The traffic buzzed, but I did not see it. Car tires pulsated against the pavement, pushing through standing water, and seemingly harmonizing with the throbbing inside my head. I pressed a finger against my temple and looked down at my watch with a sigh. My stomach churned. It was not even noon yet. Too many hours of the day remained, and without a diversion I would surely spend each second torturing myself with the finer points of what had just happened. Why Elvis had been so formal continued to unnerve me. "Business" was not his favorite subject, every fan knew this. I knew this. Historically, Elvis disliked convoluted matters.

My every step felt surreal as the question of "why" kept circling. The mystery was relentless. I walked on autopilot, muttering along in rain drops the size of tears, and spurting out ideas in a stream that was as constant as stock market ticker tape was long. Thankfully, nobody was around to hear my rambling. I walked alone, and without an umbrella, staying dry was futile. My coat was soon soaked, and my whole body was quickly drenched. I did not care.

A shiver ran down my spine while I shuffled up the entrance to my hotel. I entered and shook off the rain and cold, but my shoulders still felt weighted down. Trudging along, I walked past the bellhop who glanced casually at me, and then did a double-take.

"Good day." I said passing by the service counter, my shoes squeaking on the lobby floor and a trail of water in my wake.

Although I tried to ignore the stares of every patron I passed, their faces told me all I needed to know about my appearance. I realized that for the first time in my life, I understood the phrase about feeling worse than one looks. I pulled back my shoulders, stuck out my chin, and forced myself to walk in unhurried steady steps towards the elevator. Strands of hair stuck to my face, and I brushed them away calmly as if I had no idea why everyone could possibly be gaping.

My face flushed as I repeatedly pushed the button for the elevator. I was about to give up my vigil and take the stairs when I heard a familiar voice.

"Look what the cat drug in," said a goading tone.

I closed my eyes. Bracing myself, I turned and forced a smile in Heather's direction.

"A flight left Atlanta that quickly, did it?"

DREAM ANGEL

"I'm here, aren't I?" Heather squinted and began to walk toward me.

She reached out and touched the sleeve of my dripping jacket. Glancing down, her smile dropped at the sight of puddles around my feet. I frowned.

"What did you do, walk from Graceland in a monsoon?"

My lips pressed together in a thin line. I turned back to the elevator and continued to press the button.

"You did."

"Must you tell everyone?" I grumbled.

"You think everyone is blind?" She waived her hand in an exaggerated circle.

The elevator doors opened, and I jumped inside, turning the corner to get out of view. I hit the floor call button with zeal. The door jerked forward, and as stealthy as a cat, Heather followed me in just before it closed.

"Are you trying to leave me behind?"

"Never," I said rich with sarcasm.

I gave my wet locks a good shake and purposely flung water around the elevator like a lawn sprinkler on a hot summer day. Heather quickly shielded her face.

"You're like a wet dog." She brushed quickly at the droplets of water across her arms. "Aw, now look what you did."

When she glanced up, our eyes met only briefly before her gaze narrowed to her nose. I watched as a droplet of water trickled down to the tip and tittered.

She didn't wipe it away. A flicker of laughter gleamed in both of our eyes. History has proven that we could never be mad at each other for long, and soon we began to laugh. I extended my arms. Heather stepped into my hug out of reflex, realizing her error too late.

"Wait!" She lifted up both hands.

Before she could screech another protest, I nabbed her, and squeezed her against my wet jacket. The water gushed out of my clothes, soaking in to hers.

"Ah, man." Her body went limp.

Distracted by our game, we suddenly noticed we had reached our floor and the door had opened. Our mouths dropped open as we realized how we looked to the two young men standing across from us in the hallway, smiling lasciviously. Heather reacted first.

"Hey, get off me!" She pushed me away and stomped out of the elevator and down the hallway.

I stepped past the men and gave them a wink before leaving. As if she had eyes in the back of her head, Heather turned and glared back at me. I held up my hands in a sign of surrender. She flipped the side of her hair that was now almost as wet as mine, and grunted before continuing down the hall. I laughed and followed her to my room.

We simultaneously stopped at my door and glanced back at the elevator to see the two men still staring at us. Heather paused to bat her eyes at them before entering the room, and then rolled her eyes as she passed me. I waved before closing the door with a slam that shook the walls.

"Are we even now?" Heather asked, while shaking out her shoulder length blonde hair with a hand.

"I'll consider it." I headed for the bathroom, pausing to smile triumphantly at her before closing the bathroom door.

* * *

I was re-energized when I stepped out from the steamy bathroom, a towel wrapped tightly around my hair. I was surprised to see Heather changed and refreshed in dry clothes. Glancing around, I noticed her bags next to the unoccupied bed.

"They let you into my room?"

"The nice bellhop brought my bags up while I waited."

"What if I didn't want you in here with me?"

"It's Memphis." Heather said with a shrug.

She had a point. Memphis was a different sort of town. Life here dawdled. Even the locals seemed oblivious to the city on full tilt around them, I considered, while walking to the vanity station to brush out my long dark hair.

"What?" I said to her mirror reflection, instead of turning to face her.

Heather crossed one leg over the other and folded her arms across her chest. Her silence stung me more than our normal routine of bickering and jousting.

"You came here, remember." I lowered my gaze.

Rising from the bed, Heather crossed the room and stood next to me. We both gazed in the mirror. Neither of us wished to face the other as we each tried to find the words that would make a complex situation simple.

"How are you feeling, really?" Her voice was soft with concern.

"I have a headache." I muttered.

"Maybe you should call your doctor."

"It's normal."

"You do remember recovering from a head injury less than six month ago, don't you? A little thing called a *coma*?"

"I said its *normal*."

"Normal? Well, after seeing you back there, I'm even more worried. Why are you here?" She sighed.

"I love him."

"And," Heather knew there had to be more.

"And, I'm messing it all up." I sighed, ignoring Heather's look of confusion.

She deserved to hear the morning's events. After all, she had come a long way. How could I not tell her about what I had experienced? She was my closest friend, and up until now she knew all my secrets. I wanted to tell her. I subconsciously relaxed my shoulders just toying with the idea of confiding.

"I went to the café across from Graceland to meet with Steve after we spoke, hoping for a miracle, a sign."

DREAM ANGEL

Heather's expression fell flat. I paused to scour her face for some hint of what she was thinking, but she gave away nothing.

"*He* was everywhere, in every photo, those magnetic blue eyes always watching me." As I talked, we took a seat at the two-person table near the window.

"Elvis." Heather followed closely.

"Steve seemed to sense *him* or...or maybe it was my love for him that he could feel, I don't know," I exhaled extra hard.

"What *exactly* did you and Steve discuss?" Heather set her mouth in a hard line.

"He asked me why this man I loved so much was not with me, and..." I stopped, unsure if I wanted to share Steve's reaction to me leaving.

"And...what else?"

Heather believed me to be a little naive when it came to men. It was not too far from the truth.

"Nothing important, really."

"He's asking rather personal questions for a man you just met, don't you think?" Heather's gaze held mine.

"Maybe, but there was something comforting, familiar about Steve when we first met, and I sort of...," I paused as shame began to tighten my chest. "...jokingly flirted with him."

"You did what?" Heather's voice rose.

"I guess a part of me thought maybe..."

"Don't tell me. You believe in jealous angels?" Her tone was flat.

I exhaled, embarrassed to realize my best friend most likely saw me for what I now felt I was: a hopeless female.

"I don't know what I think anymore." I ran a hand through my hair.

"This story gets crazier every time we speak, Samantha. First a coma," Heather's voice lowered with what I guessed was guilt or regret, "which triggers a visit by an angel, and now this, a spontaneous journey chasing ghosts. Can someone please tell me where my level-headed friend went?"

Heather was on a rant, and I quickly looked away, knowing full well how this all sounded.

"I'm right here. I'm just a little…love sick." I avoided using words like "foolish" and "impulsive," though they surely fit.

"Please Samantha, let's just leave…tonight." Heather's voice softened.

"I can't. Not without him," I stood up, walked back to the mirror and began brushing out my hair in long, even strokes.

Heather watched in silence. She had that faraway look she often got in her eyes when contemplating a problem.

"What happens now?"

"He's asked that I meet him tonight at midnight," I said.

"Steve?" Her eyebrows drew together in to a scowl.

Turning, I gave her a withering look.

"Elvis. Yes, of course." Heather raised her hands into the air.

For the better part of an hour, I attempted to explain the rest of the morning to Heather. She listened as I explained how my angel at first seemed thrilled to see me, his eyes shining with love upon our reunion. Or so I thought. Apart from his natural fondness of flirting and his sensitivity to my puppy-love-like condition, his intentions seemed set on business.

"Maybe he's trying to be a good little angel," Heather rationalized. "You know, make up for practically jumping you in the shower last time he was in your home."

I rolled my eyes. It was easy for her to see things so clearly. Heather had never witnessed the charm of Elvis Presley first-hand. She had never felt those piercing sapphire eyes, reaching deep into her soul while he gave her his full attention. He had a way of treating everyone like they were the only person on earth. If there was ever a human being one could be addicted to, it was him.

"He can be "good" all he wants, as long as he stays." I mumbled more to myself.

"It's only two o'clock. What are we going to do until Midnight?" Heather glanced at her watch.

"I don't know...lunch?" I said off-handedly.

"Perfect. I know a great place to order a spectacular adult beverage."

I chuckled at my friend's never-ending quest for the world's best martini.

CHAPTER SIX

The sun was peeking out from behind the dark clouds as we sped through Memphis on the forever-renovating Highway 55. Neither Heather nor I spoke. Both at ease with the silence, Heather scanned her messages on her cell phone while I was gazing at a rainbow cast against the stone sky. So vibrant, so lively, I considered, remembering my father's bedtime Bible stories.

The Ark would have been a nice perk earlier, I smiled at the thought.

The cabbie took our exit. We wound through the streets of downtown Memphis and up Union Avenue. I kept watch on the rainbow as it followed cheerily behind. While the soft bells of a street trolley ran somewhere in the city, we rolled to a stop at the historic Peabody Hotel. I grabbed my purse and stepped out.

Returning to the thirteen-story Italian Renaissance building had my heart skipping a happy beat. Like an old friend, the hotel and I had history. Not too long ago I'd celebrated a milestone birthday here. It was a small gathering, just Heather and I, but at the time it seemed like a perfect plan. After all we were two adventurous thinking 21 year-olds with plane tickets to anywhere. The combination was hazardous, but not deadly.

Standing next to the building, I craned my neck to get a good view of the flashing neon sign perched at the top. It flashed the hotel's famous name in scarlet letters over the city. Who would have thought The Peabody Hotel, built in a time when cotton was king, and the South was in its glory, would be a fundamental adult lesson for why booze and I should never mix.

"Are you thinking what I'm thinking?" Heather snickered next to me also gazing upward.

"Probably."

"Remember when you—."

"Don't say it."

"But it was so darn funny when—."

"You promised." I sighed and then Heather laughed.

"Yeah, ok." She said.

"Ok." I walked away.

Memphis residents believe the Mississippi Delta starts in the lobby of the Peabody Hotel. It was… is a place to see and be seen. No matter the memory of my alcoholic inspired antics, best left in the past and never to be repeated, my trip was never complete until I had enjoyed her Southern hospitality at least once during a visit. I was pleased Heather suggested it.

DREAM ANGEL

* * *

As I stepped through the brass-plated French doors, a mix of old- and new-world extravagance greeted me. From the caramel-colored marble that swirled in soft patterns below my feet to the crystal chandeliers that hung majestically over my head, I felt like the belle of the ball. I imagined myself a princess, only without my prince. An inopportune problem soon to be rectified, I prayed.

Following Heather down a long sandstone hallway, I seemingly glided while admiring the out-of-season flower arrangements that decorated the corridor eventually spilling out to a grand lobby set in the middle of the hotel like a town square. No matter how many times we'd entered this crafted indoor village, my first glance always awed me. There were trees growing in over size planters, reaching upward to a lofty wood beamed ceiling, plush russet colored carpeting, and a fountain lightly showering water in to a basin at the room's center.

On this day, the hotel was all a-buzz. Patrons strolled around the perimeter, enjoying long standing businesses within the hotel each with window dressings full of colorful textiles. And, stationed in the middle of this indoor piazza were deep, comfy couches looking as though they'd been dipped in dark chocolate. My shoulders relaxed at just the thought of sinking in to their luxurious mounds.

"I see a spot, over there." I gestured and began walking toward an empty corner for four. Heather followed close behind.

A few guests were sprinkled throughout the room, spaced a socially acceptable distance apart. They spoke softly, illuminated with soft bedside lighting. Their collective conversations blended into a low, soothing murmur while soft music flowed from a black baby grand piano close by.

Sinking in to the deep cushions, I crossed one slender leg over the other, my attention drifting to Lansky's store front. I wondered if Elvis knew his favorite clothing store, once on Beale Street, had moved and couldn't wait to tell him.

"Look at that packed bar." Heather had her own idea about the important ingredients of tourism.

A large slab of hand-crafted mahogany made as the bar's top and shined from the far end of the room. Patrons sat along its glossy dark crest, enjoying expertly made potions.

"Let's order a drink." I politely waved at a passing waitress, and she nodded in return.

"One vodka, dirty, martini please, and one large unsweetened iced tea when you have time. Thank you." Heather rattled off our order before I could speak.

The waitress smiled politely as she wrote. I watched Heather with great amusement.

"What?"

"Were you thinking about that order on the drive over?"

"Hey, you bake when edgy, I drink." Heather forced a smile.

"I'm not tense." I feigned confidence, and she rolled her eyes but didn't bother to argue.

"If this chasing of angels keeps up, I'm going to need stronger therapy than booze," Heather shot back good naturedly. "Where are we meeting your angel tonight anyway?"

"*We?*"

"Surely you didn't think you'd leave me behind?

"You can't go Heather, he…," I cut my sentence short and pressed my lips together as the waitress reappeared and set our drinks to the table. I waited for her departure before I continued. "He asked me to come alone."

"I'm not letting you out of my sight." Heather took a sip of her drink and squinted.

I opened my mouth to argue, and then paused. It was useless to fight with her. I could see that glint of determination sparkling in her glare. My body sank deeper in to the plush couch. With an accepting sigh I lifted my cold beverage to my lips, my focus shifting, and my hand stalling before I could ever get a taste.

CHAPTER SEVEN

The immense lobby seemed to shrink before my eyes as my focus became glued to Steve sauntering along the outer edges of the room in which we sat. He chatted mindlessly on a cell phone. My mind spun a web of indecision. Should I pretend I didn't see him, I wondered, looking at Heather who was already following my gaze. Her eyes flickered, squinting with a perceptive glimmer before settling further in to tiny slits. I shifted nervously.

When Steve met my gaze, he paused in his conversation, and a spark of surprise turned his business-like expression into a wide grin. I gave a light smile in return, my chest swelling with remorse. I was drowning in my continence when he glanced to Heather and his happy expression cracked. Guilt aside, my curiosity peeked.

"How lucky am I to find you here?" Steve snapped his cell phone shut, and his green eyes held mine a little too intensely.

He never once looked back to Heather, who was inspecting her shoes in a display of strong-willed indifference. He was handsomely dressed, his fashion flair evident in the black suede suit jacket he wore boldly and with confidence. I could not help but admire his deep purple shirt left to drift lazily over the front of his designer jeans.

"Heather, this is the gentleman I spoke of earlier, Steve."

My cheeks hurt from my forced smile, and I prayed her Southern manners would present themselves soon. I didn't want trouble. But, with Heather one never knew what they might get. Her moods were shifty.

She coolly looked up at Steve, who extended his hand. She took it in a swift but polite shake.

"I'm sorry. Where are my manners? Please join us." I patted the seat next to me.

"Thank you. I do prefer the company of lovely ladies to work any day." Steve smiled at Heather, who remained unimpressed.

"I didn't realize you were here on work?" I nervously cleared my throat and scooted over to make room, strategically remaining out of arm's reach.

"I was here tending to unfinished business, but as of right now I'm officially on holiday." Steve dropped his briefcase to the couch and took off his jacket.

"How convenient," Heather spat.

My mouth dropped open and my head snapped to my discourteous friend so quickly I felt a neck muscle twinge in a form of self-induced whiplash.

DREAM ANGEL

"What she means is how *nice* that work was so close to Memphis." I glared in Heather's direction.

Normally a fiery look would have softened Heather's attitude, but she remained cold as stone.

I turned back to Steve and displayed the Southern belle simpleton look I had been perfecting since I was ten years old.

"What do you say we order some food?" I waved at our waitress, who was in no better humor than when we first sat down.

"And another martini please," added Heather.

I watched with great dread as Heather set her chin in that familiar challenging expression that always meant trouble.

"Sam secretly hopes food will keep me sober for when she takes me on her date later." Heather grimaced at Steve.

My mouth again fell open, and shock rendered me mute.

"Oh, you have another engagement tonight?" Steve slowly leaned back seemingly unmoved by Heathers behavior.

"It's a secret." Heather placed a finger to her lips.

"I'm meeting my friend I mentioned to you earlier." *I wish I was home making brownies.*

"Ah, the gent you were waiting for last night? What was his name?" He asked casually.

"I'll give you one guess. It starts with an E." Heather winked at him and Steve cocked his head in bewilderment.

"I-I'm not sure if he'll be there, no." My tone fell to almost a whisper.

"Will you be joining her?" He nodded at Heather, who only grinned while rolling her booze around as though it were fine wine.

Was this for real? Had I fallen into a really bad comedy skit? I found myself actually looking about for the hidden cameras.

"Heather will be joining me seeing as I can't leave her with the way she's downing martinis like iced tea," I said with a dawning realization I had played right into Heather's plan.

Heather conveniently avoided my glare by intently studying the lone green olive floating lazily in her martini.

This can't be happening; I shook my head, already scanning the area, desperate for an easy escape. A red lounge sign glowed from across the room. The hideaway called out to me like an oasis in the desert. And, I'm not ashamed to admit, I paused to consider just how long I might be able to hide amongst the white porcelain and flower scented soaps before one of them came looking for me. It could not have been long enough.

Time crawled forward in tortuous minutes, and then the food arrived, shattering all hopes of me forming an escape. An uncomfortable quiet hovered, and not because our mouths were full of food. A large elephant could have sat down to join us and nobody would have noticed.

"Have you ever been to Atlanta?" Heather finally spoke and almost craned cross the table as if wanting to not miss Steve's response.

"No." Steve said.

"You're sure?"

Steve's eyes narrowed. "I'm sure."

"Oh well, my mistake then," Heather sighed rather dramatically.

Though I was aware Heather often took months to warm up to most strangers, I had not seen her so challenging. Her instant dislike for Steve puzzled me especially when I had told her very little about this afternoon. Why was this different? The question nagged at me and yet I had to shake it off. There was no time to deal with this craziness; I had an angel in waiting.

"You know…" I laid down my food and grabbed a napkin. "We really must be going."

While I began to dig into my purse to pay the bill, I kept one eye on Heather to be sure there was no chance of her ordering a drink on the fly.

"No, here, let me. I crashed your little gathering. It's the least I can do," Steve said, as he reached into his wallet.

Heather's mouth parted to speak and daggers flew from my eyes. She wisely went back for one last sip of her drink.

"Steve, I believe I've caused enough conflict to your day, and now to your evening." I forced a polite smile to my lips, and gathered my personal effects before rising to leave.

"It's no problem, really." He stood.

"Trust me, problems are abundant these days." Heather muttered while gathering her belongings.

Steve gave no sign of having heard Heather, much to my relief. I hesitated briefly, unable to look Heather in the face for fear my anger would surface and I would cause an un-ladylike scene in public. Unlike my friend, I saw no reason for such a blatant display of rudeness. It was better to just leave, quietly.

"Well, if the lucky fellow does not show up, you ladies know where to find me."

"Steve, do yourself a favor, the next time you see me, just run the other way." I smiled before turning to leave, dragging Heather along with me.

We left Steve sitting around three plates of virtually uneaten finger foods. My cheeks burned with anger as I stomped each foot step to make my agitation known. Heather, on the other hand, surprisingly walked a straight line as we left the hotel. I observed her closely. I knew that somewhere inside that martini- fogged brain of hers, she knew something I did not.

* * *

The cab ride back to Graceland was quiet. Heather napped against the car door, and I gazed out at the flashing of street lights as Memphis blazed passed us in the night. The evening air blew cold against the glass, and I rested my head against its surface, enjoying the rousing chill on my skin.

My mind was circling around the day's mystery when we pulled up next to Graceland with a jerk that woke Heather. She rubbed her face clumsily and blinked. Heather had been so still, I had almost forgotten she was there. Her rousing woke my remembrance and a tiny flame of anger sparked again. I stared out the window, fuming while simultaneously admiring the soft glow of illumination that highlighted the dark stately manor. The driver tapped his pencil against the steering wheel.

Heather spoke first. "We're at Graceland?"

I nodded and took note that Heather sounded like her sober self. At least if Elvis did show, she would be aware enough to remember the encounter. However, my gut feeling told me that only two of us would be standing in the cold tonight. Important chat or not, he was not coming.

"Are we not talking to each other now?" Heather sighed.

Without responding, I reached over the seat, paid the fare, and let myself out. I left the door open for Heather.

"Fine, don't speak to me, but really Samantha, Steve's a vulture," Heather said, slamming the door shut for emphasis.

"How do you know?' I spun around.

"I just do!"

"Just because he's pushy in his desire to be with someone, to break his loneliness, doesn't mean he's a monster." My voice trailed off as I realized Steve and I had a lot in common.

The cabbie's tires spun against the wet pavement and he jerked out onto the empty street. We stood side by side in the still night and watched as the red tail lights grew smaller, drifting off in to the night.

"I'm sorry." Heather said.

I looked at her, but held back my words. I knew better to open my mouth when I was this upset. Nothing positive ever came out of a fiery situation. And, when I was ready to speak it would be without the urge to call her names like shit-head—I hate it when she makes me angry enough to curse—which would mean she won. For now, silence was better.

Our breath hung in small white clouds as we walked up to the gates of Graceland. Heather shivered and blew on her hands as I wrapped mine around the cold green bars and glanced into the small white guard shack to my right. A gate security guard, dressed in full uniform blues, sat sipping coffee and reading the paper. I turned and leaned heavily against the closed gate. In rechecking my watch, for what had to be the hundredth time that night, my heart skipped as the clock ticked past midnight.

"He'll be here," Heather said, as she yawned and zipped up her jacket.

"No. He won't." I exhaled.

"What makes you think he won't?"

"Because he said to come alone, and obviously I'm not alone, *Heather.*" I crossed my arms over my chest, and leaned my head back against the gate while looking up at the dark sky.

Street lights hummed over an empty boulevard. The cold cement glistened under the warm glow. Turning, I continued down the boulevard, passing a large green historic marker without stopping to read it.

"What am I, a Chest piece that everyone can move around as they please? Samantha, do this. Samantha, go here!" That feisty attitude I could normally curtail had arrived.

"Maybe something came up?" Heather tried.

"No, he's watching," I uttered mindlessly while scanning Graceland's front lawn.

No signs of life stirred. Every other tree was softly lit by blue, yellow or green landscape lighting. It gave the grounds an overall peaceful look that normally I could feel, but the more I considered my situation, the more focused on my anger I became. Once again, he was just going to leave without a word, I fumed while pacing and nibbling on the tip of my thumbnail.

"If Mr. Elvis Presley thinks I'm walking away from tonight without him, he's got another thing coming," I huffed, turned and almost bumped into Heather.

"What are you planning, Samantha?" Heather asked wearily as I walked ahead of her.

"I'm going to find the easiest way in."

"Graceland is closed, Sam."

"He told me to meet him, and if he *won't* come to me..."

Heather squinted, and then her expression fell.

"We are going to get arrested!" She screeched.

I waved my hands wildly and looked around.

"We won't get caught." I whispered.

Heather shook her head.

"Besides if protecting me is his job, let him get to doing it." My stubborn reasoning sounded simple.

Heather turned a cold shoulder to display her disapproval.

"I'm going in with or without you."

Heather studied the pavement and her shuffling feet. I bit my tongue to keep from saying too much as she looked up at the mansion towering above us. A strong gust blew, stinging my cheek.

"How do we get in?"

I smiled triumphantly.

"Let's look at it from another vantage point."

I was ready for anything. At least that's what I told myself.

"Let's get this over with." Heather grumbled as she flipped the hood on her black jacket up over her head.

We walked north up Elvis Presley Boulevard like a street gang up to no good. The quiet night echoed with the sound of our shoes, lightly slapping against the wet pavement. I did not know exactly where I was going, but my daddy had always told me, "God cannot move an anchored boat." I knew this was not what he had in mind when he shared that wisdom, but I could not allow myself to stay tied to shore while the boat to paradise passed me by. As it was, if God disapproved, I couldn't hear him.

DREAM ANGEL

Next door to Graceland, and only a block up the road, we stopped in front of a small complex of businesses. Brick and looking very much like apartments I looked about the diminutive sized property measuring-up the obstacle that stood between me and my desires. A sign posted on the front fence captured my interest. "Chapel in The Woods", it said. A thrill rushed over me.

With Heather following close behind me, I approached the building and pressed my face to the fence that separated me from my destiny. I could see the security cameras in plain sight, but I shrugged off the warning. Cameras mattered not if I was under an angel's protection, I told myself. As my vision slowly adjusted to the darkness, and even with night-blurry vision, I was still able to scan up the concrete driveway.

Plunging deeper, beyond the brick building, I could clearly observe the hint of a tiny grey church submerged in the darkness. Unlike the church from my childhood, it was not a public place of worship. Here, couples get married, and after the ceremony the newlyweds are allowed to walk to Graceland for pictures. I may not have known much about marriage, but I knew about the dream of marriage. If brides are strolling in white dresses then the walk had to be easily accessible.

"We're stopping?" Heather whispered a hint of wishful thinking in her tone.

My eyes suddenly flashed to the gated steel pressing against my cheek.

"This is the way in." I pointed through the gate, briefly sizing up the odds of scaling the fence.

I wrapped my fingers around the cold chain link, and gave it a quick, firm yank. The fortress was solid.

"What now?" Heather demanded.

I bent down and my hands flinched over the pointy edges along the metal seams of the iron gates. I stood up and let out a sigh. It just couldn't be that easy. Not for me. With my hands on my hips, I turned toward Heather and started to speak. As I twisted, my elbow hit the gate hard enough to make me wince, adding injury to the ongoing insult.

"Crap!" I spat out, not caring anymore if anyone heard.

Click.

I stopped rubbing my throbbing elbow and looked at Heather. I judged by the size of her eyes that she, too, had heard the gate open behind me. I gave it a gentle push with one finger, and it slid smoothly open.

"I don't believe it!" Heather gave me a sideways hug.

"Me neither," I mumbled under my breath.

CHAPTER EIGHT

The bottomless shadows of night enclosed us as we glanced up to the heavens. A blanket of white clouds painted the night's sky over our heads. The thick cover whisked by in a persistent stream that stirred my emotions, swelling the fervor like the opening score of an anticipated epic movie.

Heather and I watched in silence. We were like small fish dropped in to a big pond, neither of us knowing where to go first. We were out of our league. Other than minor speeding tickets neither of us had ever been in trouble with the law. The simple fact that we were standing on private property like some cat burglars should have been a sobering reality. But we were not ourselves, and both of us seemed bent on our own personal agendas. I knew what mine was, but with Heather things were a little more unclear. Granted, I had pushed her pretty hard, but she rarely did anything she didn't want to. And, if this act of insanity was strictly for me, out of friendship, how long could I keep allowing her to put herself in harms-way? No doubt, I cared about her more than I cared about myself, I thought while glancing back to the church and feeling my first twinge of sadness for the night.

"If anything *unfortunate* should happen, promise me you'll save yourself first." I spoke softly. And when I looked back, Heather's who-are-you look made me smile, if only lightly.

"No," she said.

"Then how about we run like the devil is chasing us and meet at an agreed location?" I squinted through the thicket towards the boulevard. "Like the first hotel south of Graceland?"

She grunted and then sighed. "Fine.

It was a short walk, and except for the dull sound of our footsteps, the night was hushed. No tiny eyes glowed back to us from within the shadows that circled. Even the light breeze seemed to blow without a sound. It was as if Mother Nature held her breath.

When we emerged from the woods, I stopped to admire the grand manor off in the distance. Every window was filled with an ominous darkness that aroused sadness within me despite its beauty. Just like the church, nobody dwelled inside Graceland's walls. A soft glow of light beamed up on the outside of the house illuminating it like a precious piece of showcased art.

In contrast, while the front of the manor glowed soft and peaceful the property behind the home was surprisingly bright. I wondered how I had never noticed

DREAM ANGEL

the spotlights during past visits. They shined across the pasture, highlighting the field as intensely as the light of day. And except for the trail along the fence line, virtually no shadows existed for us to hide. I glanced over to Heather who stood expressionless, dazed by the same sight.

He won't let anything bad happen, I barely heard my thoughts of reassurance over the rushing of my heart, surging an echo like that of a raging sea inside my ears.

"Let's do this." Heather suddenly refocused.

Inch by inch, we shuffled along the back of the estate, following an aged white picketed fence. Our progress was slow, and I could hear Heather breathing close behind. I had never realized how far-flung thirteen acres could feel before that night. The plan, as I had thought out thus far, was to circle around back, behind the barn, and arrive at Meditation Gardens on the opposite side, the south side, of the property.

This would prove to be harder than one might think as the ground was hard from the winter freeze, and rolled under my feet. In what seemed like my every step, I stumbled only to catch myself before tumbling to my knees. No wonder Elvis rode around Graceland in golf carts. The terrain was dangerous. Horses, go-carts, cars and motorbikes were all better adapt than strolling around the back forty on two feet.

I reached the tall white barn first. A pungent smell of soiled hay drifted over me on a breeze. Though I believed my steps to be of stealth like silence, a horse nickered from inside causing me to flinch and gasp a breath of stinging cold air in to my lungs. Instantly, I began cooing in low purring sounds but it didn't help. The animal was pounding the barn floor, expressing annoyance with every solid thud that vibrated the dirt under my feet.

Not far behind me, I could see Heather wobbling down the path I had just traveled. The sight of her stumbling, her arms instantly out at her side for more balance, made me smile. It felt like forever, but once at my side, I grabbed Heather and we both crouched down. The barn provided the only real protective shadows in which we could hide. We were almost there.

Meditation Gardens, Elvis' final resting place, was only half a football field away. And, looking out in to the wide open space between us and the gardens I felt my heart sink. It looked to me as bright as Turner field before opening pitch, and still no sign of my angel.

"This is ridiculous, Samantha. If he is *your* hard working angel, why are *we* sneaking around?" Heather hissed.

I closed my eyes and longed for that serene feeling a visit to the Gardens usually brought to me but tranquility refused to settle.

"He won't come now. You know why? Because he's pissed we broke in to his home." Heather continued to fume.

My eyes flew open. I stood straight up, alarm rising in my chest like a hot air balloon suddenly cut free from the grounding ties of safety. I looked up to the nights grey backdrop, and the clouds churned just like my stomach. Thoughts of abandoning my mission began to chip away at my bravado. I was taking one retreating step backwards when over head a white veil parted to divulge what it selfishly concealed all night—the moon.

The fully illuminated planet was high in the sky, brilliant and proud. Under this sign of encouragement, my confidence stirred. I was reconsidering my desire to retreat when the wind gusted, and a new aroma was carried in the breeze. I inhaled a fragrance as original as the man himself, and a smile spread across my face.

"Sam, are you listening to a word I'm saying?" Heather squatted by my side.

"He's in the garden." I whispered.

"He is buried there! This is crazy." Heather plopped down onto the ground. "I can't believe I'm going along with this."

I could hear her ranting, but I remained focused on a bouquet that had traveled an impossible length just for me.

We were now positioned at the back side of Meditation Garden, I could see the gazebo's stepped-brick wall, built in the shaped of a horseshoe and curving around the gravesites like a protective barricade, up ahead. It was open at either end, which made entering the garden easy. The side closest to me seemed the obvious path, but the field I had to cross to get there looked as wide as the Atlantic Ocean.

Placing one foot in front of the other, I moved towards my heart's desire. Grass crunched under my feet. As I drew closer, the sound of splashing water from the Garden's twelve-foot fountain centerpiece grew louder, escalating my anticipation. When I reached the back of the garden's brick wall, I turned and leaned heavily against its hard cold surface, my chest heaving from the thrill.

Heather followed my path across the field. I could see her lips moving as she walked. I was smiling over the sight, straining to hear her light muttering. I imagined she asked herself why she was following her crazy friend on a journey that she could never tell another living soul. She was a trooper, I had to give her that, and I couldn't help but admire her all-for-one-and-one-for-all attitude. The mere thought of her devoted friendship lifted my smile into a wider smirk. That is until I heard a thud, followed by cursing.

"Are you ok?" I whispered as loud as I dared.

"Shit!"

I held back my laughter only to hear hers let go.

"Shhhh..." I giggled out of sheer edginess.

"Oh, who cares, Samantha," Heather said, crawling on her hands and knees. "We're going to jail any minute now, anyway."

Before I could argue, the smart *click-clack* of hard-soled shoes sounded from the other side of the wall. I pushed my back flatter against the brick. The footsteps paused.

My heart pounded, and I waved to Heather, desperate to stop her progress. But she wasn't looking

DREAM ANGEL

at me. She was already up, and walked with eyes cast downward, carefully monitoring each step. My fear quickly escalated. I was straining to hear every sound in the night—a sparse rose bush rustling here, a dead leaf grazing the cement there—while also considering if I shouldn't just make a run for it, grab my friend along the way. And just as I moved, ready to take that first fleeing step, the smell of a sweet cigar floated lazily over the wall. That was no security guard on break. I knew exactly who smoked that very cigar.

"Y'all realize you're trespassin'."

That familiar drawl sent a chill down my spine.

I took one self-controlled step in the direction of his voice, and stopped, briefly reconsidering his tone. His words sounded scolding but not heated.

"Beggin' your pardon *sir* but the owner of the house will gladly make our excuses I'm sure," I said, adding an extra twang to my already southern bell tone.

"That's unlikely, *ma'am*." He mocked.

I could not help but smile even wider. I thought him adorable even when he was annoyed.

Though couldn't see him, he sounded so close. My stomach quivered, and Goosebumps broke out over my arms as I anticipated being in this handsome man's presence.

I meandered along the wall, my downed jacket rustling against its rough surface. I paused before peeking around the corner to find Elvis, at the far end of the gazebo, leaning against one of the four Ionic columns of the pergola. His majestically famous outline was unmistakable even in the shadows of night, the tip of a cigar glowing red in his hand.

"Old habit." Elvis turned the cigar around to inspect it before lifting his foot, and extinguishing its embers against the hard soul of his boot.

A golden radiance of back lighting filtered through the stained-glass and caressed his face while also highlighting something new. Was that facial hair?

"You're as spirited as ever, I see." He pushed himself away from the stone column, and that minuscule challenging grin of his was almost lost when in direct competition with the twinkle in his eyes.

In the dimly lit night, I forgot myself, and let my gaze linger down his dark slacks. When he cleared his throat, my attention quickly returned to his smirking face.

"I simply trust you to keep me safe, sire." I crossed my legs and politely curtsied hoping Elvis' humor would over shadow his displeasure.

"Smart-al-lick." His eyes narrowed at me in a playful retort.

He strode my way in smooth elongated steps that always captivated me. I held my breath as he glided in to the light, drawing nearer, and finally standing so close he was but a kiss away.

"Has anyone told you, you're mulish?" His lips molded around the word, pursing forward, and closer to my own.

Without rebuttal, I laid a hand against his scratchy two-day growth of a beard. His skin was warm under my touch. Lost in the moment, I began to caress his cheek. He placed his hand over mine, and pressed my touch deeper against his skin.

"*You* were late." I exhaled.

"*You* brought company," he returned, raising that charmingly animated left eyebrow of his.

Holding my gaze, he slowly turned into my hand and kissed the inside of my palm. My heart fluttered as his warm lips lingered, and the stirring of emotion I saw in his eyes told me he could feel the throbbing of my pulse that gave away my excitement. I have no idea how long this moment lasted, and I truly could have stood in that very spot held only by his gaze, until time ended.

To my dismay, we were jarred back to the present by a clattering near us on the gazebo's sturdy cement floor.

"Y'all are like bulls in a china cabinet," Elvis dropped my hand.

I had forgotten all about Heather and turned to see her regaining her composure from tripping up the gazebo step. Her eyes grew wider, and her mouth fell agape, as one of the most famous men in the world sauntered her way.

Soon she will understand.

"Hello. I'm Elvis Presley." Elvis extended his hand and spoke as though Heather had no idea who he was.

Unable to believe her own eyes, Heather looked at least three times from me to Elvis and back again. Elvis' hand hung in the air. Heather blinked rapidly. I could not recall If I had ever seen her completely speechless.

"Does your friend speak?" Elvis timidly rubbed the inside of his empty palm with the thumb of his other hand.

"Sadly, yes." I watched Heather's face closely and waited.

She suddenly turned toward me, and narrowed her eyes to tiny slits. I braced myself as her mouth opened to fire a retort, but then unexpectedly clamped shut. Her lips became a single line once again.

"I think she's comin' around." Elvis leaned in.

Heather's heated stare turned back only to melt like molten lava in cool ocean waters.

"You're dead!" She exclaimed.

Her outburst so startled me that I involuntarily covered my open mouth with both hands.

"Yes ma'am, last I looked, I was." Elvis chuckled and once again extended his hand.

This time she took it.

"Friends?" Elvis asked.

Heather's hand disappeared inside his two, and she looked down. I wondered if she understood she was touching an angel.

"Friends," she smiled.

The snap of a twig sounded. Heather and I both turned as something or someone approached outside the garden. Elvis let go of Heather's hand. My heart felt as if it leaped up in to my throat.

"What was that?" I whispered.

"Security," Elvis coolly folded his arms across his chest.

DREAM ANGEL

"Security!" Heather and I spoke in unison.

"I-I thought you would handle that?" I lowered my voice.

"Do my job, you mean?" His eyes narrowed. "I'll do it alright. I should turn you over my knee right here."

My cheeks flushed from embarrassment while I thought about a punishment that might actually hold wonderful benefits. Forever reading my thoughts, Elvis rolled his eyes. I smiled feebly.

"Well you... and the gate... it opened." I was babbling like a teenager caught necking in the living room.

"Honey, you would have climbed the front walls of Graceland had I not let you in," Elvis said, pointing in the direction of the famous rock walls in front of his home.

My heart sunk over the realization that I would have done just that. Justified frustration or not, I had, for all intensive purposes, broken in to his home. I might as well have thrown rocks at his bedroom window.

"I told you he'd be ticked." Heather muttered.

"Oh, hush up." I growled.

"Ladies, there's no time for bickering. Security is headed this way."

"You're going to let us go to jail?" I stomped like a child.

Elvis chuckled. "Honey, freewill gets everybody in to trouble."

He placed his hands on my shoulders and spun me around in the direction from which we had just come.

"I gave them boys a little something to keep em busy, so I'd say you have about twenty minutes."

My eyes widened as his words sank in. "Twenty minutes?" My voice quavered.

"Nineteen," Elvis' eyes danced.

Judging by his smirking he was enjoying my predicament just a tad too much.

"W-where should we go?" I huffed.

"Get out any ole way as long as it's fast," Elvis said, with a gentle push that sent me stumbling forward.

Heather raced by me without a word. Her swiftness stunned me.

"What *are* you waiting for?" Elvis asked.

"Where will you be?"

Elvis' are-you-kidding-me glare told me I was pushing him to the limits.

"Samantha, I will find you, now, get!" he slapped his hands together sharply.

I flinched but still did not move. Elvis looked down at his watch, and I then understood he wasn't kidding. As if turned loose from starting blocks, I ran. I paused just long enough at the edge of the garden to shoot a last glance over my shoulder. Elvis was still laughing.

Oh, he makes my blood boil, I stomped.

CHAPTER NINE

I suppose there are worst things a girl could choose to see at the end of her short-lived "free" life than Graceland's back pasture. At least this was what I told myself while I raced for what I believed might very well be my last moment outside of prison. I did not care how much noise I made, only that I took the shortest route to the exit. I figured I had an angel's protection for at least fifteen more minutes. Give or take a few. After that, I knew only that Elvis would refuse to intervene on my behalf. No doubt he was teaching me a lesson. I did deserve it, but I was still none the happier.

I prayed that Heather would stick to our agreement. Admittedly my route was not the shortest by any means. My hope was to simply follow the white fence behind the barn, and run as if my life depended on it until I reached the gate. How hard could that be, I silently scrutinized, and then cringed hoping nobody of importance was listening.

My feet dug in to the icy ground. I reached the corner of the barn, and like a race car sliding in to a corner I glided through it without breaking tread. Just as I cleared the white building, that same horse snickered loudly. I screamed out into the night but never broke my stride. Half way across the field, I saw Heather's athletic frame scaling the side pasture fence, near the church, and disappear into the brush. I stumbled to a stop. I'd never seen her run so fast. It stunned me almost as much the cold air that filled my chest and burned my lungs. My heart pounded. I scanned from one side of the pasture to the other.

I had been at a standstill for barely thirty seconds when, to my horror, a bright beam of light sliced through the shadows near the barn behind me. I quickly turned to face it and gasped to see not just one, but three searchlights speeding down the pasture. The way out was ahead but was still too far away. I would never make it before whoever was behind the lights caught up with me. I shrank backward into the fence, but instead of providing refuge, the fence began to buckle. Instinctively, I jumped away.

My mind worked quickly, and adrenaline flooded my veins at the sound of approaching voices. I pushed harder against the spongy section of fence and had a surge of hope. Eagerly, I ran both hands up and down the length of the fence while pushing, searching for its weakest point.

Bingo!

Two of the boards were beyond spongy and rotten all the way through. I glanced back to the Gardens, allowing the time span of a heartbeat to pass, before I turned and kicked the boards with as much force as my fatigued little legs could muster. I felt it give under pressure and I quickly bent over, pulling and pushing. I squeezed my slight frame through the crack and thanked the Lord for not giving me that hour-glass figure I had wanted so badly as a teenager.

In a blink of an eye, I had stepped off one man's private property and onto another's. Sure, I had no idea where to go next, I never had to care about this side of the fence before. I could not afford even one second to look around and get my bearings. Instead, I took off at a dead run in the first direction I saw praying I had made the right choice.

The luxuries of home security lights were almost nonexistent in this 60's era neighborhood on the east side of Graceland. Blackness engulfed me, and I was instantly running blind. I stumbled over what felt like children's toys and quickly became tangled up in line hung laundry. I was like a puppet caught up in my own strings, thrashing about, and caring not what noise I made. A moment later, my vision adjusted. Finally some hope, I thought as not far ahead, the glow from a lone neighborhood street lamp could be seen. It radiated just outside the gated yard in which I stood. And, for a moment I simply stared at the glow, as if it may hold some guidance, before lowering my gaze to the only thing standing between me and my freedom—a chain link fence. Without hesitating, I headed for it and scaled it easily.

Running like the wind I headed south down the back streets of the mature White Haven neighborhood. I stomped through puddles and felt the water as it rushed in to my shoes for the second time that day. My continence felt as saddened as my socks were soggy. Not only had I broken the law, but I had vandalized property, and jeopardized a friend's safety in making my escape.

Mother would have been so proud, I sniffed.

My stride was even and steady. The feel of the solid road under my feet and the sound of my shoes slapping the pavement helped to clear my mind. We agreed on a rendezvous point, I reassured myself as I cut through another residents front lawn, turned west—past Vernon's, Elvis' father's house—and down what I now recognized to be Dolan drive.

Heather will be there, my determination escalated. She had to be.

As I neared Elvis Presley Boulevard, I heard the scream of sirens. I slowed to a walk, warily approaching Graceland's south side, the side closest to the Boulevard. When I peeked around the corner, I couldn't help but gasp. The front of Graceland was completely illuminated by the bright blue flashing lights of at least four Memphis police cruisers and two Shelby County sheriff's cars. If this was the usual protocol to stop a couple of over-eager fans, heaven help an actual criminal!

DREAM ANGEL

Returning to Graceland tonight was out of the question. I was by far not the first woman to think she could breach their security, and they would be rightfully quick to assume I was the culprit returning to the scene. Besides the house sat too far back from the road, I knew I would see nothing from the street. If they were arresting Heather right now—I prayed not—I would be no help if I was sharing her cell. Moving away from the commotion, I crossed to the opposite side of Dolan Street, away from Graceland, and slowly headed south. I forced myself to meander as though I hadn't a care in the world.

Stalled at the cross walk, I leaned heavily against the light post. I was beyond exhausted. My stomach was churning as I had one eye on the turmoil up the road and another on a bush in case the need to get sick suddenly overcame me. As I caught my breath, I watched a bright red vacancy sign flickering from the popular Inn across the street. It was set back in the shadows, and away from the blazing street lights. I breathed deep, and on my exhale the hand flashed green. I crossed Elvis Presley Boulevard, my steps quickening as I neared the Inn. To my right, another police cruiser speed up Graceland's drive with sirens wailing and lights flashing. I turned my face.

The bank nearby flashed the time. Was it really 2A.M.? The darkness is deep at this hour, I considered as I stood in the parking lot. The shadows seemed to watch me, and my childish apprehensions returned. I had an overwhelming need to just go home. I needed a do-over for the day. A get out of jail free card, I thought while looking for any sign of my friend.

Only a few cars were parked. One silver truck to my left and a black four door import to my right, but no Heather. I took a step towards the sedan then stopped. Now, as far as I knew neither Elvis nor my friend had ever owned a car made in Japan. What now, I challenged myself, feeling the panic rising again in my chest. I was one second away from hysteria when a vehicle from behind turned on its head lights.

Quickly, I spun around shielding my eyes from the intense glare. Its engine turned over, and the large utility vehicle rumbled in the night. It was rugged like an extreme athlete while simultaneously retaining the grace of a ballet dancer. The pearly white hood glistened. I raised my hands in the air, recognizing I was going to jail. Then the car flashed its lights, once and then twice.

The tinted windows made identifying the driver impossible. I took half-a-dozen tentative steps closer, allowing intrigue to over-ride my usual good sense. The car inched forward, and the red and gold shield on the grill caught the light. The emblem glimmered and I smiled, positive the driver was indeed a friend. Who else would be behind the wheel of this purring, perfectly polished Cadillac Escalade?

With the vehicle now stopped at my side, I lightly tapped the driver's window. It slid down as if it were a scene from an old gangster movie.

"Get in," Elvis ordered.

DREAM ANGEL

※ ※ ※

I was thrilled to see Heather when I opened the door. She smiled weakly from the back seat. Her fragile demeanor reminded me of our dismal circumstances, and the happiness I had momentarily enjoyed faded. I shot a glance at Elvis, who sat stoically with both hands on the steering wheel. He stared down the street watching the drama that unfolded around his beloved Graceland. My shoulders wilted. I climbed in and reached for my seat belt. Heather and I exchanged tense glances. I reached over the seat, took her hand, and gave it a gentle squeeze. Her smile flickered.

Elvis' solemn demeanor settled over the car like an unwelcomed cloud on a summer day. My hands began to sweat under the pressure, and I imagined lightening flashing inside those stormy baby blues. Nobody spoke as he slipped the shiny Cadillac in to gear and crawled towards the main road. Elvis road the breaks as yet more police cars raced by. As his jaw muscles flexed working a stick of gum, he was decidedly displeased with the chaos I had caused. He had too much respect for the law to see any humor in this show of force over my antics.

He turned the car south down Elvis Presley Boulevard, away from the uproar. I held Heather's hand as he turned one corner, then another, winding through the back roads. Only when my hotel finally came in to view did I exhale. The car bounced over the lip of the hotel entrance, and I winced over my aching body reminding me that there were always consequences.

Elvis guided the vehicle under the brightly lit guest awning and smoothly came to a stop. A soft light filled the car, accentuating Elvis' features. I hadn't clearly been able see him, until now and once I did, I'd wished I hadn't. His expression remained indecipherable. Flat. I had ruined everything, again.

Heather opened her door first, and stepped out. I paused before opening mine, my hand stalled over the handle. I tried to find the courage to speak, but words failed me. Every time I opened my mouth to apologize, tears chocked me. I resigned myself to leave. I pulled on the handle, but before I could make my exit the door click to a lock position.

"Not you." Elvis said flatly. "You're with me."

Had this been any other time, those words would have been like a saving breath to a drowning victim. My heart would have soared back to life. But as it was, a pang of dread filled my chest. I was not ready to have this conversation with him. Not now. Not while he looked so angry. I looked out the window to Heather and smiled weakly.

"*It's ok*," she mouthed as I waved goodbye.

Stone faced and flushed with emotion, Heather watched as we pulled away. Her tall figure became smaller and smaller in my side view mirror. I inhaled deeply, assuring myself she knew where we were headed. Why else would she be so willing to stay behind? The thought comforted me, but the silence did not.

Elvis drove one handed, leaning his free arm heavily against the ledge of the closed window. I watched his profile in my peripheral vision and hoped he didn't notice. He drove aggressively, running a yellow light and then a red. His eyes fixed on the review mirror. It was not until we entered a virtually deserted Hwy 78 that his white-knuckled grip relaxed on the steering wheel.

The fact that we were not talking saddened me more than if we had been in a heated conversation. I tried to ignore the tension and pass the time by studying the shiny dark wood grain that lined the interior of the Escalade. It was beautiful, admittedly, but soon, an urge to fill the silence with mindless whistling threatened to overcome me.

"Warm enough?"

I jumped at the sound of his voice.

"Yes, thank you," I managed to mutter, while holding back the more formal "Yes, Sir," that lingered on my tongue and was more appropriate.

The night went by dreamily outside my window. Other than one shiny headlight far behind us, we were the only car on the road. I counted every mile marker along the deserted highway while Elvis' eyes continued to burn into my very soul rattling me to my core.

"This is not a game, Samantha." His words held a touch of coldness. "You could have been hurt tonight."

I opened my mouth for a rebuttal, but he shook his head, silencing me.

"Had we spoken earlier, as I wanted, you would not have been in any danger tonight."

I opened my mouth to speak and he once again shook his head rendering me silent.

"From now on, you'll do as I say." He waited and became clearly perturbed when I choose not to respond.

"Alright," I answered softly.

The car drifted from one lane to the next without even so much as a glance from the driver. His eyes were on me. I suppressed every survival instinct to remind him to watch where he was going.

"Without question," he added.

I hesitated, considering the ramifications of a promise no woman wishes to make to any man. When after a moment he raised a single eyebrow I immediately affirmed my alliance with a nod.

"Yes, ok. Whatever you say," I sighed.

His head tiled slightly.

"W-what'd I do now?" I barely recognized my whiny voice.

"Nothing. It's not often a man hears those words coming from a woman." Turning back to the road, he gave me a sideways glance. "I'd forgotten how much I like it."

I covered my face with my hands and lowered my head into my lap. He gently placed his palm to my back, caressing in slow circles.

"Can I ask where we are going?" I mumbled into my hands.

"Home," Elvis said.

"Home...as in Atlanta?" I sat straight up, my eyes flashing to the GPS display on the cars dash.

South meant Mississippi, and from Mississippi, Georgia was about three hundred miles.

"Yes, home. That is unless you'd rather we go back and you can tend to my broken fence?" Elvis spoke evenly and my shoulders slumped.

"Sorry."

He gave me an unreadable look. "You should try to sleep."

I sighed, but Elvis paid me no mind. My angel's focus was glued in the rear view mirror and a single car light that followed some fifty yards behind.

CHAPTER TEN

In the half shadows of night I raced through a dense jungle. I slapped at low hanging limbs, and jumped over fallen trees that had long ago melted in to the landscape. Light filtered through the forest's high canopy like moon beams from heaven and lit my way. Ahead, a white tiger sped gracefully through the undergrowth. His powerful paws pounded the ground, and while I lurched about, clumsy, on my two feet he floated effortlessly on four.

I longed to be one with him, to possess him. Though my desire was strong, my physical limitations made me weak. I was lagging further and further behind, a burning sensation threatening to seize my chest. When I could take no more, I reluctantly eased in to a trot and then stumbled to a stop. Without even so much as a glance back, the mighty feline disappeared deeper into the fog. I'm only human, I told myself, while drawing in deep wheezing breaths of moist woodland air that pierced my wilting lungs. I wondered how a mere mortal was expected to keep up, and then realized the answer lied in the obvious—I wasn't.

It began to rain, light at first and escalating fast. Over my head a light flashed, and I looked up just in time to hear the first crack of thunder. The rain cascaded, and like acid the water began to peel away the murky forest around me. Layer by layer Mother Nature melted before my eyes. Gone were the trees, and in their place were cold steel beams.

The reality of a man-made world surrounded me. I stood not on a woodland path but on cement. I was no longer flanked by moss covered stone, but rather metal chairs, all stacked in neat little rows around me. My state of bewilderment froze me where I stood. Then the last bit of nature melted away, and I realized I was shoulder to shoulder in a vast room full of strangers.

There were hundreds if not thousands, all looking upward to the heavens, and just as I began to pray I might wake from this eccentric dream, a spotlight flashed. It jumped from wall to wall and face to face, keeping time with a jungle-like beat that now pulsated throughout the room. The melody surged while the crowd grew tense, anticipation throbbed like the life's blood I could feel rushing my veins. I took my first step back, my mind set on bolting, when a woman next to me screamed out a name known across the world: E-L-V-I-S!

Flinching, I turned just in time to see my graceful white tiger leaping out from the wings of what I now realized was an arena. He prowled across the stage. His slithering gate transformed him until he became the Greek-like Adonis the world so loved.

He wore a white jumpsuit that opened down the middle to expose his tanned torso. The fringe that hung from the razor-sharp lines of his sleeves fluttered with his every movement. A woven belt comfortably hugged his lean waist. The spotlight reflected off of his glistening, jet-black hair. His left leg quivered with the beat as he snatched the microphone and brought it to his full parted lips.

"Y'all never been down south to much," Elvis started, and was quickly interrupted by a wave of screams.

The outer edges of my mirage remained blurry, but the exquisite vision in front of me was crystal clear. My pulse surged when his lip curled into a smile from behind the microphone.

"You just think you know what I'm going to do." He drawled and the arena roared.

Always the consummate performer, Elvis allowed the audience to simmer. He waited, with his thumbs hooked through his belt, his one leg keeping time with the bass-line beat. When he felt we were ready, he began to explain the story behind a song that everyone knew. With each word, the anticipation grew, until everyone agreed that scrumptious plant that grew out in the woods and the fields had magical powers. Everybody called it, "Polk Salad".

"Now that's a Polk, h-up," Elvis turned, drew a fist up, and with a thrust of his hip penetrated the air, "salad."

Women all around me screamed. The sight of such sexual prowess evoked their deepest fantasies. The passion that he induced from the stage was raw. He was, for all intensive purposes, making love to every woman in that audience and his little smirk told me he knew it.

My own excitement was predestined to spill over the top, and like the thousands of others, I too found myself screaming out his name. Elvis! Elvis! Elvis!

He looked down to me with an apprehensive smile that sank my heart into the pit of my stomach. His eyes were tender but they conveyed only sadness, and it was in that sadness that I saw a reflection of my own fears and grief. I stretched out my hand to him but he began to fade.

No!

"Samantha, honey," a faint voice spoke.

With my eyes closed tight, I smiled lightly at the sound of my name, spoken from lips that never failed to rouse me.

"Sam," the voice grew bolder.

My eyes popped open to reveal a smirking Elvis. I squinted as the morning sunlight filled the car. The brilliance made keeping my eyes open difficult, but I could clearly see his steady gaze resting on me.

Thank God, you're still here, I sighed, and then blushed as his smirk spread in to a wide smile.

"Sweet dreams?" He beamed.

"Yes, thank you," I said, wondering what shade of red I was this time.

Avoiding Elvis' pleased face I turned and pushed myself up away from the door panel. A twinge of pain shot down my neck. I glanced around the empty parking lot, not at all understanding where we were. Then, off in the distance, I saw it, a small painted-many-times-over white clapboard house in a court yard. It was cordoned off by many other buildings not at all from the same era. Elvis followed my gaze.

"Are we in Tupelo?"

East Tupelo, Mississippi, was only ninety minutes from Memphis, and judging by the sun's position, in an eastern sky, it had to be at least 8:00 am.

How long had we been parked, I wondered, and was not surprised to find my angel listening.

"Awhile," Elvis said, rubbing the stubble over his chin. His eyes scanned over the landscape before returning back to me with a smile. "You were resting, and I was… enjoying the scenery."

The thought of Elvis watching me sleep had my heart all a pitter-patter. The idea of him patiently waiting for me to get the rest my body needed, that his did not, made me feel treasured and special. Maybe he was not as upset with me as I had previously believed. I could only hope.

Outside my warm sanctuary, the sun looked fresh in a new day that could have passed for spring. But, when Elvis swung open the car door to exit, a crisp light winter breeze reminded me otherwise. I grabbed my coat, and together we stepped out into the day. While Elvis zipped up his waist-length jacket, I considered how he still looked time dated like a character from one of his own movies. I tried not to stare, but when he placed a felt hat on top of his head, I had to cover up my smile. He was the spitting image of 1967. My favorite year!

* * *

Nestled in the middle of a quiet neighborhood, the park named after its famous resident, was not all that large. Constructed in an imperfect rectangle, and at half the size of a football field, it was framed by some of the oldest oak trees in town. Besides the residence, the attraction offered visitors a museum, a shop full of souvenirs and two churches to explore at their leisure.

Taking my hand, Elvis led the way. The spring in his step suggested he was happy to be home, and while he was busy admiring the landscape I struggled to contain my own excitement. I was in Tupelo. No, I was in Tupelo "with" Elvis Presley! This was every fan's dream. I wanted to skip beside him, not walk.

A million questions popped in to my head. What did he think of all the changes? Does the neighborhood look different, and if so how? My curiosity was insatiable, but I held it all in. It was only in feeling my heavy stare did he glance down to me, and when he did, I returned with a grin so wide my cheeks hurt. He simply smiled back, and gave my hand a tender pat before heading for his childhood home.

DREAM ANGEL

We stood in front of the shotgun shack, a design that has always impressed me. What it lacked in size it made up for in charm. The efficient layout is long and narrow, but open and without much separation of space. Heat was not wasted, and when needed breezes sailed through in the warmer seasons. It was undoubtedly a house representing its time, and the times were rough.

Elvis let go of my hand, and I turned to see him absolutely beaming. The serenity I saw in his eyes reminded me of what my daddy had once told me about how, when we pass on, we become all knowing. And when Elvis stepped in closer to his home, his eyes shined with an understanding that said he no longer questioned why God handpicked him to be Elvis Presley. He had come full circle. And, for all the "whys" that had once haunted him while alive, he now had all the answers.

The day was young. Elvis strolled along the outer edges of the park, pausing here and there as if we had nothing but time. I should have felt at ease but I was on edge. Not wanting to be left behind, I quickly jumped in behind him and followed him up the cemented path in the middle of the plaza. I was hot on his heels. So much so, that when he turned back to see where I'd gone, he bumped in to me.

A smile flickered across his lips. "Let's, uh…just relax. Ok, honey?" He sounded with an extra measure of calm assurance that I was sure was for my benefit.

I nodded my alliance, and held back the need to remind him that people do work in these buildings, and the start of the work day was coming fast. No doubt the "real" Elvis would not go so easily unnoticed in his home town!

When he continued up the path, I remained behind in a feeble display of independence. I'll show him, I thought, but my stomach was already churning the minute he moved from my side. It was only when he stepped up to inspect a bronze sculpture of himself as a child, at the center of the park, did I manage to take my mind off of my worries.

"The rest is history, so they say." I spoke softly.

"Is that what they say?" He asked, and leaned in closer to inspect the details of the guitar.

He took a step back and seemed to ponder the small boy, destined to cross all racial lines long before he was twenty, with quiet admiration.

"I wanted a rifle for my birthday, but mama wouldn't hear of it."

"I thought it was a bicycle?"

"No, that was my second choice," he said, then glanced at me sideways. "I played excited for their sake."

To hear him speak of his family only reminded me of my own. Home suddenly didn't sound so bad. I found myself picturing my own childhood, a safe place full of family Sundays, and profound conversation around a dinner table. The memories were so clear; I could almost smell my mother's cooking.

DREAM ANGEL

Although deep in thought, I was torn from my moment by the sound of an approaching vehicle. Quickly, my attention refocused to a black Ford truck rolling up the street. I froze.

Now, a truck alone is not all-together odd, but one with oversized tires and a tow wench strapped to the grill unnerved me. It had a menacing, and even more disturbing, familiar look. What was it that rang a bell of worry inside of me? I couldn't place if it was the concern of discovery that had my hands quaking at my side, or the nagging feeling that I'd actually seen the vehicle before. I pretended to dig for something imaginary in my purse while monitoring its every move. I wanted to be sure that it didn't make a sudden turn for the parking lot. And, if it did I'd do—I didn't know what—but it would no doubt have supported Elvis' earlier belief that I was way too jumpy.

Breathe, Sam.

The truck paused at the stop sign, and lingered only briefly before turning to head out of town. Once out of sight, I let out a sigh only to draw it back when a click followed by a hum sounded from the main building. I spun around. It was only the water fountain nearby. I quickly looked for Elvis, and found him standing near the brick museum up on the knoll. He meandered showing no signs of noticing the unexpected passer-by. My heart settled a notch.

The resonance of cascading water echoed with a soothing sound. I closed my eyes. I concentrated on the smell of winter in the morning breeze. The moist crisp scent of fresh dew on the grass, and the spice from a bark exposed birch tree close by. This was a new day, a day far from the confusion and the troubles of last night. I was going to get it right today, I promised myself.

I elected not to follow Elvis. I thought it best to give him privacy, a luxury he was denied in life. Besides, simply watching him as he read a series of six-foot plaques in front of the museum was a joy in itself. The way he stood, hands behind his back and the fingers of his left hand clasped around his right wrist, gave him an air of sophistication. He was uncommonly still. His broad shoulders blocked my view so that I couldn't see which section of heartfelt sentiments, written in his honor, had captured his attention. I tried to envision the words from memory, but it had been too long between visits. As time passed he brought his hands back to the front. I smirked, envisioning him now fiddling with the ring finger of his left hand, a nervous habit I found adorable.

The tranquil sight of Elvis the angel, reading words left for Elvis the man eased my nervous tension. I was beginning to consider if I shouldn't give up my watch, and go to him, but then he turned. He headed back my way, towards the tiny shack. His blue eyes locked onto mine as he sauntered in a spellbinding strut that warmed me from head to toe despite a chilly morning.

"Come sit with me," he said, passing me and stepping up to his home.

DREAM ANGEL

He took a seat on the small two-person porch swing that hung on the tiny veranda. He sat relaxed, in typical Elvis style, with his knees set wide apart and his long legs stretched out across the deck. His broad smile was like that of a proud son returning home after a long time away.

"Well, come on now. I can't wait all day." He patted the vacant seat next to him. The bench swing barely held two people.

I looked to the "must-have-ticket" sign.

"Ah, ignore that."

He did not allow for any extra space between us when I sat, he merely lifted his arm and encircled my shoulders to bring me closer. Finally, I was in his embrace. My whole body seemed to sigh. I reclined against his sturdy chest and his warm cheek rested against my own. This was what I required, what I needed. I closed my eyes.

"Comfy?" His breath tickled my ear.

"M-m-m," I purred.

My blood warmed with ease as it always did when I was so close to this dreamy man. Slowly, he rocked us in the stillness of the morning. Of all my experiences in my young life, this moment could easily have been considered my best, my heaven on earth. Everything was perfect. We were alone. The birds were whistling a tune all around us, celebrating the sunshine that made the chill that much more bearable, and I felt safe.

This was what I wanted back at Graceland. The thought came before I could stop it.

"Are you telling me, Samantha Lynn, that after all your antics all you wanted from me was a hug?" His chest rumbled with a hearty chuckle.

I sighed. "It would have been a good start," I teased and felt Elvis' lips brush my flushed cheek.

"You do realize baby girl if we were to, uh," he cleared his throat in my ear, "indulge in our human weaknesses, our situation would only become further complicated?"

I was both distracted by his admission of having considered such desires while simultaneously puzzled over what exactly "our situation" was. I could not decide which mystified me more, why he came back or when he would leave. All I knew was his evitable departure felt like an anvil of doom hanging over my head. It swung ever so slowly, reminding me there were still so many words left unsaid between us. I'd escaped it once, but could I do it again?

The last thing I wanted to hear was an angelic version of a Dear John speech spoken from his lips. I decided right then, if I had anything to say about it, I would avoid this "talk" my angel was so frantic to have back at Graceland.

"Now Samantha, I want you to promise me, no more stunts." Elvis' voice suddenly turned serious.

"What? Of course not," I fumbled, batting my eyes and wondering which of all my actions, exactly, qualified as "stunts". Probably, all of them!

"Samantha, promise me now," he demanded, not at all distracted by my efforts to appear innocent.

I nodded, careful not to speak words that I might not be able to keep.

"No. I want hear you say it." He slowed the swing.

"Okay, okay I'll behave," I said, and secretly crossed my fingers on both hands while he hugged me tighter.

Elvis returned to swaying us once again, he began to hum a tune. I believed it to be more of a habit, a way of relaxing than anything else. Whatever it was, I loved it! I closed my eyes and listened to the reverberation of his voice. To my surprise, right in the middle of the song, he lightly kissed the base of my neck. What was that for? I pondered while the feel of his soft full lips woke my desires, and I resisted the urge to turn and taste his mouth.

"What's your job in heaven?" I strategically shifted course.

"Again with this *job* business," he muttered and picked up my left hand.

I bit down on my lower lip, watching as his hand engulfed mine, and his long tapered fingers entwined with my own.

"Well, how about your heavenly task then? My father preaches we'll all have one, you know."

"Your hands are so delicate honey, just like the rest of you." He said, now rolling my fingers over in his hand, and inspecting each one with interest.

Once satisfied, he kissed them, and then placed my hand on top of his knee. He held it there, and his leg bounced with untamed energy under my palm.

I couldn't help but imagine what all that vigor might accomplish when properly focused.

"I bet you follow God around all day singing to his every step," I added, hoping to break the spell that was spinning my head. "That's it, your God's theme music!"

My idea must have tickled him, because he dropped my hand, and placed a firm but quick peck to my cheek.

"I do sing honey, but everyone sings in heaven." He tilted his head so that he could see my face. "And, Heaven's work starts right here on earth, you know."

"I-I don't think I've been called to do anything special."

"Honey, everyone's called. It's just a matter of listening."

He spoke while wrapping dark strains of my hair around his finger. A quiver corkscrewed down my spine.

"Even me?"

"Especially you," he whispered so close his breath was hot against my ear.

What a flirt. Admittedly, I loved our easy banter. We had this game we'd play. I'd act like I didn't want his attention, and he'd try harder. It was childish, and usually reserved for the playground, but we enjoyed it. The problem was, on this day, he really was driving me mad.

"Do you know what my calling is?" I prayed that he had missed the crack of my voice.

Elvis snuggled closer, burying his nose into my hair. "Baby, you smell so good," he growled, "I'd forgotten."

He wasn't playing fair. Sure Elvis had a quirky sense of humor, but he knew exactly what he was doing to me which only made me dig in my heels more.

"You're not going to tell me, are you?" I said with a flat tone that suggestion I was unmoved, but my jaw hurt from clenching my teeth.

He unraveled me from his embrace and stood.

"Nope," His teasing smile shined down to me.

I couldn't help myself, I stuck out my tongue but he only grinned wider. With a wink, he drew in a deep, chest-widening breath, hoisted up his pants and stepped off the porch. Without looking my way, Elvis held out his hand. I didn't hesitate to take it.

"Let's get you home, baby girl."

CHAPTER ELEVEN

As we sped through the miles of predictable highway, soulful music filled the Escalade. As sad as it was, the blues guitar on the local radio station soothed me. I watched Elvis as he drove. He tapped lightly on the steering wheel with the beat and smiled playfully, but his eyes remained unreadable and shaded behind a pair of trendy aviators.

I was pondering what my heavenly job might be when my stomach interrupted with a thought of its own.

"When was the last time you ate?" Elvis turned his head toward me, but the dark tint kept his eyes hidden.

"Lunch time yesterday," I said.

Keeping his eyes on the road, he reached over and gently patted my hand. "I'm sorry. I forget about the basic needs some times."

I'm sure God likes it that way. I started to chuckle, but stopped when Elvis looked my way. I opened my mouth to protest these constant mental intrusions, but then clamped it shut. Why bother? I had never claimed to be a saint, but I had at least considered myself a lady. Modesty was proving to be difficult when my every thought was like an open book. My problem seemed hopeless. And I was about to give in when a solution as light as a feather, but with the impact of a brick, fell to mind.

A devilish smile crept across my face. One times one is one. Two times one is two. Three times one, is three, I beamed.

Slowly Elvis reached up and removed his glasses. "What are you up to, now?" His eyes narrowed.

"Trying to get through the one-sees," I turned away to look out the window. *Four times one is four. Five times one is five.*

'Follow That Dream' was my favorite of Elvis' movies. As far as I was concerned, his role as the tender but dim witted Toby Kwimper was nothing short of comedic genius. In the movie Toby used his schooling, or lack of, to keep the girls away. The more aggravated the women became with his time-table ritual, the less likely they were to hang around, tempting him in to matrimony. Toby's infuriating game was brilliant.

The concentrated look on Elvis' face told me he was busy struggling to decipher the meaning of my sudden fascination with mathematics. My thoughts were truly mine. Privacy was bliss, and it was also fleeting.

His eyes flashed with an understanding. "You never cease to amaze me, baby," Elvis' laughter skipped.

I could tell by the way he quickly clamped his lips, and looked away that he was trying not to outright laugh at me. But then unable to resist, he'd look back and started to laugh. I tilted my sharp chin higher as our shiny white chariot crossed the Alabama state line.

When the next available exit presented itself Elvis did not pass it up. He eased the utility vehicle off the highway, and rolled up to the drive-in-window of a tiny white stucco building. The smell of grease turned my stomach, but I ordered anyway.

"Can we now just get a room?" I said while picking at the only part of my food that was edible.

Completely lost in the gross-factor of my meal, it took me a moment to realize he hadn't answered. When I looked up, that Cheshire grin of his had me reaching for a napkin. What was on my face, mustard or mayonnaise? I was whipping my lips when my understanding finally cracked like a whip.

"Oh! No, I-I didn't mean I wanted a "room" with you," I said, adding the insulting air quotations as if my blunder wasn't embarrassing enough.

Elvis eyes widened.

"No! I-I don't mean you're not desirable because, well, that's just ridiculous."

Smirking, he just shook his head.

"Ah, never mind." I waved him off with a sigh. "I-I just need to shower to feel like a girl again, please."

"Ok baby, we'll stop so that you can uh," he shot me a distractingly flirtatious grin, "become a woman."

The tiny hairs on the back of my neck pricked.

* * *

"Would you and your father like one or two rooms?" The middle aged man behind the counter asked.

I looked up from the registration paperwork.

"Excuse me?"

"The elderly gentlemen with you, ma'am," he said, and nodded across the room.

I glanced over my shoulder. There sat a vigor Elvis, leg crossed and a newspaper open in his lap. I was unaware he had followed me inside. When the man at the counter cleared his throat, impatient for an answer, Elvis looked up from his read. His attention flashed to me, and then to the hotel employee. Smiling, he held up two fingers in a helpful response to a question I was incapable of answering.

"Yes sir," the man said, and then he scurried off for what I assumed were our room keys.

Curious, I inspected Elvis closely. He didn't look a day over 32 to me. What was he seeing that I was not, I was just about to ask when the worker returned. He dropped two keys to the desk with a loud clang, interrupting the moment. I made a mental note to inquire later.

With all the official guest papers signed, by me, we headed for our rooms. A hot bath was almost all that was on my mind as I headed for my hotel room. I say almost because I'd be lying if I said the sight of Elvis carrying my bag, accompanying me to a private room, didn't spark a longing. Though a line had been drawn months ago,

DREAM ANGEL

I still wanted him in every way that a woman wants a man. And it didn't matter that we'd been down this road before, unsuccessfully. The electricity between us was instinctive, powerful, and sadly forbidden.

Two times one is two, two times two is four, I had graduated to the two-sees.

"Are you going to do the times tables every time you want to shut me out?" He asked as he fumbled with the room key.

"When you stop reading my every mental blurb, I'll stop doing multiplication." I entered the room, chin set, and frustration surging.

I inhaled his spicy cologne as I passed. *Two times three is six, two times four is eight.* I could feel Elvis' eyes following me. He dropped my bag on the bed and walked to the adjoining room. My heart sank.

Watching his reflection in the vanity mirror, I searched for a reason, a suitable plea, for him to stay. Intimacy was not my lone motivation. I simply didn't want to be alone, but I couldn't bring myself to speak such seemingly childlike feelings out loud. Instead, I watched him reach in to his pockets, searching for another set of keys that would take him away from me for the night. When he looked at me, I sheepishly averted my eyes.

Two times five is ten, two times six, is twelve.

The door creaked as he opened it. At first, he made no move to leave. I could feel his gaze from behind, but I couldn't look at him. I was half woman and half child. My love for him was like a weight to my chest. I dare not breathe too deeply for fear it might sink further and suffocate the life right out of me.

Why in my life did pain always seem to walk hand in hand with love? I had learned that lesson the day I buried my mother, and now that familiar heartache had returned. Only this time things were different. There was no wall around my heart. My angel had dismantled it months ago. I was defenseless.

With my eye downcast in a mix of grief and confusion, I did not see him as he approached me from behind. He laid his palms on my shoulders, and my body awakened under his touch.

Two times seven is fourteen, two times eight is—.

He drew me against his chest. "Sixteen," his velvety voice whispered in my ear.

I looked up to him in the mirror and wished I hadn't. His lips fluttered briefly, sensually, with a smile before settling in to a more solemn expression.

"Samantha, please don't hide from me." He pulled me gently around to face him.

"No, don't." I rested my palms against his chest and pushed but he held firm. "I'm not myself. I'm weak."

"This too shall pass."

I could feel the gentle rise and fall of his breath under my touch. His heart beat was escalated, and my own seemed to match it beat for beat. Images of our last night together flickered in my mind like clips from a tragic love story.

"Why, why are you here, really?" I whimpered, searching for answers in the depths of his crystal blue pools.

"Because you need me." His voice sounded thick.

"And you'll leave, when?"

"When, you ask me to." His knowing eyes grew misty as he reached up and swept my hair away from my face.

"That won't happen." I muttered, my own tears now swelling.

A corner of his mouth lifted in a sad replication of that iconic grin. "Yes, darlin', it will," he uttered, drawing me closer, and like a child longing for comfort, I clung to the safety of his embrace.

His body softened as he drew me deeper, his arms crushing me to his chest.

"Love, that's the key to the world," His lips swept over my hair in a light kiss. "It's God's perfect plan."

"If it's so perfect, why does it hurt so much?" I asked, still resting against his shoulder.

"Good love always does, baby. Good love always does," Elvis repeated with a soft sigh.

He shifted only slightly and lifted my chin. My lips trembled as he gently wiped away the tears I could no longer hold.

"You're so pretty, honey," he muttered, while cradling my face with his hands. "I look into your eyes and I see a love, I saw only from a stage. It's as intoxicating now as it was thirty years ago."

A peaceful smile slowly adorned his face, and his attention shifted to what I believed was some distant moment in time. I wondered if he was reliving the memory of a love he had spent his life time trying to understand. His fans love. A love he was drawn to, even now. And when his tempestuous blue pools cleared, he still held my face within his palms. His interest shifted to my mouth.

Please God, let him kiss me, just once, I silently prayed, and saw his smile flicker with a sensuous grin.

A single moment was counted with a heartbeat, and then I his lips melted against mine. I skyrocketed to heaven. At first his kiss was timid and tender. He merely skimmed over my lips, pausing after each purposeful taste to gaze into my eyes before flashing me a bashful grin and kissing me once more. The space between us gradually became smaller. Our gravitational attraction was like that of the sun's pull on the planets. We nearly melted into each other's arms, our bodies exhaling as one.

The kissing, once soft and innocence became urgent and hungry. Fervently, he reclaimed my lips, demanding I give him all I had. I opened to him eagerly. The long-missed taste of him washed over my tongue evoking a burst of passion that shot through my body like a meteor shower on a clear summer's night. My knees buckled and his grip tightened.

With an arm around my shoulders, and his free hand pressed firm against the curve of my back, he drew me determinedly against his body. All delicious ingredients of him, both soft and hard, molded perfectly with my own. The familiar terrain of his body ignited a primal instinct so deeply buried inside of me even I didn't know it existed. I was ravenous to touch him.

My hands trembled along his torso, crossed his slender pelvis and slipped downward. His breathing skipped over my touch, and we panted mouth-to-mouth. He shifted, allowing me room to experience him, enjoy him. I was kissing his neck, moaning, while he was shuddering. The realization that he wanted me as badly as I wanted him had me so crazy, I hadn't notice he'd pushed me hard against the edge of the vanity station. Its pointed edge dug in to my back.

"God, I crave you," he moaned, and slid his left hand down my right thigh.

My body liquefied. Impatient, he drew my leg upwards. And with the same hip thrust that had fascinated a generation, he pressed his pelvis firm into mine. Filled with wanting, I trampled the traditional spirit that existed inside of me. I'd forgotten about the woman who normally believed in marriage before sex. And, neither his blasphemy nor our forbidden love-making could snap me from this fog. The barricades of principle had melted.

Elvis unlatched his own belt while I snapped off every button on his shirt, and plunged my hands deep into the soft brown hairs that decorated his torso.

"Lord, help us," he hissed through clinched teeth.

The significance of his plea slammed against my heart. Like a slap to my face, my focus cleared. I looked to my angel, and sucked in a breath of surprise. His face was contorted with fury. His once passionate blue waters now churned with contempt. He looked at me with an empty gaze. And when I placed a gentle touch to his heated face, his eyes cleared.

Wordless, we stared at each other. It was as if we were seeing each other for the first time, and tears swelled in both of our eyes. He drew me all the way in to his arms, hugging me and squeezing me tight.

"Baby, oh baby, I'm so sorry," he said hoarsely.

The tears flowed. We clung to each other, our bodies shaking with emotion. He pealed himself out of my embrace, and I crossed my arms over my chest. I hugged myself tighter, but still the shame swelled. Elvis marched across the room with his eyes cast downward, and grabbed his jacket.

"Where are you going?" I sniveled.

"Out," he said flatly and flung the door open. It slammed behind him, and my body jumped with the finality of the moment.

I peeked out the window, and watched his long, rushed, strides carrying him down the walkway. He shoved his right arm inside his jacket sleeve, while the other flailed about, struggling to find its mark. The ends of a shirt I had virtually torn apart with my own hands blew in the breeze.

I watched until I could see him no longer. Once he was out of sight, the damned gates opened and more tears fell. I turned and raced for the one place I could grieve in private—the shower. As I'd done in the past, I jumped in fully dressed. I sat on the cold tile, knees drawn up tight, and allowing the warm water to shower over me. Curled up in to myself, I wailed.

* * *

Wrapped in a towel, I sat damp and steaming on the stiff bed. If the clock was right, it was noon. It was too early for a long, deep sleep, but I needed a few hours. My eyes burned, and I rubbed them as I yawned. I glanced to the doorway. What kind of woman can so easily tempt one of God's angels? I scowled. Tossing the towel to the floor, I crawled into the fresh sheet. Goosebumps spread over my bare skin in a cooling rush. The crisp, cold sheets were comforting. And when the heat from my body began to melt the iceberg linen, I shifted, searching for yet another frosty landscape in which to lounge. This routine continued until my exhaustion overcame me and my eyelids, too heavy to hold, closed.

I slipped off to a blissful sleep. The soft, but distinctive scent of lavender my mother wore filled my senses. I inhaled slowly and deeply over and over, as if breathing in her very essence. I opened my eyes and found myself standing in a field of flowers. Purple petals on green strands surrounded me. I reached out and softly laid a finger against waxy petals.

This was a field made for my mother, and everything about it was as real as could be. I slowly turned in a complete circle, fully expecting, needing, to see her standing before me. She was nowhere to be seen. I squeezed my eyes closed and held back more tears of disappointment. The ache in my heart was no less than the day she died. I whispered an inaudible prayer to leave this place, and the field slowly melted away. I mercifully sank back into deep slumber.

CHAPTER TWELVE

I woke to the gentle strumming of an acoustic guitar. Each melancholic note enamored me, supporting my mood like a sympathetic friend. At first I refused to open my eyes, afraid the beautiful serenade would fade away. Eventually and only when I felt ready to face the world, did I reluctantly peek.

To no surprise, I saw Elvis sitting across from me in the room's only easy chair. He had changed clothes, and looked refreshed in a navy blue suit, his white shirt crisp and stark against the dark fabric. With his eyes closed, his long fingers finessed each note. A single swatch of black hair drifted lazily across his forehead. I dared not breathe, for fear of disturbing the moment.

"Rested?" His soft baritone all but hummed the question.

"Yes, except for the dreams." I stretched under the covers.

"Hmm... yes." He struck a bluesy twang on the guitar.

"You watch my dreams too?" *Where did he get the guitar?*

"From a store down the street," Elvis answered, abruptly stopped playing and rose from the chair. "I have something I'd like to show you."

He laid the guitar against the chair and crossed the room in three strides. I sat up, my mouth poised with an apology, and or question. I couldn't decide. I never got a chance to sort it out, as he interrupted with a sudden about face u-turn back in my direction.

"Listen, honey, about earlier," he ran a hand through his hair, pushing back that stray strain to its rightful place. "That wasn't your fault."

A tear collected in the corner of my eye. "Yes, it was."

"No, sweetheart, it's not. Look, w-we just got caught in the middle of a rivalry older than time, that's all."

I only knew of one battle older than human existence, and instantly visions of tormented souls swarmed my imagination.

"And that sadistic bastard, he loves to use our weaknesses against us," Elvis' words rattled with rage. "He's just waiting to catch me off guard."

His eyes were scanning over the room and I found myself looking as well, fearful of what I could not see. My heart pounded and my stomach turned. The mere thought that Lucifer, the first fallen angel of heaven, had inspired such insatiable lust was almost too much to comprehend. It was other-worldly. I didn't want to believe it, but I knew what Elvis had said was true. The devil was real, and he was forever close.

"W-what does he want, me?"

"Oh, he'd love that," Elvis chuckled and began to pace the room. "No darling' he's taunting me and laughing about it. He wants to see me fall to my desires and prove myself unworthy."

His words tumbled out on seemingly one breath.

"But, he forgets he's nothing but an occupational hazard to me, that's all." He said, holding his arms straight out at his side, palms up and in a challenging gesture. "I'm not the same man!"

My eyes were fixed on the dark corners of the room. I wanted to scream at him to keep it down. An angelic battle was not what I wanted to see. I was fragile human flesh!

When he refocused to me, his temper simmered but only a notch. Red from the neck up, he was fuming just under the line.

"It won't happen again," he growled.

Overwhelmed, I managed only a nod.

"I'll give you a few minutes to ready yourself." His voice was softer, but he pointedly slammed the door behind him when he left.

As if someone yelled "Go!" I sprung off the bed and grabbed my travel bag. I wanted out of this room! I dug out a pair of jeans and a blue cashmere sweater. I held them up the mirror. This was just going to have to do. It was far too cold for anything more feminine.

I almost poked my eye out with the tip of a mascara wand when a knock at the adjacent door startled me.

"Samantha, are you decent?" he called out impatiently.

"Coming," I hurried to add the finishing touches.

I yanked opened the door and raced to get my knee-length black jacket. I could feel him watching me from behind. He stood, his weight shifted to the right, in a stance more relaxed than before. I was happy to see he was not wearing ancient Roman armor, geared up and ready to slay the three headed dragon that I feared was still hiding in my room. And me, without a Mr. Jigs!

In one erratic motion, I jammed one arm through a sleeve while leaning precariously over furniture to reach my scarf.

"It looks cold outside," I said, as I straightened my jacket's lapel and fastened the buttons.

With a toss of a dark red scarf around my neck, I was finally ready. My chestnut hair flowed across my shoulders. I turned and almost bumped into Elvis.

"Ready?" He extended his hand to me, an easy smile flickering across his face.

I took his free hand while he carried a black wool coat, matching gloves and hat in his other. His jet black hair combed perfectly straight back. Not a single hair out of place. I pondered why God would create a man so handsome, tell me not to touch him, and then say it loud enough for the devil to hear? Even I knew Satan couldn't resist opposing God. I was sure the dark angel was having a good laugh at how easily I was led astray.

Elvis was right. The fight between good and evil was like a game of cat-and-mouse. And, it went so far back one couldn't help but wonder if anyone really knew what they were fighting about. The point was lost to me, I thought as we exited the room, and I watched Elvis pull the hat down low around his face. The Bible says the Devil loses in the end, I reminded myself. I guess Satan doesn't read, I chuckled and then looked around.

"Where are we going?" I moved closer to my protector.

"It's a surprise."

* * *

In the faint afternoon light we strolled. I leaned against his sturdy frame and followed his even strides not bothering to watch where I was going. Instead, I looked up at the sky that hung over our heads like an abstract work of art. I felt safe by his side, and became lost in the colorful strokes of orange and purple signaling the sun's last hurrah of the day. Soon the night's shadows will have their turn at splendor and judging by how quickly the sun was sinking to the horizon, I will enjoy it with an angel.

God is a talented artist, I thought. And I was considering if I had ever walked in a more prefect evening, with a more wonderful escort, when my cell phone beeped. Elvis dropped my hand. I shoved my hand inside my bag, aware of a mix of curiosity and impatience radiating from his direction. Though he had owned one of the first cell phones, I don't imagine he would ever have guessed they would one day be small enough to get lost in a lady's purse. I was flipping my cell phone open even before it was fully exposed. The word "Steve" flashed in and out of focus. I hit read.

You leave town without a word?

My heartbeat skipped. Instantly, my thoughts flashed to that unidentified car drifting so unassumingly in the shadows as we fled Memphis last night. And if that wasn't enough to rattle me there was always Tupelo.

"I-I will return this later," I looked around, forced a smile, and snapped the phone shut.

The park was only a few short blocks. At my side, Elvis' gate was more of a march then his normal easy glide. My mind spun with worry. Ahead, I saw the cemented path, lined with trees, and filled with pedestrians. He headed straight for it.

"Who do people see walking next to me?" I hoped to discuss anything outside of Steve or the happenings back at the hotel.

"They see what they want to see," he said pointedly.

It was impossible to miss the vibe of a troubled Elvis. Alive, he wore his emotions on his sleeve. Though he was an angel, this hadn't changed. His mood was dark, and I knew better then to push. We were well in to our walk before I finally felt his arm muscles relax, and that centered angelic demeanor returned.

Around us, cars filled the streets. They whisked by as workers, freshly released from cubicles all over town, got a reprieve for the day. And just like in Tupelo I couldn't help but tense up. I kept repeating under my breath, God is in control—another one of my daddy's tips—and after saying it ten times, I finally began to feel a circle of warmth. Dang, if he isn't always right!

A sweet smell of a tulip poplar tree filled the early evening air. I drew in a deeper breath. My senses relished the comforting scent of nature. I heard raised voices. Like the teenagers who loudly played field games in the last moments of daylight.

"In case you're wondering, Steve is a man I met while looking for you back at Graceland," I explained. "He's a fan of yours."

"I'm aware of who he is." Elvis paused and turned to face me. His face looked grim, worried even, and I held my breath in concern, but our moment was cut short by an object that fell from the sky.

We both jumped as a football wobbled at our feet before settling onto its side.

"Hey, mister, can you get the ball for us?" Cracked the voice of a tall boy from across the field.

Smiling politely, Elvis bent down and picked up the football, rolling it around in his hands. Gripping it like a pro, he leaned back, and with a whip of his arm, sent the ball flying through the air. A crowd of teenage boys scrambled to catch it, all falling short, and miscalculating the power and distance of the throw.

"Ah, man," they collectively moaned.

Elvis smirked, his satisfaction obvious as he bent over to pick up his stylish hat that had tumbled to the ground. Placing it firmly back in place, he grabbed my hand and guided me away from the game. In light of all that had happened, explaining Steve was never more important. And I tried to broach the subject with him, only to be shut down with talk about the weather and the distance of the drive that still lay ahead. I gave up. What was one more day? It could wait till tomorrow. Our time together was precious and it was such a lovely evening.

* * *

Centered in the middle of town, the park was larger than I imagined. Of course that was of no concern for Elvis. Once inside the park, he knew exactly which way to travel. At every cross section, he moved without hesitation, and every turn always led to yet another well maintained path and another direction. I was beginning to wonder if he had a destination in mind until we finally arrived at a tranquil picnic area with a small lake just off in the distance.

Water gently lapped at the shore. A few couples lingered. They huddled close together for warmth and strolled along a tree-lined path around the water's edge. They looked happy, and in love. My heart skipped. I was happy to share the last remaining hours of the day with my love. A romantic at heart, enjoying the sun as it slips below the horizon sounded like heaven.

A green park bench sat at the edge of the moderate shore line, and Elvis motioned for me to take a seat. I looked around for my surprise. He let out a grunt and sat down by my side, lifting his arm around my shoulder. A light breeze tousled my hair, and his. I looked over my shoulder at the children playing in the sandbox behind us and smiled. Each child sat digging with the passion of tiny gold miners. One turned our way.

"What is so special about this lake?" I continued to watch as one shy little princess stepped out of the sandbox.

Her long blonde ringlets bounced, giving her the air of purpose as she walked. She only briefly glanced at me as she circled around to her intended mark. Elvis' eyes widened in surprise as the little miss crawled up on to his lap without so much as a word. Smiling broadly, he gave her a helping hand.

"Well, hello, sweetness. What can I do for you?" Elvis looked behind us.

I nodded toward the direction from which she had come. She lifted her tiny little hands over her mouth, and leaned in closer to whisper something into his ear. Elvis' smile brightened, his teeth shining white against the paleness of her doll-like skin. The tiniest of whispers hummed next to his ear.

"She did?" Elvis beamed.

"Yup," said our small guest, folding her hands in to her lap.

"Well, I'll be." Elvis' eyes widened as if the sweet child had just told him the most wonderful news.

"And..." The little blonde girl looked at me as if considering if she could say what was on her mind.

Giving it a second thought, she leaned back in to continue her conversation with Elvis in private.

I instinctively longed to have a child as lovely as her one day, and I could not help but want to hold her. Elvis' laughter burst out into the evening, interrupting my dreams of motherhood.

"Ok darlin'. I'll be sure to do just that." Elvis hugged her to his chest and her little arms clutched his neck.

"Grace!" A distressed call came from behind.

The little girl's eyes got wide as she slid off Elvis' lap. I extended her my hand, but she sprung down all on her own. Glancing over my shoulder, I could see what I assumed was little Grace's mom, displaying that look of fear all parents get when they cannot find their children.

"She's over here," I waved to a relieved looking woman who picked up her pace and trotted toward us.

"Sorry!" The woman called.

"It's quite alright. She's a doll." I yelled back.

Pulling her knee-length jacket down like a well trained little southern lady Grace circled around the bench. She walked back to mom slowly, which only caused her name to be bellowed in a tone that made me flinch. I couldn't help but chuckle as Grace skipped along, not the least bit worried.

Having gone just a few steps, Grace suddenly stopped, spun around, and raced back towards us. My heart skipped as she ran toward me, not Elvis. Out of breath, she stretched up on her toes to reach my ear.

"He smells like candy!" She whispered excitedly, before turning back, her steps quicker now than before.

"What'd she say?" Elvis poked me.

"She said you smell as sweet as candy," I laughed and Elvis smirked while blushing.

"Well, you are awful sweet, you know," I reached over and pinched his cheeks.

"Ah… stop fussin' on me now. Look… the mom, she's comin' back."

I glanced up to see Grace's mom dragging her off the playground by one arm.

"No, she's not." When I turned back, he was already up and walking down to the lake, his laughter echoing in the breeze.

"Oh, you're a brat." I raced after him.

My intention was to pass him, but with reflexes like lightening, he snatched me by the waist and pulled me back into his arms.

"Come here, you." He spoke through clenched teeth while encircling me from behind.

Laughing, I rested my back against his sturdy chest.

"What did little Grace share with you?"

"She asked for me to give her grams a kiss for her when I get back to heaven."

"She knows you're an angel?"

"Children see much more than we give them credit for." Elvis pressed his warm cheek against my cool face. "And, they rarely miss the miracles."

Standing at the lake's edge, wrapped in his strong embrace, I watched the water as it stirred; gently moved by a cold night's breeze. Heat radiated from Elvis' body and I snuggled closer to his warmth as though he were a campfire.

"Was Grace what you wanted to share with me?" I spoke softly, hesitant to break this peaceful silence.

"No, your surprise lies here." Elvis pointed towards the water.

As if on cue, the wind stopped. Strands of my hair fell softly to my shoulder.

"Watch closely, baby girl." His breath felt hot against my ear.

All was still. My breath slowed in anticipation of Elvis' gift. Even nature held its breath. Not even a leaf fluttered in the trees. When a small swell began to spread over the glassy surface, Elvis loosened his embrace. I leaned in for a closer look.

CHAPTER THIRTEEN

As though an unseen rock had dropped into the calm surface, the water began to ripple. The circles grew larger, and slowly a familiar reflection came into focus. I watched as the two people I love most, my mother and my father, walked hand in hand. The sun was high in the sky over their heads, and as bright as any Atlanta day in June. Like a mirror to the other side, I imagined this beautiful scene to be a glimpse into heaven. A lump grew in my throat. My heart longed to join them.

But when my father turned and placed a soft kiss on my mother's lips, I felt a rush of concern.

"My daddy, is he... he's not..." I dared not utter the word out loud.

"No baby girl, he's very much alive. He's only dreamin'." Elvis gathered me back in to his arms, encircling me from behind, and I exhaled my relief in to the cold pre-dusk air.

I closed my eyes and fell back against Elvis' sturdy frame. My rapid heartbeat slowed, and quickly I reopened my eyes not wanting to miss one blessed moment.

"This is the type of love God wishes for you Samantha," Elvis uttered close to my ear.

His words sank in deep, stirring my thoughts as I watched my parents holding each other.

"A God sanctioned love, blessed in this life and the next."

My heart was listening, and I understood his meaning, but my attention was locked onto my mother. It had been more than two years since I had seen her. Tears swelled in my eyes as I remembered how tired and frail she looked on her last days on Earth. She looked so happy here, resting in my father's arms, no sign of the ravaging cancer that had taken her life.

Oh, how I'd missed her.

I was pondering my life without her when my mother's eyes turned to look out from her watery stage right into mine. I jumped back against Elvis' chest, and his arms tightened around me for comfort.

"Easy, honey."

"Did you see that?"

The same gentle smile that had calmed me as a child glowed. My father's lips moved silently as he chatted by her side, unaware of our connection. Mother watched me while she quietly listened.

"Your mama is quite the lady." Elvis spoke as if he knew her firsthand. "She wishes for you the same happiness she had with your father. We all do."

The lake began to stir again, and the forms of my parents became blurry, and then began to fade. My mother's smile widened, in one final goodbye, just as the doorway to heaven closed.

"Mama told Daddy they would never be apart."

My mother's bedside promise to my agonizing father was still vivid in my mind. I could clearly see my father, kneeling beside her, holding her as she took her final breath.

"She is a wise woman." Elvis kissed my temple.

"How did she know?"

"She knows God."

"And love?" I was beginning to understand.

"Baby, if a man and a woman have God, they have everything."

A bird struck up a tune somewhere in the park.

"Have you always believed this?" I asked and a long pause followed.

"My mama preached it, but I guess I thought my situation was too complex to practice it." He pondered for a moment, "Had I a bit more time, I would have done things differently."

"Too bad you can't go back."

Elvis turned me around to face him.

"No. It's too late for me." His eyes were soft as they scanned my face.

He rested his palms gently against my cheeks, and the warmth from his own soul seemed to reach down to mine.

"Are we having "the talk"?" My eyes narrowed, and he began to chuckle, light at first, and growing by the minute.

When Elvis laughed, he laughed with his whole heart. It was hard not to join in.

"God has a great plan for your life, Samantha," his chuckles settled, "And, let's just say that I was sent to ensure you get over a few bumps, "safely", and get on with it."

I should have felt happiness to hear that God had a plan—Lord knows I didn't have one—but my wide smile faded. I'd hoped these bumps were long behind me.

"So… about these challenges I have to "get over". Is one of them you?" I asked. I knew I was right when I saw that sideways smile of his.

* * *

A light mist moistened the night's air as Elvis and I walked along the now-empty streets, our footsteps echoing in the night. A soft glow from the street lamps lit our way. The city had gone to bed. We strolled, both of us content in the stillness.

Keep God at the center, Elvis had preached back at the lake. My parents had set a great example of love transcending time, but I had never experienced anything close to what my angel was suggesting. I had been more than a little left behind in the love department.

I pondered my forever-single situation the whole way back to the hotel. When Elvis released my hand to open the door to my room, the separation from his touch woke me from my thoughts. Standing in the open air corridor, rain drops, the size of marbles, began to fall. I watched as each one, unique from the other, splashed to the ground outside the shelter overhead.

"I'll be in my room if you should need me," Elvis said softly.

"But..." I was interrupted by the seemingly always impossibly timed ringing of my cell phone. I made no move to answer it.

"You should take *this* call, honey." Elvis looked pointedly at my purse.

Sighing, I began to rummage around. I was just about to give up when my fingers stumbled over their mark.

"Hello," I grumbled.

"Samantha?" My father's reprimanding tenor fired in my ear.

A smirk slipped over Elvis' lips as he stepped to the doorway.

"D...Daddy?" I stuttered like a child caught sneaking out of the house.

Elvis pushed the door open and stepped aside. I hurried past my angel, nibbling absorbedly on the tip of my finger nail.

"Where are you?"

Silence.

I prayed this would be the time I could quickly deliver an acceptable response to my father.

"Sa-man-tha." He spoke my name in broken syllables which was never a good sign.

Elvis chuckled and reached over to gently remove my finger from my mouth.

"I'm here, Daddy."

With a soft kiss goodbye, Elvis began to take his departure.

"Where in the world are you, baby girl?"

I watched Elvis cross my room toward the adjoining door that led to his. For once, I did not dwell on the emptiness of his leaving. Instead, I was taking too long to give my father an answer, and could think of nothing he'd want to hear that wasn't a bold-faced lie.

Elvis paused briefly, watching me in sideways glances. Only the truth will do, I realized. Elvis nodded in satisfaction and stepped through the door, closing it behind him with a smile.

"I'm in Alabama?" My confession sounded more like an inquiry to what I hoped was a good answer.

"Alabama?" Daddy's voice rose.

"See, daddy, it's complicated, but I had gone to Memphis and..."

"Yes, yes, Heather mentioned that. Why are you *driving* back to Atlanta, Samantha?"

I suddenly realized his phone call wasn't random at all. Daddy had called Heather and that action alone sparked a dozen red flags. Heather and my father rarely spoke. They were opposites, often agreeing to disagree. Suddenly, I was listening very carefully.

"I appreciate everyone's concern daddy, but I just needed some time to myself."

"Well, I don't think a female should be driving that far alone." My father grumbled.

"I know you're worried, but I will call you first thing tomorrow morning. I promise."

"Well, I suppose that'll have to do."

"Daddy, were you napping earlier?" I casually shifted the subject. I knew good and well how much he loved his ritualistic afternoon nap.

"What?"

"Did you get your nap today?"

"Why?"

"Was it a pleasant sleep, Daddy?"

"A pleasant sleep?" He repeated my question slowly, after a noticeable pause.

My father was never at ease discussing things of the heart, unless it was in the safety of the larger church congregation. I held back my snicker.

"Did you have sweet dreams?"

"What does any of this have to do with you driving alone across the country?" Daddy's voice rose once again.

"Nothing, I was just checking to see you were getting your rest."

There was no need for me to question further. My father's inability to share his dream told me all I needed to know. He had indeed been dreaming, just as Elvis had said. I smiled, happy to prove my angel was right: love reaches to Heaven.

"I have to go now, Daddy. I'll call you soon."

"But..."

"I love you."

"What?"

"I said, I- love- you." I chuckled.

"I love you, too, baby girl. Be careful, please."

"I will," I said in close, and hung up the phone, flopping gratefully onto the well-worn hotel bed.

My father was worried. It warmed me, but it also concerned me. It was unusual for Heather to involve my father in my crisis. It went against the best-friend clause! Something was out of place. I vowed to get to the bottom of it.

CHAPTER FOURTEEN

At the window I mindlessly twisted my hair, watching the rain pelt the roof top. The sky sparked with a flash, and a moment later, a loud crack sounded. I almost jumped out of my skin. The clock by the bed displayed the default time of 12:00.

This storm could last all night, I moaned, and glanced at his closed door. As much as I wanted to knock, I had to consider if it wasn't best that we stayed apart for the evening. My heart sank at the thought. Then again, if he invites me into his sanctuary, I might actually sleep.

I tilted my eyes to the heavens, "I promise to behave," I told the Lord, and then smiled. Who would have thought that shy little-me would actually be considered a threat?

Staring at the four beige walls around me, I half expected God's response to appear like with Moses and the burning bush. Absurd, I let out a chuckle, but then quickly held my breath to listen. Nothing. Shrugging, I opened my travel bag and dug for my sleep wear resigning to a night alone.

I lifted my cherry-red silk night gown, and could not help but frown. How presumptuous of me. I should have brought my flannels! I stood in front of the vanity mirror and brushed out my long dark hair, stealing a glance back to the door between me and my angel with every stroke. Daddy always did have the worst timing, I pouted. Elvis all but ran to the solitude of his room.

I slipped on my night-gown and sat down on to the edge of the bed with a sigh. The long shiny fabric reached to my feet. I noticed my toes matched the garment perfectly. The irony of such a thought-out detail, made me laugh. And then in looking down to my low neck line, I also rolled my eyes. I flopped on the bed.

Unease sank in. Lying on my back, I counted the tiny flakes that sparkled inside the aged plaster of the ceiling. I stroked my stomach in small comforting circles, shifting the soft fabric on my skin with the palm of my hand.

What was he thinking leaving me here alone? He knows I'm a big chicken. *I should go over there and knock on the door,* I craned my head to look over at the barrier.

It seemed to glow red with a forbidden do-not-enter sign. Sighing, I lifted one shapely leg into the air and pointed my toes upward. The fabric fell to my hips. I had my mama's legs, I considered, slender yet shapely.

"Samantha!" A voice bellowed from next door, and my startled scream filled the room. I slapped my hand to my mouth, and jumped off the bed.

What'd I do now? My bare feet padded on the worn carpet as I drew near the door. I laid my head on the aged wood.

"Come in, Samantha."

Grimacing, I cracked the door and peaked in. I spotted Elvis' long, lean frame lounging across the bed, his gaze focused on a thick book he held in his hand. My mind switched channels, and the seductive entrance I had many times rehearsed in my head in preparation for just this opportunity was useless here. Besides, he was reading the Bible, and probably the King James version.

He was fully dressed, right down to his well-shined boots. I stood momentarily paralyzed, both wanting and feeling unworthy of his attention. His eyes rolled up from the good-book and settled on me. I fought the urge to tug at my nightdress.

"I-I was lonely in there all by myself," I pointed back to my room, where oddly I was ready to return at any moment.

Elvis pursed his lips and nodded.

"I was!" I set my jaw, all too aware of the message my alluring attire must be suggesting.

In what looked to me like slow motion, he closed the imposing black book calmly inside his two hands. Unable to maintain my insolence, I dropped my stare to his boots, which were as still as the wind before a striking tornado. That nervous energy he always seemed unable to control was gone. He seemed to be having a moment of – I didn't know what— an evaluation of his own emotional condition or contemplation over my motives, but I compulsively began to nibble on my finger nail.

"Alright, get in." Elvis said, and I could have sworn I saw his lips twitch before he quickly regained his control.

With the Bible still in his strong hands, he folded his arms over his chest and watched me as I became comfortable in my new environment. I wriggled into a comfortable position. The golden etched bindings nearly glowed in the dim lamp light.

"Situated?" His eyes danced.

"Yes, thank you."

"You should be the one reading this, you know."

"I read the Bible." I said rather smartly for a woman who didn't want to sleep alone.

His eyes widened. "Oh? Was it while you were planning your, uh... attire." His eye brows quivered like a Marx brothers' movie. All he lacked was that cigar.

"Funny. If I make you uncomfortable, I can leave." I said and sat up.

"No," he grabbed me by the arm with a chuckle. "I-I think I can handle you."

He was joking, but I could feel his hand trembling as he held my arm. The struggle we were destined to share was painfully real.

"Your virtue is safe anyway, I promised The Boss." I tried to lighten the situation further.

He drew in a deep breath through his nostrils, evoking a sensual snarl while holding his chuckle for a fraction of a second before letting it slip into outright laughter.

"Was the promise made with or without crossing your fingers?" His humor skipped as he tried to catch his breath.

I shook my head at him. "You just can't help yourself, can you?" I said with a smile that only grew wider the more he laughed.

"Well, if you weren't so cute mad," he brushed the bridge of his own nose with his hand in an attempt to hide his amusement. Another habit I found adorable.

"Very funny. Why don't you be a good angel and read me something from the Bible?" I slipped my hand under my pillow and settled in.

Elvis regarded me with great interest before opening the thick book. His eyes searched around the delicate pages as if trying to decide what was best.

"Here, lets read like my daddy used to when I was small," I leaned over and placed a finger randomly on the page. "I'll pick, and then you read."

He watched me, his eyes full of humor, and then he looked down and began.

"My God sent his angel and shut the lions' mouth, so that they may not hurt me."

When he was done, his face softened in the same peaceful way my father's used to when in awe of God's perfect timing. I rested a soft touch to his arm. No words were needed to describe the feelings that lingered under all of our jousting.

"Come' ere, let me hold you." A sensual smile flickered across his lips.

"I gave my word." I sighed and enjoyed his exaggerated scowl.

"Get over here, woman," his eyes widened as he reached and pulled me in to his arms.

Side by side we lay. Inside his embrace, a different kind of love stirred. It far overshadowed the physical passions between a man and a woman. We were bonded by something stronger than the flesh, and I knew he wished more for me than a single moment of passion. He wished for me what he could not give me—a lifetime, my lifetime, of love.

If only I could convince my heart.

CHAPTER FIFTEEN

I opened my eyes slowly, briefly unfamiliar with my surroundings. In all my years as a flight attendant, and all the successive mornings of waking up someplace different than the day before, this feeling of disorientation should not have startled me. However, on this morning, one thing was pleasantly different. I was not alone. Heat radiated by my side. At first I had not noticed his presence, having forgotten whose bed I had fallen asleep. When my mind cleared, I realized that my angel was sleeping only a few inches away from my side. I slowly rolled over to see my living dream.

He slept with his back to me, one arm tucked under his pillow. He looked as peaceful as a sleeping child, his shoulders rising and falling in peaceful rhythm with his every breath. He wore no shirt, and for a moment I fantasized about what else was missing, and then remembered the promises and realizations of last night.

I inched closer. Slowly, and pausing often to see that I had not disturbed his slumber. I held my breath and leaned over him to gaze at his face. To see his pouting lips with a hint of a curl, even present as he slept, made me smile. I longed to wrap my arms around him and cuddle him from behind.

Deep in sleep, he sighed and shifted slightly on his pillow. A patch of blue-black hair covered his left eye. My hands shook as I reached out to gently brush the hair away and unblock my view. He stirred, and his eyes fluttered open like an oyster displaying the pearl gems inside. Slow to come out of his dreams, he glanced around and seemed to be unfamiliar with his own surroundings. I had never considered that angels would suffer that same confusion.

"I thought angels didn't sleep," I whispered.

His head turned to look over his left shoulder, towards my voice. He inhaled deeply, taking in his first deep breath of the morning, and rolled over. My temperature rose when our bodies touched under the covers. His lips shifted into a slow, easy smile.

"I'm making up for all those years I couldn't," he took my hand, and lifted my fingers to his mouth for a good morning kiss before returning my touch to his bare chest.

His soft chest hairs felt like silk rose pedals under my touch. I resisted the urge to lower my nose to his sweetness and inhale his scent.

"Catching up on lost winks?" I kept the conversation light.

"Something, like that," he yawned, and his nose wrinkled so adorably that I laid a finger to it.

I giggled as he looked from my face to my finger and back again. A mischievous look flashed in his eyes and I braced myself.

His reflexes were fast, and I barely flinched when Elvis shifted his weight and repositioned himself over me. Flat on my back, the weight of his body pressed heavily against my small frame. His belt buckle dug into my stomach, proving he was indeed still dressed from the waist down.

"Hasn't anyone ever taught you how to give a man his proper good mornings?" He asked, while grinning ear to ear.

I enjoyed the round- and- a-round nature of our teasing games. It seemed flirting was all I was going to be allowed to enjoy, but there was one problem. Elvis played to win! One could be sure there'd be no mercy, and cheating was never completely off the table.

"I know how to greet *my* man in the morning, yes." I played my part perfectly.

"Well, then?" He smiled over me.

"You're not *my* man."

His only response was the shifting of his gaze to my lips.

"Y-you're my, uh…angel and all, but." My game plan was getting blurry.

"You talk too much." He paused. "Just kiss me."

He asked for it. I reached up and wrapped both hands around his neck, pulling him to my lips. I kept my eyes open long enough to see his rising in stunned surprise, his complaint muffled by my lips. He jerked way and licked at his bottom lip. I let loose a burst of laugher.

"A-ha, a-ha, a-ha..." He mimicked.

"I always wanted a crazy stage-side kiss," I laughed.

"You...," was all I heard him say before I felt his teeth nibbling on the side of my neck.

I screamed, and my squeals mixed with his outright laughter. He held my hands firmly over my head with one hand while tickling me with his other. Pinned under him, there was no escaping, even if I had wanted to. My body went limp, exhausted from the tear-shedding laughter. Elvis laughed victoriously and relaxed his hold.

Our humor slowly subsided, and soon all was quiet in the room, save our labored breathing.

"You're silly," he panted, our noses touching as we caught our breath.

Though my watery eyes blurred his beautiful features, I could sense his lips were just a kiss away. Without thought, I turned my head and lifted my mouth to his. He drew in a breath of surprise. Dropping my hands, his palms slid down to the sides of my face and his eyes drifted close.

Elvis loved to kiss, and he was a master at it. He kissed with the eagerness of a teenager, and all the patience of a man. His lips were supple and soft like the South's finest spun cotton. I made good use of his tendency to linger, and shifted my lips, attempting to enjoy every scrumptious curve of his full mouth. He pulled away first.

"Better?" I purred, and enjoyed a stirring look of melting self control in his eyes.

"Hmm, almost, perfect." His grand smile was broad and dazzling but I frowned anyway.

"You have to leave room for improvement, baby. It's better that way." He placed a quick peck to my nose and then slid off the bed.

Barefoot, shirtless and wearing only the pair of trousers he had on from the night before, he strolled across the room.

"We need to get on the road." He ran his hand through his tousled hair. "Your Daddy is waiting."

I opened my mouth.

"No arguments now." He pointed at my abandoned room as he walked into the bathroom and slammed the door behind him in one smooth motion.

I knew it was silly to pout, but I could not help it. I kicked at the bed sheets, flinging them off of me. When that didn't relieve all my frustration, I thrashed against the mattress until I was tired.

* * *

The drive from Alabama to Georgia was less than 300 miles. Amazingly, Elvis managed to drive it in less than three hours. He drove as if on autopilot.

My hesitations about returning home began to melt when the towering skyscrapers of downtown Atlanta came in to view. A sense of peace rushed over me. Maybe I had finally accepted God's plan for me, or maybe Elvis' laid-back demeanor those last hundred miles had rubbed off, I cannot say. But on this day, as we passed the city, headed for the more urban side of Atlanta, my excitement grew. The feeling was warm and welcoming. I was finally, in the truest meaning of the word, going home.

Elvis eased the Escalade off the freeway and into my neighborhood. Georgia's graceful live oak trees—iconic of the old south—lined my street, its evergreen branches seconding as a canopy over head. Through the rain-splattered car window, I admired each familiar yard, still brown from winter freeze. We turned the last corner, and my heart fluttered when I could finally see my white brick beauty.

He turned the sleek Cadillac into my driveway and parked. Without a word, I stepped out into a light mist. Automatically we fell into our roles. Elvis raced to the back of the car to fetch my bags, and I ran to unlock the front door to my home. We moved so easily in each other's company, as though this could have been our lives in some other realm of time. I placed my key inside the lock, pausing when I heard my name.

"Ms. Samantha." Mrs. Jefferson, my elderly neighbor called out while waving clutched items in the air.

Mr. and Mrs. Jefferson had lived in this neighborhood for more than fifty years. Well in to their eighties, and with all of their children living outside Atlanta, Mrs. Jefferson had all but taking me in as her own. The admiration was mutual.

DREAM ANGEL

"What have you got there, Mrs. Jefferson?" My upbringing did not allow me to call her by her first name.

I left the door unlocked for Elvis and stepped down from my porch. Elvis glanced up from the trunk of the car.

"Some mail darlin', I thought it not safe to leave it stacking up in your mail box." She wobbled precariously, but with determination, toward me.

"Thank you, ma'am...please, I'll come to you."

Mrs. Jefferson did not have the best of vision, but I did not want her getting a good look at the dream I was parading into my home.

"I can walk. I'm 80, not dead child," she fussed.

We met half way, neither of us shielding ourselves from the rain. I took the mail from her hand.

"Oh, and before I forget, this note was left on your door this morning. I thought I better get it, least it blow away," she said while shoving her hand into the side pockets of her long dress and pulling out a folded piece of paper.

The familiarity of the hand writing caught my eye, but I couldn't right away place it.

"I see you have a friend with you today, Sam."

I heard her speak, but I was busy examining the folded white note with the blue inked word "Samantha" smeared from rain down the front.

"Hello there young man," Mrs. Jefferson said to Elvis, not waiting for an introduction.

Elvis had reached the front door and paused. "Ma'am," He nodded his head, his hands full of bags, before gently nudging the door open with his foot and entering my home.

"Oh, he's a handsome fella alright," she squinted but I was not too worried.

"Yes, well..." I stuttered, resisting the urge to tear open the note and read it right in front of her.

"Child, I'm not totally blind. I know a hunk of a man when I see me one!" She said, than added, "even if he is a little young."

My attention flickered. I slowly looked up to her grinning face, and a heated flush crept up my neck.

"I'm sorry, come again ma'am." I said, leaning in closer.

"Oh child, that boy looks like he just broke loose from his mama's apron strings. I bet he's spirited, too! Those young ones always are." She turned and with a wave of her hand, promptly marched back to her house.

The rain dripped down my head while Mrs. Jefferson's step quickened with surprising stability as she raced to get out of the rain.

"Don't you worry, your secret is safe with me," she called over her shoulder.

I smiled. Great, first I'm accosting the elderly and now I'm cradle robbing. What's next? I shook my head. Shoving the stack of mail inside my jacket, along with the note, I ran across the lawn to shelter. I bounded up the painted white cement stairs, skipping the last step, and in reaching for the brass antique door knob, I paused. I looked to my left, and then to the right, unnerved by what I imagined were the eyes of the world watching me, or worse. Welcome home, I thought, and stepped through the threshold.

Right away, I scanned the room, half expecting something further to be out of place. Everything appeared just as I had left it, neat and orderly. I noticed my bags lay abandoned near the phone station. A blinking red light captured my attention, announcing a message waited on my phone. It was probably Heather. I elected to check it later.

With Elvis nowhere in sight, I could hardly wait to open the note. I was taking off my jacket, and unfolding the paper at the same time.

Unsigned, it read: *I must see you*

A mix of fear and fascination swelled. In my mind, there was only one person who would have left such a desperate note. But Steve didn't know where I lived, and we had just arrived, I rationalized. I flipped the note, front to back and then face forward again.

"Samantha?" Elvis' baritone called out.

I folded the paper in to a wad and shoved it deep into my pockets. Running my hands through my hair, I pulled back my shoulders and heading down the hall. I was just about to pass my office when I spotted him and came to a sudden halt. He was standing in the only light available—the daylight that seeped through a crack in my binds. He had his back to me, and he was staring at my white bare walls.

"Are you redecorating?" He bent over and picked up a framed photo of himself stacked neatly on the ground by his feet.

My insides curled into a knot.

"No." I entered the room, my hands conveniently buried with the note inside my pocket. "I took down your pictures."

I went to his side, but he didn't acknowledge me. He just gazed at the vibrant young image of himself, seemingly captivated by a time in his life when he held so much in the palm of his hands.

"I-I just couldn't look at these beautiful photos every day not knowing if I'd ever see you again." I said, and to be sure I had his attention, I reached out and gently touched to his shoulder.

When he looked to me, his gaze was piercing.

"You're stronger than you think, baby." He said with a concentrated look that suggested he knew a secret.

When I said nothing in response, he let out a sigh.

"Surprisingly, I'm not bad with a hammer." He waved the photo my way with a playful smile that made me chuckle.

"I may take you up on that one day," I said and as I reached for the photo, a beep sounded from my home computer.

Elvis spun around. I thank the Lord for changing the subject.

"That's a letter, or rather email." I pointed at my obsessively organized desk.

"This generation and all its gadgets," Elvis said with a hand over his heart.

"It's pretty handy."

Walking over to my desk, I took a seat. I gave the mouse a little shake and the computer screen lit up. My wallpaper was a lovely photo of Elvis.

"I see I didn't get taken off of everything," he said as he sat comfortably on the corner of my desk.

"I hadn't gotten around to it yet," I smiled, and he glared at me sideways.

He flipped his hand over, and motioned for me to proceed. A little yellow envelope blinked at the bottom of my screen. I moved the curser over it and with a click, up popped my unread mail. 'N.B.N headed your way', the letter head read. My eyes widened.

"So, this is a letter from, Melissa?" Elvis moved closer, reading her name from the display.

I nodded and let out a defeated groan.

"Melissa is... a fan of mine?"

"You know, this can wait," I reached for the mouse, but was stopped short by Elvis' hand.

"Why don't you want me to see her letter?"

"I...I didn't say that." My cheeks burned.

"Show me the letter," Elvis patted my hand.

"But..."

"Samantha." Elvis' voice grew stern.

Melissa and I had been friends for years. We shared one thing in common, a love for Elvis Presley. I paused, knowing full well the attachment icon would not be meant for mixed company. Melisa has a quirky personality. I sighed and clicked the file. It only took a second before the surprise popped up.

"I'll be as son of a..." Elvis stood up to get a better view.

The file opened to a photo of Elvis, shown dancing to a number called, "The Walls Have Ears" from his movie, "Girls, Girls, Girls." The song was by far the least interesting association the photo carried. The shot captured Elvis, completely by chance, in a state of arousal.

"Nobody will see it, Boss, they said." He smiled with sarcasm and walked away.

"It's uh... hard for a girl to miss."

He turned. "Are you saying women are passing this around?"

"I—"

"What does N.B.N. stand for? Wait, I'm not sure I want to know." Elvis raised both hands.

"Naughty but nice," I blurted out and Elvis paused, his hand still held in the air.

Our eyes met and his lips twitched with a smile. I dared not move. Elvis cracked first, and his outright laughter engulfed the room.

"Naughty but...," Elvis struggled.

"Nice." I finished for him.

He collected himself long enough to steal a glance at me, and then doubled over once again.

"So, let me get this straight. 'Little Elvis' here has been shared with women all over the world?" He wiped tears of laughter from his eyes.

Little Elvis? I'm not touching that one!

"Yes, I suppose you could say that." I was chuckling myself now.

"And to think, all those years, I was doing it the hard way!" He slapped his leg and went into a new round of guffaws.

Just as I was thinking this little distraction could not have come at a better time the phone rang at my desk. I looked twice in surprise at the caller ID. As though given a cosmic cue, it was my friend, Melissa. We both reached for the phone, but Elvis beat me to the call. His eyes glimmered triumphantly as he brought the receiver to his ear. I gestured wildly and begged for him to give me the phone.

"Hello, you've reached naughty but nice headquarters, this is Elvis, please leave a message after the tone," Elvis said before sounding a shrill beep and dropping the phone into my hands.

A muffled voice called questioningly from my palms. I brought the phone to my ear. Elvis sat back down on the corner of my desk to watch.

"Hello?" Melissa said.

"Yes, I'm here."

"Sam? Where did you get that message, it sounded just like him! I can't believe you found one that actually said naughty but nice." Melissa rambled excitedly

"I...uh...had an impersonator friend record it for me a while back," I shrugged, and Elvis grinned like an alley cat that finally had found some cream.

"You're a clever girl! Hey, I'm calling you to see if you're going to the tribute concert tonight in Atlanta."

I hadn't heard about any Elvis-related concerts in my home town. I glanced at Elvis, who simply raised his eyebrows.

"No, I wasn't planning on it," I said.

Elvis shook his head otherwise.

"Oh? I was hoping you'd pick me up a t-shirt. I really like this guy."

"I-I had no idea anyone was in town."

Elvis sighed and rested his chin pensively on his right palm.

"Listen, Melissa, I have company, can I call you back another time?"

"Oh, did you get the photo I emailed you?" Melissa suddenly asked.

Elvis grimaced and reached for the phone.

"I really have to go!" I practically shouted as I spun my chair away from his grasp.

I hung up the phone, not waiting for goodbyes. I would find a way to explain later. I exhaled in relief. I turned back around only to find Elvis glaring at me, his eyes tiny slits.

He had hopped off of the desk and was leaned back against it. His easy posture would look relaxed on anyone else, but his legs, stretched out in front of him and crossed at the ankles, telegraphed irritation with constant jiggling.

"You mentioned a concert?"

CHAPTER SIXTEEN

An hour later, and in a turn of last-word-irony I was dressing for the evening show. To say Elvis is persuasive is like saying the ocean is wide, but there was more to this evening than just my accommodating nature. I wanted out of the house. I had been trying to convince myself all evening that "anyone" could have left that note on my door, but my continence wouldn't rest. All I could see was Steve' pleading eyes at the café, and Elvis reminding me that God's children were historically bad when making decisions alone. The consequences for my sins felt long overdue.

Sitting at my grandmother's antique vanity, I was dabbing perfume to my wrist when the phone rang. I almost dropped the bottle in my rush to pick it up. The word "daddy" flashed on the screen.

"Daddy!" I had forgotten to call as promised.

"You were supposed to call."

"When I got home, yes sir," I squeezed my eyes tight. "I'm sorry." I knew better then to make excuses.

The line went silent. I turned the receiver around to see if we were still connected, and we were so I waited.

"You arrived safely then." He said curtly.

"Y-yes, sir." It wasn't so much a question, but I answered anyway.

"All right, goodnight."

"Goodnight."

Still holding the phone to my ear, I listened to the dial tone. I felt as disconnected as the line. My father deserved better. He had suffered through so much heartache. He didn't need me twisting the olive-branch of his life, he needed peace. But, I was human too, and a lot had happened on those three hundred miles home. I needed to talk to someone. I called the one person I knew I could count on.

She picked up on the first ring.

"I'm glad you called." Heather said, skipping the more mundane "hello".

Just the sound of her voice did wonders. "I'm home, and I'm fine." I beat her to the punch.

"Are you sure? You sound...funny."

I heaved a sigh, got up, and went to my closet.

"To be honest, things are...strange here." I considered a navy blue dress then disregarded it.

"W-what do you mean strange?"

My heart strings tugged over the worry I heard in her voice. She was like a big sister to me. The urge to tell her about the last twenty four hours surged but I held back.

The battle of good and evil didn't serve well over the phone.

"You know, it's been odd." I picked out a pair of black ankle strapped heals and tossing them to the bed.

"Odd, covers a lot of ground, Samantha!"

"Please, don't shout at me. Daddy's already mad, and I don't think I could handle it if you were too. I'm ok. I'm home, and Elvis is here, but I do need to talk to you. Can you come over tomorrow morning, it's sort of," I was extra careful, "important."

I could hear her breathing.

"Are you there?"

Heather had been in the trenches of life with me for so long, I wouldn't have blamed her if she hung up. But she didn't.

"You're right, we should talk."

That was easy.

"O-ok...good, tomorrow it is then," I said.

"See you in the morning, sleep tight," she said, and with that she promptly hung up in my ear.

The dial tone shrieked, and a silly smirk came over me. Heather's atrocious phone etiquette was back. Surprisingly, I had missed it. I longed for the good ole days, my old life.

* * *

I adjusted the cuffs of my long sleeved dress, and considered myself in the mirror. My chestnut hair fell soft in lengthy ringlets around my face. I was dressed all in black, a simple but classic look. Though worn off the shoulders, and exposing just the right amount of skin, my intentions were in fact more of an innocent nature tonight. I wished to tantalize not tempt. Leaning in closer, I wondered if my eyeliner was just a bit too heavy, and then just as quickly disregarded the notion. I felt sexy.

The heels of my shoes clicked against the wood floor of the hall as I joined the night. It's funny how a pair of shoes can boast a girl's confidence. Tonight, I felt poised enough to look my angel right in the eye and speak my heart. My excitement sparked as I walked, chest out and shoulders back. I imagined an invisible trail of perfume lingering behind me as I entered the living room, butterflies in my stomach, and looking for my prince charming.

Elvis was nowhere to be found. I dropped my hand bag to the brown suede couch with a sigh. I took out my necklace for the evening and fumbled with the clasp. I failed to hear my escort when he entered the room.

"Let me help with that." Elvis' Mississippi drawl roused a quiver across my shoulders. I glanced up and froze.

Across the room, dressed in a pair of sharply creased black slacks and pale blue shirt, was a man of worldly sophistication. And as he sauntered my way, I was mesmerize by the sight of the Presley strut reduced to a slower swagger. Was this Elvis Presley at the age of 70 or 75? I couldn't decide, but I dare not blink for fear I'd miss something new. Like the neatly trimmed, stark white mustache and goatee he sported, for one! His blue eyes shined a beautiful backdrop to his tanned skin and faded hair. He was the image of his aged father, but with the fuller soft features of his mother.

With steady hands, he took the jewelry from my grasp, and in looking at me, that familiar grin slipped across his face.

"What's the matter youngin, cat got your tongue?" He laughed.

I admired the lines of aged wisdom that deepened around his eyes. "You're beautiful," I sniffed back my tears, and crawled into his arms.

He encircled me in his embrace. "Careful now, this ole body hurts."

"You do? Where?" I instantly felt the need to mother him.

"Everywhere."

"Can I help?" I rubbed his arms surprised at how stout he was even at this stage in life.

"Nah, it's just a few too many, 'Polk Salad Annie's', I'm afraid." He chuckled.

I laughed with him and carefully hugged him once more. He was so beautiful. I would have happily sacrificed years from my own life to have seen him experience this stage of his.

"Let me get a look at you, darlin'." Elvis took my hand and stepped back.

He lifted my palm in to the air, and in turning his head slighting that little boy grin shined. He admired my face, then my hair, and his eyes sparkled with approval. I felt special. And I didn't have to look in the mirror to know my cheeks were multiple shades of red.

When he reached out with his free hand and wound a bent finger inside my curls I giggled like a teenager.

"Look at you, so beautiful." His easy smile was just for me. "And, I'm in no position to do a damn thing about it."

Even at this advanced age, he was still capable of stirring a deep desire within me.

"The tiger is tamed?"

"Tired, is more like it." His smile widened, deepening those adorable dimples.

Unable to resist touching him, I placed a light touch on his face. He quickly took my hand and brought it to his lips for a kiss.

"Turn around, let's put this on."

I had been so involved with his transformation that I forgot he had taken my necklace. I turned around, lifted my hair, and felt him slide the chain around my neck. He clasped it with surprising accuracy, and then resting his open palms to my bare shoulders, he leaned down. His lips gently glided over my skin in a light airy kiss. A vision of a much younger Elvis ran through my mind.

"You're too old for me, you know?" I teased, and enjoyed the sound of a deep chuckle in my ear.

* * *

The drive to the Cobb Galleria Centre was short, but traffic crawled. A light mist fell. The city lights sparkled in distorted watermarks across my windshield. I could feel an excitement in the evening air, a charge. It was the kind of thrill one can only find in a city the size of Atlanta. The night was alive, and I was dressed for it. I wanted to grab my handsome escort and show him all my favorite spots across town. Yet here we were, stuck in traffic with only the slap-slap sound of the wipers for company.

Talk about a downer, I looked down. Great, even my curls were drooping. I frowned.

A stream of vehicles filed past us. It seemed the whole town had showed up, and I counted three cars before someone let us in. If people only knew who was sitting in this car, I mused, the effort to park would be less painful. I circled once, twice, and then found a spot.

At first neither of us moved to exit. I watched Elvis' face flood with astonishment over the size of the crowd. I had to admit even I was shocked. There were fans everywhere! Some were dressed for an evening out, while others displayed their loyalty on a tee-shirt, but all unknowingly passed their idol in the car.

"Are you sure, you want to do this?" I asked.

He didn't answer right away. He was busy watching two women screaming and running to each other, arm's out and in full stride. His eyes widened as they collided and hugged as if it had been years. Smiling, he gave a chuckle. He was shaking his head while nibbling on those legendary lips. I was just about to repeat the question, when he suddenly spoke.

"I'm sure."

Examining his profile, I willed myself to see anything but Elvis Presley. I failed miserably.

"You're sure nobody can *see* you?"

"They *see* what they—"

"Want to see...I know, you told me." I sighed.

His attention snapped my way. "Let's just enjoy the evening, Samantha."

"Ok, however, you still look like," I started, and his eyes squinted at me. I held my hands up, "I'm just saying."

He inhaled a deep breath, and calmly reached into the breast pocket of his jacket. He pulled out a pair of thick black glasses usually reserved for glaucoma patients, and slipped them on. Turning my way, his expression was blank. A second passed and then he flashed a smile.

"Better?"

The glasses engulfed his face, hiding his famous baby blues, but his features were still hard to miss.

"I vote we leave." I said flatly.

I knew every romantic spot in the city. This wasn't one of them. What I wanted was privacy, alone time, with the most charismatic man in musical history. I wanted to find a cozy restaurant and cuddle up in a corner under candle light. I didn't care if he was old enough to be my grandfather—I stole a look—literally! And when I turned, bent on suggesting it, the passenger side door opened.

I took that to mean any proposal of a change would be vetoed. Disappointment flooded my heart.

Even as a much older man, Elvis remained a solid figure, but still moved in a slow and calculating way that matched his new age. I could not help but stare as he picked up each leg with his hand and encouraged it out of the car. I jumped out and raced to help him, but he waved me away with a scowl. Normally he'd tower over me by at least four inches, but tonight I was wearing my big girl shoes, and easily grew three inches. And though I tried to help by slipping my right hand around his left forearm, he promptly swapped our hands. Always a man's man, he would escort me not the other way around. I should have known.

We stepped in behind a crowd. Elvis' gait, though slowed to quarter-speed, still held that hypnotic strut. I was aware of how distinctive this walk of his was, perhaps to the degree of imagining double-takes from others around us. I paced us slower, allowing for more space between Elvis and his devotees.

"You need to change your walk," I whispered.

"What?" He said a bit too loudly.

I stopped and waited for the crowd to move further along.

"I know you don't realize this, but your style of walking is like the drug of choice to us fans. That impersonator inside has probably spent years trying to copy it perfectly!"

Elvis looked down to the ground with a smile.

"Can you change how you walk?"

"I-I don't know any other way to walk, honey."

"Think, Sammy Davis, Jr., John Wayne, or anyone else for that matter. You're an actor, improvise."

"Ok, I'll think of something." He gave my arm a reassuring pat.

We started once again and this time, his body leaned heavily against mine. The sheer weight of him caught me by surprise, and I heard myself grunt like a man. I fully expected a teasing comment to follow. Thankfully, none came.

With his arms draped around me, his shoulders slouched, and he walked with a limp in his right leg. A war wound, maybe? I had no idea, but he played the age card perfectly. Had I not known better, I would have rushed to get him a wheelchair.

* * *

The red brick galleria of Atlanta hosted an array of events. It was a multipurpose venue, used not just for the benefit of entertainment but also conventions. A newer building, it was rectangle in shape, and looked out of place when in comparison to the more mature establishments that flanked it. Course, the oddly shaped glass pyramid set on top didn't help. The building looked as if it wore an oversized birthday hat, and I couldn't help but snicker whenever I saw it.

The walk to the entrance was a bit of a distance, but eventually we caught up with our crowd. A woman threw us a look, one that suggested she found it odd that such a tiny woman could really second as a leaning post for a six foot tall chunk of man, no matter the age. I realized we must look ridiculous. Even in heals, I was miscast in my part.

Once inside, people were elbow to elbow. I was overcome by the pungent smell of floor cleaner and tangled cologne from the crowd. The chattering was so loud I could barely hear myself think. How they managed to visit I'll never know. But when a small group of people split off to admire the extravagant décor, the space they left behind helped to ease my sudden case of claustrophobia. My ability to breathe improved, but I still wanted to flee. Then Elvis patted my arm, and reluctantly, I pushed forward.

We parted the sea easily. People would see us coming and politely move aside. Maybe it was a respect your elders thing, but all I cared about was finding unused air before I passed out. And when my view was finally not the back of someone's head, I saw a group of people moving down a side hall. The sign read "Ball Room". We jumped in to join them.

The current flowed steadily. The shuffle-step-stop repetition allowed my attention to wonder. In fact I was so busy examining the glass roof—it didn't look half as silly from the inside—I was unaware we stepped through two absurdly tall solid oak doors. And when I woke, I felt transported back to the Peabody hotel. The room was breathtaking. With three crystal chandeliers over head, the ballroom was deeper then it was wide. Round tables, decorated in fine linen, were evenly spaced throughout the room.

"Over there." Elvis pointed to the farthest corner.

With a burst of vigor, he gave me a yank. To my shock and dismay, he headed for a table occupied by three young women.

"Mind if we join you young'uns?" Elvis asked in the voice of a 90- year- old man that had even me doing a double take.

Three heads, a statuette blonde, a brassy brunette and a mix of both, turned. All three women looked first from me and then to Elvis before nodding their approval with weak but respectful smiles.

Had I not been busy feeling so conspicuous I would have appreciated Elvis' thought-out seating arrangements. Having us sit with women barely out of high school was genius. A younger flock of women would be more likely to ignore a man as old as their grandfather. It was a perfect plan. We settled in, ready for the show.

"Where y'all from?" Elvis' accent twanged as he yelled at the girls, who were talking amongst themselves.

"Macon," the blonde, wearing a size too-small tee-shirt, said.

"What's that?" He cupped his ear with his hand.

People around us began to gawk.

"He doesn't hear too well." I mouthed, pointing to my own ear. I held back my laughter when I saw all three of their faces take on the look of dread.

"Y'all like this Presley feller?" Elvis asked, and the ladies eyes brightened at the mere mention of his name.

"Oh, he's wonderful," The brunette gushed with an accent that sounded more East coast then of a Southern decent.

"He's dead. Ya'll know that, right?" He blurted out.

All eyes, including mine, now glared his way. None of the young women spoke. They were seemingly unsure of how one responds to such a statement.

"Ah, just the same, I never cared for all that wigglin' anyhow." Elvis licked his lips as if the mere thought of it had left a bad taste in his mouth.

This was apparently the last straw. All three women stood, grabbed their bags and marched away from our table. Elvis watched them leave, his lips twitching with humor.

"Was it something I said?" He joked, sounding very much like his old self.

He crossed a boot over his left knee, and gave me a wink.

"If they only knew," I muttered as I watched the ladies walk away.

Elvis glanced back over his shoulder, and the mischievous twinkle in his eyes softened. "No, it's better this way," he said, and the room lights dimmed.

As if someone had flipped the volume switch, a room full of chatter dipped to a low buzz. The room shuffled, glasses clanged and people hushed each other around me. The air was thick, pulsating with excitement. The audience was ready.

An orchestra rumbled from the stage. Even with my vision impaired by the sudden darkness, I could see all heads were turned forward. All eyes but mine, that is. I was busy watching the restless stirring at the tables around me. The excitement was especially visible in the women. Some were hugging the friend next to them or holding hands. They waited impatiently for the man of the evening.

When a short burst of excitement sounded from the opposite side of the room, Elvis slipped off his glasses. I considered how even in this low light, his silhouette announced his presence. Beneath the canvas of a 75 year old man sat a living legend, whose knee bouncing told me he wanted nothing more than to take that stage. He was fidgeting so badly, I half expected him to leap out of his chair at any moment. My attention was so focused, that when the horns sounded with the opening of 2001 Space Odyssey, my heart jack hammered inside my chest.

"Elvis!" A woman shouted somewhere in the darkness.

"I'm here, baby, I'm here," he whispered, and shifted to the edge of his seat.

He was holding my hand while that famous crescendo swelled. The percussions blasted, and his grip tightened. I winced. The drummer crashed his symbols and the band ignited. Elvis was clearly transfixed. He didn't even notice that I had slipped my numb and tingling hand out from his death grip.

A spot light hit the stage. The crowd went into a frenzy of applause, and Elvis clapped too. But when four women stepped out from stage left, followed by four males, he all but elevated right out of his seat. I had my hand out, ready to grab him at any moment.

"Well, alright," he said with a brilliant smile.

When all performers were in their rightful places, the intro came around again, and the man of the evening took the stage. A round of applause filled the room. I sat up tall, but my view was partially obscured by a few hundred bobbing heads. It was only when the artist moved to center stage that a beautiful replica of the famed 1973 American eagle jumpsuit came into view. My focus flickered as the stage lights reflected off the red, white, and blue rhinestones in an almost blinding ray of light. The artist strolled across the stage twice, and then stepped up to the microphone. When the theater lights hit his face, the crowd gasped. And I could tell by the wide-eyed look on Elvis' face that he was as surprised as I was at the likeness.

Though not as strikingly handsome as my angel, I had to admit this man was close. In fact, the resemblance was eerie.

"Well, I said, see, see, see rider." The song began.

The screams only got louder as his voice echoed. The crowd was caught up in the moment. And when a woman directly behind us screeched, Elvis and I both turned. It was dark, but I could clearly see him watching her as she waved her arms, unaware the man she "really" wanted was right in front of her. He turned back to me, perplexed and slightly amused, but I could only shrug. I'd never been to a show quiet like this, and her reaction stunned even me.

Worried at first, I considered mentioning the man on stage was doing him a great honor. But then a woman stood up from her seat and rushed the stage. That's when everything changed.

"Come on." He grabbed my hand.

Focused on his virtual double, Elvis headed for the stage. He followed the outer edge of the crowd, pulling me in his wake. Determined to get a closer look, he stepped around tables, and dodged couples dancing in the aisle. I was struggling to keep up, while also looking for a safe place to hide.

A storm was coming; I could see it brewing in his eyes. His heated gaze was locked on the stage, and to my horror, I realized he was marching in full Elvis fashion no longer caring about the illusion of his age. As though on a mission, he took rushed elongated steps that were agile even for a twenty year old. I frantically scanned the room, but nobody paid us any mind. And when he stopped a few feet from the stage, and I accomplished a virtual face-plant against his back without acknowledgment, I knew I was in trouble.

"Everyone's having a good time, don't you think." I said loud enough to be heard over the music.

He said nothing. He simply stood with his arms crossed at his chest, his gaze shifting from the man on the stage to women waving their hands in the air while their husbands rolled their eyes. It was not a secret that Elvis the man never understood his fans devotion, but he did count on it and even needed it. And while this love he counted on was being showered onto another, the look of worry on his face told me, he feared losing it.

We had to leave. I opened my mouth, an excuse already prepared, but I never got a chance to speak it. I was silenced by the first few bars of "Love Me Tender", or as I liked to call it, the kissing song. I cringed. Surely God will come to our rescue, I prayed, and when he answered, I was never happier.

"He's good, but he's *sure* not Elvis." A woman said to another as they walked by without seeing the man she spoke of so ardently.

"Oh how I wish he were!" The other said, and not a moment too late

Elvis' fiery eyes cooled. Even standing in thick darkness, I could see the light smile that now softened his features. In the time frame of a single heart beat, he went from looking like the loneliness man in the world to the most beloved. Grinning, he stepped back in to the shadows. He leaned against the wall, left knee drawn up and his boots heal propped up behind him. His gaze was focused on the women as they continued up the aisle, and I internally exhaled.

"Love Me Tender" swelled. As was the tradition, the passing out of kisses started at the stage. But unlike Elvis' show, the party soon moved to the floor, and scarves flew around the tables with zeal. Playful fans snatched them up. The man of the hour move quickly. All appeared to be business as usual until his eyes met mine.

Caught off guard, I quickly averted my gaze. My attention fell to a tall but average framed man, standing on the other side of the room. He was statute and motionless, a contrast to the commotion around him. And though he was cloaked in the shadows, his attention appeared fixed. It was as if he looked right at me. My stomach instantly coiled into a knot. My body went cold, and I had to look away. The moment I did, I wished I hadn't. What if he moves, and comes this way? I wouldn't see him. Quickly, I looked back. He was gone.

The song was drawing to a close. Behind me Elvis had pushed away from the wall. He stood erect and stiff. I pondered his alert posture. Had he seen the man too? Was he thinking what I was thinking? That the note and this man were somehow linked? That likely all pointed back to Steve, and the mess that "I'd" started back in Memphis? Trying to calm myself, I drew in slow and even breaths. Elvis didn't know about the note, I reminded myself while I looked back over my shoulder at him. Or did he?

The kissing drew closer. Small beads of sweat rose on my upper lip as the handsome man headed my way. The theme from "Jaws" echoed in my ears. I took a step back, but stopped when a blinding spotlight hit my face. The artist was suddenly before me, and I found myself squinting into a pair of emerald eyes like that of the Caribbean Sea.

Without missing a note, the performer extended me his hand. In it he held one silk blue scarf. Having never been given such a gift before, I was unsure if the offer was really meant for me. I nervously looked around. And when nobody stepped up to claim it, I reached out.

The silky treasure merely fluttered across my finger tips before it was snatched away.

"Easy, now," The artist said with a chuckle to someone behind me.

It funny how vital an object becomes when you think someone has "taken" it from you. Scowling, I spun around to…the real Elvis. He stood ridged, scarf in hand and a sneer on his face. Leisurely, he wadded the gift into his palms and promptly shoved it in his pocket. His glare was steady, and didn't ease until the entertainer wisely moved on. When his eyes meet mine, his frown lifted into smile.

"I'll give this to you later." He winked.

* * *

When the first few bars of "Can't Help Falling in Love" began, I grabbed my coat, took Elvis by the hand and all but dragged him out of there. All I could think about was getting outside in time to spot any sign of "the man" or Steve…who ever. Not to speak to him, but to prove to myself that he actually existed. That up to this point, I hadn't imagined it all. After all, in my life coma's and day dreams seemed to be common place. And though

I didn't give him much choice, I was surprised Elvis went so willingly. Course he trudged along refusing to give up the charade. I wanted to scream at him to hurry, but I just kept pulling and he kept resisting. I'd look back every few steps, irritated with our pace, and his little swaggering grin would spark my temper.

With Elvis on my hip, I blasted out the lobby door and into a frigid night. Once outside, the cold air rushed over me and I sucked in an icy breath of surprise. I looked left and then right. No Steve. All I could see was a sea of red tail lights in a convoy to the exit. If Steve had been here, I'd missed him.

CHAPTER SEVENTEEN

The drive home was dreary, void of inspiration. Only the light humming of the car's engine filled the space between us. The cities lights flickered through the cab, highlighting Elvis' stone- like features. I tried not to stare, but it was impossible. He was so silent, and I was worried. He sat gazing out the window, his thumb lightly resting against his mouth and a distant look in his eyes.

A mix of regret and guilt swelled. For months now, I had felt estranged uncomfortable in my own skin. Since the accident, my emotions my moods, everything had changed. I'd spent months ignoring it, making excuses. But it wasn't until this night, an evening spent evading my own self made demons—with an angel no less—that I began to question my own reality. Up till now, I had accepted many truths that most would find unbelievable, but even I was starting to have doubts. Had someone told me I was simply going insane, that none of this was real, I would have been relieved. Insanity at least made sense!

"He thinks he loves you, you know." Elvis suddenly spoke. It was the first words he'd uttered since we'd gotten into the car, and the first time his voice didn't elevate me to great heights.

Stopped at a traffic light, I strained to see his most telling feature—his eyes.

"No I don't know that." I said carefully. "What I know, or rather what I believe is that Steve and I just met and suddenly he's infatuated." I left out that Steve's attentions were provoked and instigated by me. That it was my fault, but I was sure he knew.

He smiled lightly. "You do make a lasting first impression."

I stared at him. "I've done nothing but cause chaos at every turn and you're making jokes. Unbelievable." I turned back to the wheel with a heavy sigh.

"You would feel better if I was mad?"

"Yes!" I spun back to him. "At least I'd understand that, it would make *sense*, and..." I was just about to explain why I deserved his wrath when a car honked behind us. Looking up, the light was green. I grumbled and hit the gas.

"Women," he chuckled.

I merged onto the freeway, but drove five miles under the speed limit. Cars were passing me, sneering and gesturing. Elvis would smile big and wave, only to then drop back to a serious expression once they'd passed.

DREAM ANGEL

"I need to find him, and try to explain. If he's here because of what happened in Memphis then—"

"No."

I pulled my eyes from the road, analyzing him. That's it, just no? I was supposed to just settle for that? I moved over to the fast lane and gunned it.

"So, I wasn't imagining it? He is here?"

"Samantha, do you trust me?" His tone sounded fatherly, but then the allusion of his age helped.

Why is it nobody can give me a simple yes or no answer?

"Immensely." I drew in a steadying breath.

"Then we'll take care of this tomorrow, together. Until then no running off half cocked." He was nodding at me, pointedly, insisting on my compliance.

I'm sure the analogy fit, but I didn't like how it sounded, so unthinking so reckless—so me. I agreed.

The subject was dropped. By that I mean we stopped talking about it. Again, the quiet came. It felt like torture. If music was good for the soul, then silence was the Devil's only friend. I needed to settle my mind, and I knew only one way to do it. I reached over and flipped on the stereo. Preset to my favorite channel, "Burning Love" bounced from the speakers.

Every since I was a little girl music had always been my escape. Right away the guitar strumming intro lifted a weight from my soul, and put a flicker of a smile on to my face. Desiring more, I headed for the volume but Elvis beat me to it. With the push of a button he changed the channel. A gospel standard suddenly echoed. Granted this was not the singer of my choice but I didn't complain.

Inside these beautiful words of praise, I felt my spirit stir. My heart simultaneously pounded with delight and pain. I was a bundle of mixed up feelings. On one hand, it was not lost to me that I was spending my days with one of God's angels, and yet I hadn't given God himself a moment of my time. Sure we'd read the bible together, I'd even prayed out of desperation. But as I once vowed, I had not sat quietly in God's presence. Yet, the Almighty comforted me. The uplifting music enveloped me. It was as if God himself had wrapped his arms around me, lifting me to new heights. His unconditional love was good for my troubled soul.

When I was sure I couldn't get much higher, Elvis began to sing. My heart leapt over the sound. His voice was variable, unpredictable, and often brilliant. The very sight of him enveloping himself in song was a spiritual experience in of itself. I watched him drift deeper into song. His eyes were closed and his facial expressions were so soft one just knew he had reached heaven, if only in his heart and mind.

We were but a mile from the house when I picked up the pace. I zipped around the last corner, and coasted into my drive just in time to catch a glimpse of that lip curling upward as his baritone lifted into a soft tenor. Expertly he controlled his voice as it smoothly rose into an eyebrow rising falsetto. He held the arrangement without strain. I was entranced by a voice that had sung with the angels long before he was one.

The song ended and so did the moment. At first, nobody moved. I barely even breathed. Elvis sat with a look of satisfaction on his face. He all but glowed. There was no doubt that he had been created to touch people with that voice—his mission accomplished. And when he turned to me with a humble grin fixed on his face, I returned with a smile of my own, only double.

"Thank you." My voice was thick. "If I could hear that every day, I'd go to heaven right now."

He studied me. "That's sweet honey, but you have your whole life ahead of you, don't get in a rush," he said with a soft smile before opening the car door.

Elvis reached the house first and I passed him the keys. He held the door for me to enter, and I couldn't resist placing a tender kiss to his lips as I passed, enjoying the sight of his eyes narrowing over my forwardness.

"Would you like a snack?" I dropped my bag, unraveled out of my jacket, and headed for the kitchen.

"I could eat." He followed close behind.

I smiled to myself. I knew he didn't really need to eat. He didn't need to sleep either. He simply enjoyed participating in the tiny pleasures in life. But we'd missed dinner, and I was famished. I craved a devilish treat, something I had been considering long before the evening started. It was a small request really, a perfect end to the evening.

With Elvis hovering close by, I opened the refrigerator and pretended to look for something truly desirable. I shuffled items from one shelf to another, stalling for effect. And when I felt I had his attention, I grabbed two sticks of butter and turned. His eyes twinkled with curiosity.

How do I get what I want, I ponder. Maybe I should just ask? No. That would be too easy and not nearly as much fun. Composed, I walked across the kitchen, and headed for the pantry. He watched me closely. And I almost laughed out loud at how quickly he jumped into step. I brought out a jar of peanut butter and slapped it onto the counter. Then I grabbed a single ripe banana, and turning, I swung it in his direction. He looked quizzically from the peanut butter jar, to the fruit, and then back to me.

"U-huh, no!" He waved his hands in the air.

"Ah, come on, just this once?"

"No-o-o...," he said, shaking his head.

As if to make a point, he turned and sat down at the table. He crossed one leg over the other, ankle to knee, and that foot of his went to jigging with nervous energy. I pouted, but it was no good. He wasn't about to budge.

"You won't even make me one little bitty peanut butter and nanna sandwich, just for fun?" I asked, already collecting the other ingredients I remembered from heart.

"No, it's been way too long, Sam."

"Ok, then, I'll make one for you." I willfully banged two pans together, drowning out his protest, but he only chuckled.

"I read how to do this, once."

Elvis' lips twitched as I fumbled with the skillet. If there's one thing all women know, it's how to get a man to take over a task. First I began, vigorously and completely in error, spreading the peanut butter on an untoasted slice of bread. Second I worked extra slow, dragging it out. I peeked periodically to see if my angel was paying attention. He sat, forehead to index finger, studying me in silence. I "sliced" the bananas and placed them on top of the nutty mixture. Then purposely, I dropped two bread slices into the skillet, unbuttered.

"Ah man!" Elvis said, jumping up from his seat too quickly for a man of his age. "I don't know what you've been reading darling, but you can't skip the butter."

"Oh?" I stepped aside.

"You toast the bread first, honey, *then* you mash, *not cut*, the bananas," Elvis grabbed the fork from my hand and began creating the treat that was almost as famous as he was.

Smiling triumphantly, I took a seat. The sight of a domesticated Elvis cooking with his sleeves rolled up, and a towel tossed over his shoulder was a stunning sight. He forearms flexed, and he moved with such ease it was obvious the passing of time had not tampered his memory. I couldn't help but admire those long tapered fingers as he worked. He had great hands, smooth yet strong. At just a glance, a woman knew those hands were talented. I especially loved that one pinky finger, bent from an old football injury. It was so manly, an injury he would no doubt have suffered, famous or not.

When he began to tell me the story behind his favorite treat, I forced myself to refocus and hung on to his every word. He said his mother had made the treat to pacify her little boy's request for sweets. And like the other children in his neighborhood, they couldn't afford extras such as jelly so the banana's made an easy replacement. He thought it was poignant that what was essentially a poor man's sandwich had become so famous.

"Now you take the butter...like so," he said.

The bread sizzled when he released it into the skillet. Steam from the hot butter floated lazily up from the pan. It drew my eyes to the clock for the first time that night. It was 11:00 pm, and I didn't want the night to end.

When Elvis turned, sandwiches in hand, I was already holding my fork. His smile dropped, our eyes met, and we both began to laugh. Shaking his head, he dropped my plate in front of me and took a seat.

"That's a dirty trick," he waved a finger at me.

Smiling happily, I dug in.

"Baby girl, you don't eat this with a knife and fork." He grumbled.

I looked up, appalled that he actually suggested I eat something so greasy with my fingers. A clear violation of the distinctly Southern way my mother had raised me.

"Your mama's not here." He picked up his sandwich and took a bite.

"You're sure about that?" I glanced around.

He could only nod his affirmation as he busily savored a gooey mouthful. I looked down at the hot treat, and with a hesitant smile, I picked it up to take a bite too big for any woman. Might as well go all the way! Elvis' eyes widened and he began to chuckle. I covered my mouth.

"Goo," was as close as I could come to a compliment as peanut butter mixed with the light taste of fruit stuck to every corner of my mouth.

Elvis' laughter quickly turned to hysterics. Soon he was slapping the table top in his amusement. As always, I found myself laughing so hard that I was close to choking, which only made it that much more hilarious to Mr. Presley.

* * *

I washed and Elvis dried. The night was winding to a close, whether I liked it or not.

"I think it's time for you to get some shut eye," he said casually while drying the last pan.

I glanced over, considering what argument might work this time, though none had in the past. It was a shame too, I thought. I was just getting use to this new "advanced" look. With his caramel skin, a gift from his Indian ancestor, glowing handsomely against his white locks I felt oddly comforted with this display of aged wisdom.

"Thank you." I whispered.

"Ah, it was nothing. Just don't forget the butter next time."

"No. I mean, thank you for tonight."

He looked at me, grinned, and reached for my hand.

"You're welcome, baby."

I brought his cold damp fingers to my lips and kissed them, lingering longer than normal.

"I don't know what I would have done without you with me tonight. You were," I paused before clarifying, "are...you are a true gift to this world and to me."

His gaze lowered, "Oh, I-I don't know about that, honey," he said.

His modesty remained his most endearing quality.

The evening—and our time together—was coming to a close. I could feel it. Even now it's hard to explain "how" I knew, except to say the moments we shared were like a slow burning candle glimmering softly to its end.

"Do you realize how much you're loved?" I asked softly.

He didn't respond, but his intense look urged me to go on.

"You once said it's hard to live up to an image? Well, what you saw tonight was a whole lot of people still loving the man, not the myth."

His eyes quickly turned misty. It never failed to surprise me how easily he could be brought to tears. How under the shell of this sturdy man beat the heart of the most compassionate human being I'd even known, or ever will know.

He drew me into his arms, inhaling a breath that seemed to have no end. "Thank you," he muttered on the exhale, while still holding me firm.

Tenderly he pushed me out from his arms so that he could look into my eyes. As was his habit, he held my gaze for the longest time allowing his attention to drift over my features. The air sparked, and that familiar pull tugged at me.

"It's late, I better go to bed," I sniveled, realizing it was best.

He leaned in, his lips lightly brushing over mine in an innocent kiss goodnight. "Sleep tight, baby girl."

His lips were so very close. I could feel his breath, and yet taking my cue, I turned to exit.

"Oh, uh, honey." He called out. "You forgot somethin'."

Turning back, my heart soared at the sight of a blue silk scarf dangling in the air. I had all but forgotten about his promise. I raced to claim the gift I had always wanted him, and only him, to give me. Reaching out, I grasped a corner, and excitedly gave it a yank. The fabric pulled taut as Elvis had held firm to his end. How sweet of him to play this game with me, I gushed.

Though I knew he would not let go until he was ready, attempting to take it was part of the fun. I pulled again, and as I had predicted, he was resolute. His smile beamed. I sighed dramatically to which he only chuckled. After a few more attempts he let go. I snatched it up, and brought it to my heart.

"Now get to bed," He ordered.

I considered stealing one more kiss, and then thought twice. I didn't want to press. I knew if I kissed him, I would want more. Though my heart was breaking, I dramatically whirled the scarf over my head and took my departure like a queen. I could hear Elvis chuckling all the way down the hall.

* * *

My swift entrance stirred the air, and a light scent of lavender—my mother's favored scent—surrounded me. The aroma was strong enough to imagine that I only had to turn and I'd find her waiting for me. The mere thought was heavenly, but I knew better. Mother wasn't here. She'd been gone for years now, yet the loss was still so fresh. Some days, I'd wonder if the pain would ever lessen, and then worry that such a reprieve would mean her memory may fade with it. I suppose a daughter always needs her mother, I thought, and before I could stop it the first tear fell.

Weary from this constant emotional rollercoaster, I headed for my bed. I was kicking off my shoes, unzipping my dress, and just about to take a seat when a pile of clothes, discarded haphazardly across my bedspread, stopped me. I hadn't realized I'd left such a mess, I snarled. Whipping away a tear with the back of one hand, I snatched up a hand full the garments with the other and tossed them over my shoulder. Still not relieved, I grabbed another and another. On and on it went until clothes were scattered all about room. Panting, I fell to my bed like an exhausted pile of human flesh

While I lay there I was visited by a third and final emotion—shame. It snuck up on me like the ghost of Christmas past, and a weary understanding crept in with it. I realized much of what was wrong with my life had everything to do with my insistent need to do everything my way. It was a flawed plan that I kept beating, desperate to make it work. Worse, God had expressed to me what he wanted, even sent an angel, and I still wasn't listening. How hard headed could one woman be? I was like a tornado of disaster blowing through everyone's life, including my own. Nobody was safe!

When was I going to grow up, and do what I knew was right?

On a mission, I grabbed my leather bound journal from the table next to my bed. I hadn't written a word for weeks but with pen in hand, I waited for that all over warm feeling that my father had always told me meant God was close. My heart was unsettled, so I prayed while I waited. I don't know how long I sat, it could have been two minutes or two hours, but when that warm rush finally came, I was ready.

Dear God.

I won't make excuses for my behavior. I only ask for your forgiveness, and take comfort in your compassionate nature.

For 300 miles your angel spoke of your beautiful plan for my life. He told me that great blessings can be found in a single act of obedience.

I believe I finally understand. I'm ready, and I submit to your plan. I pray for the strength to follow through. My angel belongs with you.

Clutching my journal to my breast, I crawled into bed. I wanted to do as my angel asked, as God wanted, and move forward. I longed to be worthy of this special gift God had sent me, and accept what had once been unacceptable. I wanted to let go.

When will you leave, I heard my own voice ask as I drifted off to sleep. I squeezed my eyes tighter. *When you ask me to*, Elvis' words replayed.

CHAPTER EIGHTEEN

Clink-clink-clink! The sound flooded my subconscious. It was obtrusive and uncalled for like a neighbor pounding a tool at 8:00 A.M. There was nothing worse than starting your day with the urge to strangle someone. And now it was going to take me two hours and a pot of coffee before I could find my better disposition.

Clank-Clank-Clank!

It was no use. I rolled over and buried my head under my pillow. I played like a turtle until finally curiosity got the best of me. I peeked to the clock. Was it really 10:00 am? That's not early that's late. My face heated, and I felt foolish for being so cranky.

Outside, rain softly tapped against my window in a constant drizzle. It was another dreary day, perfect for the task that lied ahead. Letting go, I snarled and then sighed. I'd been delaying the inevitable for so long, it seemed unbelievable that tomorrow had become today. I wasn't even sure how this worked. Do I just tell him, it's ok to leave? That I understand he can't stay and hold my hand forever? And what about Steve, was he still out there? The questions were endless, and to stay calm I had to remind myself that Elvis would know what to do. Shoot, he'd probably be thrilled, happy for me! I frowned.

Turning over, I yawned and stretched but that all over good feeling never came. Might as well get on with it, I thought and jumped out of bed. I slipped on my purple fuzzy slippers and puttered to the bath. I took one look at myself in the mirror and gasped. My hair was sticking not up, but out on both sides. I looked like a rock groupie—worse—from the 80's. I couldn't help but chuckle at the unsightly mess. It was either that or cry which was a real option at this point.

Ambidextrous as a child, I wielded a hair brushed with one hand while tending to my teeth with the other. Good manners dictated that I should have been up long before my guest, and with one strike already against me, I skipped my normal routine. In fact the only makeup I allowed time for was mascara—the one thing mother said never to leave the house without. Well, that and lipstick.

Ready in a jiff, I pulled my knee length robe closed with a yank, and with a deep breath stepped out to the day. The aroma of roasted coffee beans drifted down the hall, rich and robust. For a moment I considered running for my favored morning beverage, but chose to linger instead. Savoring the moment seemed best. The very thought of Elvis brewing my favored treat, anticipating my morning routine, made me smile. It was my first for the day. Maybe I should just keep him? I smiled. No, I had to follow through. Do as he wanted, what Elvis himself had predicted. *Stick to the plan Samantha,* I was lecturing myself when that blasted noise came again.

Clink-clink.

The sound was sharp, and I simultaneously jumped in place. Quickly, I realized the noise was coming from the hall bath—our very first meeting place. I smiled with the memory. Slowly I approached, my eyes locked on to the door. I could hear the sound of water running as I drew closer, a trickle not a steady stream. I sighed with relief. I wasn't sure I could handle the sight of my angel back where it all started, naked and enjoying a shower. I would have surely caved to such a temptation.

The door was cracked. At first I hesitated, but finally I did what all hot blooded women in my position would have done—I peeked. It was only a reflection, but the sight of a 30 year old Elvis, bare-chested and wearing only a towel, made me instantly flush. And as if the fresh-from-a shower look wasn't inspiring enough, he was shaving and with a pink razor to boot. He held it awkwardly like a whittled down pencil in an over sized palm. On every downward stroke he'd pause and tap the sinks basin with the bladed edge.

Clank-clank! I smirked devilishly.

I should have moved on, but my feet simply refused budge. I was frozen; convinced any sudden movements would alert him to my position. It was better to remain still—all day if I must. It was a sacrifice I was willing to make, I thought before sneaking one more look.

He worked slowly. I couldn't help but notice the tiny pieces of tissue stuck to his chin and almost openly laughed. Seems he was out of practice, clumsy, but breathtaking just the same. With his hair slicked back and water droplets still glistening on his skin, he was like a perfect piece of art, and should have been standing in an open aired castle rather than my cramped bathroom in Georgia. But of all his outward qualities nothing shined like his inward beauty. He all but smoldered as he stood there so relaxed and natural enjoying this time to himself.

How was I going to let him go? I still didn't know.

As I sent up a silent prayer for guidance and strength, I saw his hand pause from inside the mirror. His gaze shifted, and I quickly fell to my love for arithmetic. *Five times one is five. Five times two is ten.*

He flashed me a big smile. "Well, don't just stand there lurking," he said with a chuckle and a push to the door.

I headed for the only seat in the room, the commode.

"I, huh, normally prefer an electric razor, but this was all I could find, hope you don't mind." Elvis inspected the device with repugnance.

I nodded happily as he went back to the task at hand, seemingly unmoved by my presence.

There's nothing sexier than watching a man shave. The sight of him jetting out his lower lip, giving careful consideration to his next move, had me feeling as sultry as the moist bathroom air. Without thinking, I pressed my own tongue inside my lip as if offering him helpful hints. The urge to wrap my arms around him, and run my hands up that tempting chest swelled.

On more than one occasion, I had to remind myself to breathe. I'd become distracted with something as simple as his bare feet, seemingly bigger than a size eleven, and actually forget to draw in a breath! I was lost to a visual tour that started at those knees—he thought knobby but I found adorable—and ended at the towel wrapped around his lean waist. By that time my lungs were so wilted, they all but begged for a breath. And when I finally drew in one, I gasped so loud, I couldn't believe he didn't hear.

"Damn woman, if you don't make love to me with your eyes," he said, with a quick shimmer of his shoulder, "gives me Goosebumps every time."

"I-I don't mean to stare." I was giddy and slightly mortified.

"No need to apologize, honey, I like it." He gave me a wink from inside the mirror.

I tried to laugh away my all-over blushing, but when he suddenly announced, "Heather's here," and a second later I heard the knock, I raced from the room.

"I'll get it!" I had forgotten I'd asked Heather to come by, but I was glad she was here.

I didn't stop for a security peek I just opened the door.

"I'm so happy you came." My warm smile widened further over the sight of the morning treats she held in her hand.

"Good morning," she said, cradling a tray of bakery goodies and eyeballing my attire. "I hope I didn't interrupt anything."

"No, I just got out of bed."

"Did you?" She giggled as she passed me, headed for the kitchen.

"You know it's not like that," I said hot on her heals.

"Well, thank God for small miracles. Besides, I hear sex is better if the person is actually "alive". Heather said in her typical forward tone.

At first I scowled, but then I chuckled. It was sort of funny.

"Where is the hunk this morning anyway?"

She sat down at the table and began to pass out the designer coffees. Mocha, my favorite! The smell alone had my mouth watering. Or was my mouth watering before she got here? I inwardly giggled and my face blushed.

"He's in the hall bath, shaving." I reached for my drink.

"I bet that's quite a sight." Heather lifted her cup to her lips for a taste.

"It is."

Her first sip stalled in mid air as she stared at me over the rim of her steamy brew.

"Tell me you're not spying on him, Samantha."

I rolled my eyes. "I was invited to watch, thank you very much. Besides, we were only talking."

She smiled lightly. "Good."

DREAM ANGEL

Suddenly, the morning felt lighter in the presence of a friend. It was an odd mix of contentment with a bit of silliness, but it felt good.

"We were just catching up since, you know, we didn't get much time to talk on the drive home." I said under my breath, enjoying Heather's scrutinizing expression.

"W-what do you mean? The drive is over 300 miles."

I nodded and sipped my coffee.

"Well, if you didn't talk, what did you do?"

I shrugged. "Stuff."

"You're kidding, right?" She laughed hesitantly.

This was too easy. Heather wanted to hear that Elvis was the stud the world had always imagined so badly, it almost took all the fun out of teasing her.

"Well you know," I looked around, "a man like that can have a lot of pent up energy after thirty years."

Heather choked on her coffee. Quickly she grabbed a napkin and pressed it firm to her mouth. She was coughing and gagging, while my smile remained strategically hidden behind the lid of my drink. After awhile, I began to worry she couldn't breathe. And I was just about to get up and swat her on the back when she gasped a breath. She's alive! My laughter exploded.

"You, you, witch!" She hissed.

Call the newspapers she's watching her language!

"Bitch."

So much for that!

I slapped the table as I laughed. It truly was a rare moment of giving Heather some of her own medicine.

We were laughing, enjoying the easy banter that came with our special kind of friendship, when the man of the hour entered the room. We both sat up straighter as Elvis stood before us, dressed all in black with the cuffs of his sleeves flipped up and his eyes wide in curiosity.

"Well, hello there big boy," Heather said in her best Mae West impression.

Elvis' I-don't-get-it smile fluttered, and we both busted up again. When it became obvious we weren't going to calm until one of use left the room, it was Heather who excused herself. She shot pass Elvis so fast she practically spun him in place. I heard her giggling down the hall and a second later, the slamming of the bathroom door.

"Is she sick?" Elvis pointed in the direction she fled.

"Most definitely," I said, chuckling and dabbing tears.

Nothing was more prefect than sharing in a moment of silliness with the two people I cared for most. Granted, it didn't help to lessen the pain of what lied ahead, but it was none-the-less a perfect moment in time. One I will relive forever.

"W-what'd I miss?" His eyes sparkled as he sat down.

I knew he hated being left out of anything, especially if it was a secret, but there was just no lady-like way to share the details with him.

"We were, uh, talking about a private matter that," I paused to rethink.

"Hold it." Elvis held up his hands. "The rooster doesn't always need to know what the hens have been up to."

"Well, you didn't miss anything, just girl talk." I stood up and walked to the edge of the kitchen.

Looking down the hallway, the bathroom door was still shut. I could hear water running on the other side. Any minute now, my life would change. But not before Heather returned. No, she needed to hear what I had to say, I told myself as I stepped into the hall and began to pace. I needed her with me. Only with her by my side could I broach the subject that weighed down my heart.

"I don't know how y'all drink this. It's not coffee." Elvis said from the kitchen.

I turned back, and found him standing there with a cup of modern day brew in his hand and a look of disgust on his face. When our eyes met I forced a smile, but he didn't smile back.

"It's an acquired taste." I averted my gaze.

There was no avoiding "the talk", I knew, but the irony that I was now waiting on it so ardently didn't escape me either. My life was just crazy enough for this moment to appear normal, I thought and took another look down the hall. What was taking Heather so long?

With my heart pounding like a jack hammer against my chest, I resigned to start without her. And I managed to take only two steps towards the kitchen before that red flashing light from the night before stopped me. Now, stalled by the phone station, my attention flickered. When had I last checked my messages? Was it before Memphis—no—before my accident? Again the answer was, no. In fact, I realized, I couldn't remember ever checking it. And I can't say why—possibly to stall the inevitable—but it seemed important that I do it now.

"Honey, are you feeling—" Elvis' words drifted off as he stepped into the room.

I looked up to him, and I'm not sure what perplexed me more, the look of dread on his face or how quickly he curbed it.

"A-are you ok?"

I didn't answer.

"I think I broke your toilet, no joke, because it just keeps running, and I've been jiggling the handle for," Heather's rambling was cut short when she too entered the room.

Why was everyone looking at me as if I had my hand over the button to World War III? Shrugging, I pushed it.

The answering machine clicked on with a hum. The first few messages were from my father. They echoed loudly, and I quickly hit the forward button. I skipped through doctor reminders and rescheduling requests, desperate for answers. I had no idea what I was looking for, and yet my heart raced. On the fourth message, I understood why.

"Hello love, I was calling to see if you had made it home from Boston." Steve's voice blared. "Guess not. Well, ring me when you do."

Steve? My mind skipped. Did he just say Boston? I fumbled for the next message.

"I hope you're reconsidering my offer, Samantha. Remember, I love you." Again it was Steve's voice.

I looked up and the sight of Heather, misty eyed and pale, escalated my confusion and my fear.

"I-I don't understand." I turned to Elvis, hoping he would explain, but he was monitoring the floor.

I was reaching out to him, pleading for him to just look at me when Heather began to explain.

"You've known Steve for some time, Samantha," Her voice was barely above a whisper.

At first, I wasn't sure I'd heard her right.

"No. I-I barely know him." I said, convinced this was a misunderstanding.

As if on cue one last message blared, cementing the facts further.

"I'm growing tired of this game, Samantha. You *better* call me." Steve's normally jovial tone rumbled with anger.

The room spun, and I took a wobbly step backwards, bumping into Elvis.

"Whoa baby," he said, steadying me while guiding me to the couch.

My body trembled. My head pounded light at first but escalating fast.

"I-I'm so sorry, Sam. I didn't want you to find out like this," Heather's voice cracked.

Sitting on the couch, I felt numb. I was staring at her while also scanning through my memory bank like a movie stuck on rewind. Every encounter I'd had with Steve replayed. Try as I might, I couldn't recall anything prior to Memphis. Nothing that could explain a way this nightmare, and or stop the look of worry on Elvis' face.

"I don't remember." I whimpered helplessly.

"I know." Heather spoke those two words so matter-of-factly, my breath caught inside my chest.

"What do you mean you know?" My voice began to quake, and tears quickly pooled as the ramification of her words sank in. "How long?"

"Only a few days, I swear. I had no idea Steve was even back until you called me from Memphis."

Back? I shook my head, unwilling to believe, yet the tears steadily flowed and my gut churned over the truth.

"I rushed to you as quickly as I could, but when I got there and saw he was playing this game, acting like he'd just met you, I freaked out," Heather began to pace. "I didn't know what to do."

A barrage of feelings flooded forward. Everything, from humiliation to betrayal hit me at once. The idea that Heather had raced to Memphis at the mere mention of Steve name frightened me. That she'd known and yet allowed me sit at the Peabody hotel, and share a drink with him like he was some new found friend, enraged me!

"How is this possible?" My anger surged.

"You dated Steve for a few months, at best, then broke it off two weeks before Boston, before the—"

"The accident," I finished for her. "You're saying he's been out of my life for almost eight months?"

For that matter, how long had he been in it? This can't be happening! An inferno blazed inside of me.

How dare he play this little game, scaring me, harassing me with texts and notes, who did he think he was? What did he want?

"What did he mean by, reconsider? Reconsider *what*?" I snapped.

"Marriage." Heather just blurted it out.

Bam! My world stopped spinning. *Marriage*, I eternally repeated. I will not faint, I will not faint.

"He'd asked you to marry him, Sam, and you said... no."

Next to me, a solemn Elvis took my hand. He gave me a tender squeeze. His touch woke me from my trance, and I looked at him. His eyes were filled with such compassion I couldn't imagine a force strong enough to make me forget how much I loved him.

"Steve wanted to marry me?" I looked at Elvis, but my question was directed to Heather.

"*Wants* to marry you, Sam, as apparently he still does but..." Heather began, and my attention snapped to her so quickly she took a step back.

"But, what?" I growled.

Heather glanced to Elvis. My attention shifted, and I watched as my angel gave her an affirming nod. A fear of a conspiracy began to swell inside of me.

"He didn't take it well." Heather ran a hand through her hair. "He was following you to work and showing up at your house. When you tried to reason with him, he became angry."

I was barely listening; my eyes were steady on Elvis.

"Steve," Heather shifted her position as if trying to gain my attention, "he left harassing messages on your phone."

I refused to look at her. Since when did my friend need anyone's approval to speak? *He knew*, the thought rolled around in my head. My face was hot and my hands shook. He knew, and he'd known all along.

"At one point, I suggested you take out a restraining order. But before you could, he disappeared."

My thoughts raced back to Graceland and the "business" my angel was so eager to share with me.

"What is it, honey?" Elvis asked, completely unaware of the storm that was about to hit.

"You knew this whole time?" My words were rich with accusation.

His expression went blank. My insides went cold. Before I knew it, I had strapped myself in to that same emotional rollercoaster ride I'd been on for months. This time, I sat upfront powerless to stop it.

"Samantha, this isn't his fault." Heather was quick to his defense. "He wanted to tell you, but I pleaded for him to bring you home so that I could tell you here, myself."

A vision of Heather and Elvis, sitting in a Memphis hotel parking lot, plotting their plan behind my back, while I raced through the back neighborhood of Graceland had me seeing red.

"Sure, I understand." I jumped to my feet, strangely comforted by the startled look on Heather and Elvis' face. "You're both here to set the record straight."

The flood gates opened. Months of raw emotion rose to the surface. He didn't come back "for" me, he came to "handle" me. I had been a fool. Anger spun and I was like a tornado undecided where it might strike first. Nobody was safe.

"H-honey, I-I think you should sit back down."

At my side, Elvis placed a touch to my arm but I shrugged him away.

"Don't' touch me!" I growled and he quickly recoiled.

My heart pained, but a frantic need to order him out of my life overshadowed my true feelings.

"I thought you came back because you loved me, but you came back to finish the"—I almost chocked on the word—job."

"What? No...I," he started and then paused. Fire sparked in his eyes. "Now wait one damn minute."

"Wait, for what? It's simple, either you love me or you don't?" I was lost to hurt and frustration. "Which is it?"

"It's not that easy and you know it." Elvis spoke through clenched teeth, and his tempest blue eyes churned with a storm that quickly matched my own.

My heart felt like it was in a vise, every beat brought a painful breath.

"It is just that simple, to me."

"A-h-h," he growled, turned his back to me, and stomped to the other side of the room.

"Samantha," Heather tried again. "Why would he go through all this effort if he didn't care? Remember it was you who was being so difficult that day at Graceland, you told me that yourself."

The truth made me flinch, but only for a second.

"No, you don't understand. Today was planned. He predicted it himself. He's been following a time line, knowing it would lead me here."

In hearing my accusing words, Elvis whipped around to face me. His beautiful face was contorted in anger.

"*Don't* do this Samantha, not now." He shook his head, his lip curling with a snarl.

"Why? I'm home, your job's done." I shrugged.

Glaring at me now, he extended a shaky finger my direction. I braced myself for a just retort but none came. We just stood there staring at each other, both of our eyes misty with emotion.

"Please leave." Even as I spoke the words, I wanted to take them back.

He was as still as stone. My heart was in my throat as I waited for him to say something. Finally, and without one word more, he turned and headed for the door. He muttered something I couldn't hear as he grabbed the knob, and jerked it open so hard it slammed against the back wall, leaving an impression in the plaster that remains to this day. Then with a kick to the screen door, he exited out in to the early morning rain.

A cool breeze gusted into the room, swaying the door on its hinges. My body quaked. I held my hand firm to my mouth, while keeping an ear to the wind. I heard no starting of the Cadillac, no brief parting of the sky. There was no sign that he had left. He was just gone.

CHAPTER NINETEEN

"Samantha, can't you see he only agreed to my plan because he loves and cares about you?" Heather begged for me to listen. "Not because you're a case number, but because he wants to help."

I couldn't respond. I couldn't even catch my breath. Who was this person spurting ugly words? Where did so much anger and nastiness come from? Even at my lowest, I'd never felt so warped and unrecognizable. Had I really just accused Elvis of being the one thing he had never been in his life, insincere?

"Hey, where did you go?" Heather's voice broke into my thoughts.

I turned to her, stunned like a survivor standing in the middle of the road after an accident. You should be dead and yet you're breathing. Her eager expression pleaded for me say something, but I was all talked out.

"I love you, but I don't want to talk anymore."

Calmly, I wiped the last tear from my cheek. My mind floated around in a haze. I couldn't stay, not alone in this house. Not tonight. I needed a safe heaven, someplace or somewhere I could go to think. As my thoughts bounced, my gaze landed to a family snap shot taken at the cabin on Carters' lake. I smiled weakly. The lake had always been a happy place. Just looking at the photo gave me a sense of calm serenity. More than ever, I needed to find that woman in that photo. She was inside of me somewhere, lost but not gone.

I spun around, "I have to go!"

* * *

Nestled in the Blue Ridge Mountains, just an hour outside of Atlanta, is Carters Lake. Inside well over three thousand acres of mostly government owned park land lays the area's most popular getaway. Camping, boating and hiking are just a few of the activities to be enjoyed.

My father bought the cabin back in 1985, when I was old enough to appreciate its beauty, and yet small enough to pester with "Are we there yet" too many times along the way. Always overeager, I could barely wait to run wild along the caramel beaches and dive into its warm surface. We spent every holiday at the cabin, except Christmas, huddled together in nature's beauty. Now, my father rarely returned and I only visited in my dreams.

As I sped down a wet abandoned highway, an over casted sky followed over head. I felt like a horse racing

DREAM ANGEL

for the barn with blinders on. I just had to get there. I was scared. And thanks to my recent antics, I was alone.

A fog hung low, shielding the beauty of the rolling hillside, painted with barren maple trees and stark pined boughs, outside my window. It didn't matter, I passed viewpoints that awed and inspired without even seeing them. I drove by memory. And except for the slapping of windshield wipers, I had no company. Not even music played.

I used the drive to process the news that had hit my life like a wrecking ball, leaving pieces of myself strewn about everywhere. How was I going to tell my father his little girl was sick? And though I knew better, I couldn't help but wonder if my angel would be waiting for me at the cabin. The thought made me laugh out loud, in a warped comical way.

By the time I had gone over every piece of new information, twice, I was headed up the cabin's gravel drive. I slowed the convertible. This last stretch was notorious for pot holes, and I was squinting through a blurry windshield maneuvering my car like a tank through a mind field. At times, I drove on the grassed shoulder which I noticed had been cut tight to the ground. I smiled to myself, aware that the manicured condition meant my father had finally visited.

When I parked, I didn't get out. For a while I just sat, listening to my car's rag top fluttering in the gusts and gazing off into the distance. From my location, I could see the lake. The water churned, and the waves rushed to shore and crashed against the rocks. It looked dark and angry, just like I felt.

The clock on my car's dash said 12:00. It was dark for noon, I thought. And when I was ready, I grabbed my bag, threw open the door and ran for the house. The rain pelted me as I leapt up the front steps, two-by-two, and landed with a loud clomp on the front porch. Shaking off the rain, I dug in the flower pot by the door praying my father's habits hadn't changed.

Jackpot!

The door groaned when it opened. As I stepped through the threshold, the sound of the door closing echoed back to me and I flinched, still on edge.

The cabin had only the barest of necessities. There was a small living area, one bedroom, one bath and a made-for-one kitchen. Against my mother's better judgment, she conceded to my father's decorative tastes—rustic wildlife. The color pallet was mostly earth tones, and included one fish pattern couch with pillows that said "cabin fever". I remember my father was like a kid decorating his tree fort. Mother and I could only watch and laugh.

The cabin was perfect solitude, but it was cold. With no wood for the fireplace, and the only light available was what filtered through the windows—one in the living room and one in the kitchen—I worked fast. Because it was twilight, I raced for the lights first. I dropped my bag off in the bedroom, and got busy flipping on the breakers. It took a minute, but the tiny house moaned to life.

DREAM ANGEL

A soft glow filled the room. It cascaded over the wood paneling highlighting one familiar item after another. Mother's favorite reading material remained neatly stacked by her favorite chair. And the red and white afghan she'd sown by hand was strung over the back of the couch. All of it sparked my remembrance. Like how mother had spent hours working on that blanket for my father, and how he loved to cuddle up with it on long afternoon naps. The room was a virtual time capsule to my life, and time away had not dimmed its beauty.

I sat down on the couch, kicked off my shoes, and stretched out. The heater vent hummed over my head, diligent against the cold. Thanks to the room's diminutive size, it didn't take long for the air to warm. It was by far not cozy, but it would do. As my internal temperature rose, my muscles thawed, and the shock that had had my stomach jumping eased.

I had cried no tears since leaving Atlanta. Maybe I was tapped out, I didn't know, but I was tired. Still fully dressed, I rolled over with a sigh and closed my eyes. I could hear the rain striking the metal roof over my head. The rhythmic sound soothed me. And when a gentle shiver rushed through me, I reached for my father's favorite blanket and pulled it close. Daddy won't mind, I thought and I settled in.

The last thing I remember seeing was a photo of me at the age of eight on the wall across the room. I looked happy, but I couldn't remember why.

CHAPTER TWENTY

I was standing on a jetty. A thick fog surrounded me, and my hair was damp from the mist. The planked floor below my feet gently swayed with the rhythm of the water as it lapped the sides of the dock. The air was fresh, and I felt revived. I was unfamiliar with my surroundings, but I was not scared.

I started walking. Slow at first, dawdling really, then an overwhelming sense of urgency overcame me. What world lay at the end of this plank? From my position, it seemed endless. Intrigued, I walked faster—a trot now—cutting through the dense fog like a boat moving steadily up a river, smooth and on course. As my body warmed, I kicked into a full stride, arms pumping the air and legs extending fully forward. I found a comfortable pace and held it.

The brisk air stung my cheeks and my lungs burned. I had to get to the end. And just as I started to question if the path even had an end, I saw it. The light was brilliant, like a beacon in the night guiding the lost at sea. I ran for it as hard and as fast as I could. Only focused on the light, I was oblivious to what was happening beneath my pounding feet. Before I knew it, I raced right off the dock, arms stretched out at my side and my head tilted upward to the heavens. I landed on sand, hard, and stumbled before catching my stride.

I raced along the water's edge. The dense, gray fog had melted away, and rays of summer sun sparkled over Carter's lake like diamonds against glass. Its beauty was awe inspiring. So wonderful, I trotted to a stop, gasping for a breath, and enjoying the suns warm caress on my skin and the rustling of the trees around me.

"I thought I might find you here young lady." Her words were carried to me on a breeze.

I dare not move. I dared not to hope. With my excitement barely in check, I slowly turned to see my mother walking along the sandy bank. She strolled, holding the hem of her violet colored dress away from the waves that splashed over her feet. She was as beautiful as her last healthy day on earth, laughing and kicking at the water like a child at play. Strands of her chestnut hair—long and with a gentle wave like mine—lifted in the wind. Her eyes were filled with such joy; she out-shined the vast beauty around her.

Crying, I ran to her.

"Shush…baby girl, don't cry." She said as she drew me into her arms, cooing and hugging me tighter. "Let me look at you."

Tenderly, she pushed me out of her arms. She looked at me in that adoring way that always made me feel like I was her greatest miracle.

"You're so beautiful." She crushed me once more to her chest.

I hung on tight, afraid to let go. Inhaling her essence deep into my lungs, I never wanted to forget how she smelled, how she felt—so alive and thriving. After so much time apart there should have been so much to say, yet neither of us spoke. No words could have made the moment more special. We simply walked arm in arm along the water's edge. And it wasn't until we reached the picnic bench on the far side of the grassy knoll that my emotion's settled enough that I could find my voice.

"Daddy and I miss you so much." I said, while lying in her lap, cheek to her thigh and looking out across the lake.

"I'm with you both, always." She spoke so softly, I strained to hear her over the sounds of nature.

She braided the ends of my hair as we talked just like she used to when I was small. I loved it then and I loved it even more in this moment.

"Things have been hard since you—" I couldn't bring myself to say it.

"Died? It's ok to say the word Samantha."

"I'd rather not." I rolled over and gazed up at her.

My spirit soared at the sight of her rosy red cheeks. Her skin was creamy and flawless, and showed no signs of the sickness that had once plagued her. She was beautiful, perfect.

"What *would* you like to talk about?" Her green eyes sparkled over me.

I frowned like a reluctant teenager, and she returned a motherly insightful grin.

"Elvis, maybe?"

I groaned with real pain.

"You were pretty hard on him, don't you think?" She asked, allowing a moment to pass before continuing. "You know, sometimes life changes directions, Sam, but God always has a plan."

"What's God like?" I switched gears, needing to work up to the subject of Elvis.

"That's a big question."

"Well, is he a man or is he a woman? Is he from the North or from the South?" I kidded, and we both laughed.

It felt good to laugh.

"Baby girl, he'll be whatever you want him to be," she leaned down and kissed my forehead.

"I knew you'd say that." I sighed dramatically.

"You did, did you? Well, the important thing is that you know he loves you, no matter what."

"I love him too." I hadn't said those words out loud since I was a child, but I did mean it.

Now looking up at a sky as real as any on a clear summer's day, I admired the deep blue that was streaked with a few stark white clouds. And I could smell Georgia's wild ginseng lingering in the breeze. It's amazing what God can do when given a blank canvas, I considered and hope flashed.

"Is this real, mama, are you really here?"

"Oh, baby girl, sometimes God uses our dreams to reach us, and other times it's just our imaginations."

I grinned, aware that mother was being as cagey as my angel.

"Elvis told me about your visits with Daddy in his dreams."

"Did he? Well, you know how he can't keep a secret." She lowered her voice as if wanting to keep this knowledge just between the two of us.

"Oh mama, I treated him so horribly." I covered my face. "I was so angry, so hurt, I don't know why I said all those nasty things. I wanted to do everything right, and I ended up doing everything wrong."

"Now, now, Mr. Presley will recover." She sighed. "Besides I warned him you could be a handful."

I dropped my hands. "Mama!"

"Oh, baby girl, he knew what he was getting into." She swept the hair back away from my face. "We have more important things to talk about right now, like Steve."

Steve! I sat up, eager to hear what she had to say. The mere mention of his name triggered alarm, but nothing brought me more worry than the look on her face. Her eyes were cold, her expression flat. She no longer looked at me but rather through me. When I softly touched her arm, my hand pressed almost through her as though I was pressing on cloud. She was beginning to fade away.

"Promise me," she started to say in a distant voice.

I reached out for her, grabbing her hand, but her fingers slipped through my gasp. She was gone.

CHAPTER TWENTY ONE

The unwelcome sharp slam of a nearby car door penetrated my subconscious. I fell through the gap of time, tumbling and landing to the ground with a thud. A spasm shot though my hip. I had fallen off the couch, and whimpered from the pain. All was pitch-black except for a single beam of light piercing through the living room window.

Light flooded the room, flickered, and then went out. I strained to listen, but heard only the rain pelting the metal roof. Nothing more stirred. I had no idea how long I'd been asleep, but I guessed more than a few hours, though it felt like only minutes. After a quick physical inventory, I stood. My vision had not fully adjusted, so I moved cautiously and with my hands out. I told myself the car lights were nothing more than a lost tourist, but I knew better. People just didn't accidently end up here in the winter, lost. If someone was here, they were here for a reason.

My palms began to sweat ever so slightly. Shuffling to the window, I parted the blinds and peeked. The storm had escalated. Dark clouds blackened the sky, and the rain came down in sideways sheets. I could see a dim reflection off a small lake that was forming in the back lawn. I grimaced. Looking to the opposite side of the property, I saw only trees and low woodland shrubs thrashing in the storm. I could see nothing that would account for what had seemed to be headlights coming through my window. So I believed, until I looked west towards the dark churning waters of the lake. Movement caught my eye.

At first it was but a vaguely outlined figure on the move. As it drew closer, I could see by the build that it was a man. I quickly calculated that I had four more seconds before he would be knocking on my door. I sucked in my breath and drew back from the window, and a rush of adrenaline flooding my body. I felt dizzy, and for a moment considered if I wasn't still dreaming. This had none of the usual comforting qualities, though, and my fear was far too vivid for this to be a dream.

My imagination ran wild. What do I do? What can I do? I'd seen enough horror movies as a teen to guess what happens next. Bottom line, the woman never makes it! She just runs around screaming and tripping over her own two feet.

On the verge of full-out panic and two second away from succumbing to tears, I leaned in for another look.

The stranger bounded up my front steps, his body in full motion as he flipped off his hood. I held my breath as he stood for a moment just out of the shadows. It was Steve. Automatically, and without much thought, I exhaled a sigh of relief. When one feels as if they're hanging over a 100-foot drop, they don't question the person who holds out a hand. They see only a chance for help.

After all I knew, I should have questioned Steve's presence that night, but I was overcome with a sense of reprieve that he was not the midnight killer I had imagined. To me, he was a man whom I had just been told had asked me to marry him. Most importantly, he was the man with all the answers to my many questions. Only he could tell me what I no longer remembered.

Still, I hesitated to answer his knock.

"Samantha, we need to talk." He knocked again. "If nothing else I think you owe me an explanation, and I'm not leaving until I get one."

He was right. I did owe him something, didn't I? If anything I owed him an apology. My hands shook as I released the lock and opened the door. A warm familiar grin greeted me.

"Thank you." He glanced past me, hesitated, and then entered.

As he walked past, I paused for a moment in the doorway, staring out into the unsettled night. Even in the dark of the storm, I could see the shapes of trees as they bent at the fierce wind's supremacy. Just at the edge of the forest line I caught a glimpse of an old, black truck decorated with too much chrome. It sat menacingly in the dark, occasional glints of light reflecting off the metal grill.

Now fear rose up like a cold wave inside my chest, and I squelched a scream. Though not a sound escaped, I still covered my mouth. Like a freight train on a collision course, the pieces from the last 48 hours crashed together in my mind. The headlights that followed me outside of Memphis, the lingering truck in Tupelo, the notes and text messages all formed a very frightening puzzle. And I had just welcomed the last piece through my front door.

"H-how did you find me here?" Though I tried to appear calm, my voice shook.

"You brought me once, two summers ago."

I had no memory of that trip, but for a fleeting moment the knowledge gave me comfort. To have shared such a treasured part of my life suggested a sentiment that I no longer remembered, but must have felt for this man. What happened that change my mind?

The lights were still out, and the fact that we were engulfed in shadows didn't seem to bother Steve. He removed his jacket, tossed it on to a chair, and moved deeper into the room. Considering the circumstances, his self-assurance baffled me. I waited until he took a seat, and then opened the fuse box near the door. This was not a candlelight moment, and prayed the storm had only tripped a breaker. With a flip of a switch the lights came on. I breathed a sigh of relief.

I turned to discover Steve already relaxing on the couch, legs crossed and admiring my mother's handmade blanket. My face flushed at the sight of him handling my mother's things.

"Here let me get that out of your way." I took the blanket, clutched it to my chest like a shield, and sat in a chair across from him. My reaction surprised and worried me at the same time.

"Your mother made that, I remember." Steve muttered in what was his first sign of wavering confidence.

"I wish *I* could remember." I stared at him desperate for a clip of a memory but none came.

Steve looked terrible. He hadn't shaved for a while, and his green eyes were red around the rim as if he hadn't slept in days. He wore a pair of tired old blue jeans. Until this moment, I'd never seen him look anything less than stellar. His disheveled appearance unnerved me.

"Prior to Memphis, I have no memory of you." I cut to the chase.

"I gathered that, yes." He ran his hands through his wet and matted blonde hair.

I waited, hoping he'd take the lead, but he neither spoke nor looked at me.

"So, you knew yet you said nothing?" I could feel my anger rising, that rollercoaster ride ready by my side.

"At the time, I didn't see the point." His gaze rested on me, cold and scrutinizing.

I ran a hand through my hair attempting to calm the blaze that burned hot in my chest "How did you know I'd be at Graceland?"

"It was January 8th." He said simply.

The predictable habits of a fan, I'll have to remember that, I told myself.

"I had gone hoping we could talk, but obviously that was out of the question. Was I that easy to forget?" he asked coolly.

As if a bucket of water had been dumped over my head, I instantly unruffled, and averted my gaze to my hands, clasped in my lap.

"I wish I knew how to answer that, but I-I don't understand it myself."

When I looked up to Steve, his expression was hard. I empathized, recognizing that dull look of heartbreak. Sadly, we were similar. We both were chasing something that was clearly out of our reach, only he resented what he couldn't have, and I had accepted my fate.

"Yes, well, it's possible this other gent has clouded your mind," He sighed, stood, and began to walk around the room.

I wanted to bombard him with questions and accusations, but my intuition told me to choose my words carefully.

"Heather says we parted ways weeks prior to my accident, long before I met—" I caught myself just in time, "the new man in my life," I added.

"Heather talks too much," he paused to straighten a photo on the wall, and then stood back to consider it, "I wasn't privy to any *accident*." He added with a hint of cynicism.

It was in this display of disinterest and genuine disconnect, that lay my first hint of hopelessness. It was clear that only I was interested in finding some common ground to our problem. I stood and began to move towards the kitchen. I wished to allow for some space between us, while still hoping a resolution would present itself.

"I-I'm told we weren't in contact at the time that I was ill, so I suppose you wouldn't have known, " I tried, "but I'm sure if I could just explain—"

"No!"He suddenly snapped.

Steve slowly turned around from where he had stopped pacing near the front door. He shot me a seething look that chilled me to my core. Nobody had ever looked at me with such pure rage. I could hear his ragged breathing from across the room, and his fists clenched and unclenched at his sides. I couldn't stop myself from looking beyond him at the small table where I had carelessly tossed my car keys earlier.

"No explanation is needed," he said, "because nothing has really changed luv, now has it?"

Every muscle in my body instantly tensed as Steve reached behind with his right hand. He pulled out a pair of worn, black leather gloves from his back pocket.

Methodically, and never taking his eyes off of me, he worked his right hand into the first one.

"You tossed me aside once, and it seems you've tossed me aside again. Old habits are hard to break, are they?"

I was standing in the kitchen still wondering what he could possibly need gloves for. It took a moment, and then I realized by his expectant stare that he had asked me a question.

"I-I'm sorry if it appears I've tossed you aside, but if I owe you an apology for anything it's for allowing you to initially believe that I was available." I'd hoped to de-escalate the situation, while instinctively inching towards the back door. "My behavior in Memphis was not my true self, and I genuinely hope you can forgive me."

"Well, it's all water under the bridge really, I mean we might have had a chance to start anew in Memphis, but then Heather showed up and everything changed," he paused to tug the cowhide low around his wrist, "I reckon she told you about me, did she?"

I paused in my retreat, looking at Steve incredulously as in three short sentences his accent completely transformed. He was almost smiling now, and without raising his head looked up at me as he continued to adjust the glove. A breath caught in my chest. At first I thought I must have heard wrong, and then he spoke again.

"The way I figure it, darlin', she told you I'd been *harassing* you, *stalking* you," He kept one eye on me while he worked to put on the other glove. "She never did take a shine to me."

My mouth fell open.

"Ah-h, the accent. Yes, well, your reaction was similar the first time," He fluttered his gloved hands in the air, eyes wide with crazy, "shock and dismay."

The blood drained from my face. I couldn't believe what I was hearing, or what I was seeing.

"Oh s-u-r-e I played the game for months, trying to fit in with your high falutin' friends, always the perfect gentlemen. Boring! You wanted a saint not a man, and I ain't your daddy."

Steve kept his head down now, and obsessively tugged at one glove, then the other. He had begun taking slow, stilted steps toward me, and at least for the moment was clearly putting more attention into his ramblings than where he was going. I shuffled towards the back door. Though my heart was in my throat, I moved in firm but measured steps.

"So the way I figure it, honey, I should get something for all my trouble. Don't ya think?"

Steve sighed deeply, and then slapped his leather clad hands together. I flinched and tried to keep my heart from beating out of my chest. I was almost to the back door, eager to make an escape, when Steve slowly lowered his hands to his sides and raised his head. His face was almost unrecognizable to me. My options were limited, but obvious.

I spun around and flung the door behind me open. My gaze flickered out into the night, to freedom, and for a split second hope surged. I took that first step at a dead run. I got one foot out the door, and a hand grabbed me from behind. My head snapped back as I was jerked to an almost instant stop and swung around by my blouse. Steve slammed me, back first, up against a solid object in the kitchen. Pain discharged across my collar bone.

"It's not polite to interrupt when I'm talking!" Steve spat in my face.

"Please..." I whimpered.

His body was pressed against mine, and his breath was heavy with the smelled of alcohol and mint. I turned my head away, but he roughly grabbed my chin and turned my head back to face him.

"What I'm *trying* to say baby doll...is," he pressed harder into me, "you owe me and I'm here to collect."

"Get off me." I croaked as his hand tightened around my throat.

I drew in a quick breath through my nose and on the exhale spat in his face. Grinning menacingly, he closed his eyes, and allowed the wet substance to drip down his face.

"You ought'n have done that. See, I hadn't made up my mind what I was going to do with you when this unfortunate business was over," Steve paused to lick my spit from where it hit near his mouth. "Now, I have."

As my need for survival swelled, the world around me muted. I could hear only the sound of my heart pulsating in my ear. Desperate and determined, I lifted my foot, and drove my knee into Steve's body. Like the key to my shackles, his hands fell away from my throat. I drew in a life renewing breath as he shrank away clutching his groin. He swore venomously, but I never heard a word. I was already out the door.

A mix of rain and snow fell. The slush soaked into my clothes and I was instantly drenched, cold to the bone. My breath blew out as steam in the night. I ran barefoot across the back yard. I trampled through the pooled water, slipping once but catching myself. I hit the gravel driveway at a full sprint oblivious to the numbing pain of tiny pebbles digging into the bottoms of my feet. I jumped over partially frozen pot holes, clearing some and missing others.

I glanced back. Steve was up and headed down the back steps. I pushed harder. Part of me wanted to keep an eye on his every move, but that was silliness I knew. It was unlikely that his intentions had changed. He was surely headed my way, and as scared as I was my steps were solid. Endorphins rushed through my veins like a drug. I could have run until dawn, but vast acres of forestland stood between me and help.

For a moment I considered if I shouldn't just run into the dense woods. I no doubt knew this area better than he, but if I was wrong and he caught me, I feared my father would never know what happened to me. I couldn't put him through the never ending pain of not knowing and hoping I would one day return. There was only one place to go.

I reached Steve's truck, praying that he had left his keys in the ignition, ready for a quick exit. My hands were so cold, I could barely grip the slippery door handle on the driver's side. Using both hands, I yanked the door open and immediately felt around for the ignition. My heart sank. I flipped down visors and yanked open compartments. My heart pounded with the knowledge that Steve had to be drawing near. I couldn't look. I shoved my hands under the seat, my fingers fumbling around. When I skimmed over something cold, I gripped it as best I could and quickly brought it out into the dim light. It was a key! I came back up just in time to see a flash of movement at my side.

Instantly, I lunged over the console. He was swiping at my legs while I was kicking at his grasp. It was hopeless, and before I could get out the other side he had his hand wrapped around my ankle. With incredible strength he flipped me flat to my back. I landed, head first to the passenger side door and the impact rattled my senses. My vision blurred. I was seeing two of everything. I screamed and when I did the back drop of night rippled just over Steve's shoulder. Convinced a greater evil had just arrived, I screamed louder. Like a time warp in space, the atmosphere flexed and elongated. I held my shriek in a long, agonizing note. Steve smiled with satisfaction. He was completely oblivious to what throbbed like an invisible life force just behind him. "It" hovered while he paused to enjoy the power he had over me. Doing so would be his downfall.

The space around him furrowed, and a flash of lightening sparked. I wordlessly pointed behind Steve, but he paid me no mind. In the blink of an eye, Steve's weight was lifted off of me. His face quickly changed from intense anger to wide-eyed shock as his six-foot frame was sucked backward out of the truck and flung to the ground. He hit so hard I felt the reverberation.

Curled up in a fetal position, I was too scared to move. My eyes were locked to the spot I had last seen the ripple. Whatever just happened was powerful and invisible, a force that I couldn't identify as friend of foe. I feared I'd be next. Without having to move, I could just see Steve. He was face-down in the mud and not moving. I could clearly hear him moaning and groaning. Just the distance and impact of his fall should have kept him down for good, but it didn't. The sight of Steve pressing his hands into the mud and pushing himself upward sent me into complete hysterics. I was sobbing, my body quaking as he struggled to get up. He had made it to his knees when the air ripple again and picked him right up off his feet.

Suspended in the air, he fought for his life, fists slicing the air but connecting with nothing. It was as if he fought a ghost, each attempt only provoked another strike. It was all happening so fast and was so unbelievable, that my only reaction was to keep screaming. I was completely unable to collect a rational thought or take command of my terror. To my horror, Steve's body was hurled in my direction. He landed in front of me, face down in a disheveled heap on the vehicle's hood. The truck rocked from the impact.

All went quiet. Even the sleet stopped. I lay as still as a statue for a full two minutes, barely able to breathe. The storm passed and clouds began to split. Only a partial moon dared to peek through a less disturbing sky. I held my breath, my senses sharpened by my desire to survive. We were not alone. The air around me pulsated with a life, a tangible energy. I couldn't see it, but I could feel it. I didn't know when the next flutter was coming, or if it would come after me, I only knew that "it" was still here. I slowly turned for the passenger side door. I placed both feet to the ground and stepped out. My knee's instantly buckled and I landed face first into an icy mud puddle. Splashing around, I dug my bare feet in and pushed myself up. I told myself not to look back, just run, but a moan from Steve stopped me in my tracks.

I cautiously glanced back over my shoulder in his direction. Steve raised his head up from the dent he had made in the truck's hood. He looked at me with his right eye—his left one had been pounded shut—and drew in a rattled breath. He opened his mouth to speak, but only made a gurgling sound. Before he could begin to form a word, the air cracked with thunder. Steve's head jerked back and he moaned even louder. As horrible and surreal as this was, it wasn't Steve I was watching. An image was forming behind him, a figure that faded in and out of visibility, but whose outline pulsated with energy.

Though faint, the energy took the form of a man. Flickering the whole time, the outline slowly gave way to the entire person. He was tall and luminous. There was nothing demon-like about him as I had imagined, but his face was dark with anger and his eyes sparked. He had Steve suspended by the back of his jacket and dropped him back onto the hood of the truck with a thud. He kneeled down and pressed one knee hard into Steve's back. Steve closed his one good eye and went limp. The man leaned down and hissed in his ear.

The face of my angel flashed. It was only a side view, but that chiseled nose and iconic profile allowed me draw in my first full breath. I wanted to run to him, but I couldn't feel my feet. I wanted to scream out his name, but I had no voice. The adrenaline that had once sustained me subsided. My knees were locked. Between that and the waves of shivering from the fear and cold, I was unable to move.

Elvis picked up Steve as if he weighed no more than a feather, and with a kick to the truck's door, slammed him into the driver's seat. It took only a moment before Steve realized he was free. He sprang to life, and scrambled for the key's I'd left dangling in the ignition. How he managed to move was amazing to me, but I understood the look of desperation in his eyes. His own survival instincts had kicked in, and a moment later the truck roared to life. The engine surged and the tires spun.

The truck hopped in the mud before it grabbed solid ground, and shot forward like a canon down the drive. All I could see were the crimson tail lights blazing in the night.

With my arms wrapped protectively around myself, I gently rocked back and forth on unsteady feet that I could no longer feel. I was terrified, exhausted, and just wanted to hide.

"Samantha." His soft tenor was like a whisper in my ear.

My angel was now standing before me. His face had softened back into that of the man I knew and loved. He stood with his hands on his hips, weight shifted to his right, and water from the storm still glistening on his face. I saw a warrior of God, a guardian of human life. When he extended his hands to me, palms up, I ran to him, broken and fragile.

"I gotcha, baby girl," Elvis said, swooping me up in his arms.

I don't remember the journey back to the cabin. All I remember is the feel of strong arms around me as I sobbed with my head buried firm against his chest. He carried me into the cabin and pushed the door closed behind us. The warmth inside immediately began to revive me. But it wasn't until Elvis began to peel me from his arms that I found my voice.

"No, no, no!" I clung on tighter.

"S-h-h-h, honey, take it easy," he said tenderly while slowly unraveling me from his body, one limb at a time.

My every muscle was rigid from the cold. The minute my legs touched the ground, my knees buckled. I started to fall, and Elvis quickly gathered me back into his arms.

"I'd put you in a hot shower, baby, if I thought you could tolerate the pain." Elvis said while marching me down the hall.

He tapped the bedroom door with his boot tip and gingerly laid me on the bed.

"I'm sorry honey, but we need to get you out of these wet clothes."

He did not wait for permission to undress me, he simply went to work. There was no shyness, no moment of hesitation. I tried to help but he shooed my hand away. The light from a bedside lamp cascaded a soft glow across his concentrated features as he worked. Had our situation been one of intimacy, I would have found that wisp of dark hair low across his brow erotic and sensual, but I only briefly considered it. He moved fast, fumbling in all the areas you'd expect a man too, but accomplishing the task on his own. Soon, I was completely naked. He kept his gaze low and began to rub my legs with hands that felt hard on my skin. I bit back my tears.

"I'd heal you if I could, baby, but I'm no Jesus," he'd say, and then exhale a heated breath onto my feet, messaging and encouraging circulation.

To say he had magic hands is an understatement, but this was not quite the special attention I had always imagined. The process was torturous. I'd cringe, anticipating the pain as his long fingers wound around my calves. He'd knead my muscles, and just as the agony would subside, he'd shift to a new area and it would start over again. As painful as it was, relief could not come fast enough. And though my toes tingled, and my knees were no longer locked, my core body was like a block of ice.

"T-t-too slow," I managed through chattering teeth.

"Ok, baby girl, hold on," he sighed deeply, while muttered something about having to do this the old fashion way.

Standing up, he jerked his wet shirt tails from his paints and unbuckled his belt. He was undressed before I could process what was about to happen. He joined me on the bed, and while supporting his own weight, he gingerly laid his long naked frame over mine. Carefully, his body sank deeper until my petite frame virtually vanished and an all over heat seeped into my bones. I moaned openly from the reprieve.

He looked down to me with a playful smile. "I-I don't know about you, but I imagined this moment differently." He was teasing, but the lines of worry were still present on his brow.

I forced a smile. "A-a-are...y-you...cold?"

His face softened. "No, baby, I'm fine," he said with that caring tone that always made my heart swell.

My eyes flood with emotion. There was no hesitancy, I let the tears flow.

"I-I'm so sorry," I said weakly.

"Shush, now," His own voice cracked and his eyes grew misty as he stroked the damp hair away from my face. "I'm sorry too, honey. I'm sorry I couldn't get to you sooner."

"Y-you were distracted?" A vision of him throwing darts at my photo popped in my head, and I chuckled but stopped when it hurt.

"Something-like-that, yes" he said, and leaned down to place a tender kiss on the tip of my nose. "I just can't take my eyes off of you for one minute without you getting yourself into trouble."

"W-what a girl will do for your attention, huh?" I said and enjoyed that famous smile widening over me.

As we lay together, cocooned in each other's arms, the stillness that enveloped us was like the calm after a storm, tranquil yet electric. I let out a shaky breath, and he drew me closer laying my head to rest over his heart. Nuzzling his chest, I was hypnotized by the rise and fall of his every breath. And when he stirred, attempting to become more comfortable, I startled inside his embrace and he merely held on tighter.

"I'm here, honey, I'm here," was the last thing I heard him say.

CHAPTER TWENTY TWO

A blanket of white covered the ground. Snow in Atlanta? It happens, but even I couldn't remember when. I was standing at the kitchen window that next morning, coffee in hand, and struggling to see any sign of last night's nightmare. Not one track, not even from the smallest animal was visible. Mother Nature had simply wiped the earth clean. I closed my eyes, and thanked God for at least the illusion of a new day.

I had fallen asleep in the arms of an angel and woke alone, blurry eyed and groggy. Right away, I noticed a note pinned to my pillow. I read it first thing. It started with, he had gone to make sure our "new friend" hadn't mistaken last night for a bad dream, and ended with: You know where to find me.

He was right, I realized. I did know where to find him, and I couldn't help but laugh mockingly at the knowledge that it never required a plane ride to Memphis. The solution lied in the simplicity of one question. Where do all good little angels go at the start of every day?

* * *

The drive back to the city always seemed shorter. To this day I believe it's a holdover from my childhood, a time when I couldn't get to the lake fast enough, and then sulked notoriously when it was time to leave. This time, I was ready. Real life had come crashing down around my childhood memories. Never again would I look back to the lake through the eyes of innocence. Steve had taken that from me. And after a quick shower and a change, I was packing to leave. I loaded up the car and paused only briefly before sealing up the cabin for what I knew would be another long absence.

The roads were clear, and the journey home allowed me time to think. My mind worked on what I would say when I saw my father. I was aware he'd want to know where I'd been, and what had inspired this early morning visit in the first place. I decided not to tell him about Steve. The details were too horrible, the outcome too hard to explain. Besides when it came to my angel, my father only knew pieces of this amazing tale. He was aware of the dreams I'd had while lying in the hospital. I had told him the story myself. In his religious convictions, he had rationalized that God had provided me with a distraction, a reprieve from the pain while my body healed. It was a simplistic idea to a complicated reality. One, I was willing to let him believe.

All around me, the rolling hills looked sprinkled with a snowy powder. Sadly, and just like the day before, I didn't bother to admire them. Once out of the mountains, the soft beauty of woodland nature slowly gave way to the harshness of steel and skyrocketing high rise buildings. The city buzzed like a beehive. Car's lined the roads and pedestrians packed the sidewalks. I exited the freeway, and immediately saw the white cross from the steeple up ahead. I was almost there.

My heart was pounding as I pulled in. I parked near the administrative building and I sat, edgy and easily overcome with emotion. This was not how I wanted my father to see me, shaken to my core. Closing my eyes, I prayed for strength and protection, half expecting a rebuttal answer from the Devil himself. But it wasn't long before a sense of peace rushed over me. I didn't want to waste the confidence this all-over good feeling gave me, so I grabbed my purse and raced for my father's office.

I had noticed the parking lot was empty, but that didn't surprise me. After all, it was the middle of the week. However, I was stunned when I entered and found Nancy, my father's secretary, absent from her desk. I looked down to my watch, 10:00 am. Maybe she was late? I crossed the room, and hesitated briefly before knocking on my father's door.

When nobody answered, I peeked and saw my father fast asleep on the couch. For a moment, I felt as if I was the intruder. I almost turned to leave, but then I wondered what lovely moment he might be sharing with my mother and decided to wait. Content, I sat down in an empty chair by his side, and settled in to enjoy an odd case of role reversal. For once, I'd watch "him" nap just as he used to watch me.

My father was quite the sight. At six foot three, and all curled up on his side, he all but swallowed up the average sized couch. I couldn't help but snicker at the way his black wing tip shoes dangled off the sides like a little boy wearing his father's shoes. My laughter slipped into an internal sigh, as I admired his pallid hair, giving him a touch of aged wisdom, and I silently commended my mother for her impeccable taste in men. He was stunning, in a fatherly sort of way.

The moments passed in the slow rise and fall of his every breath. As if feeling my presence his eyes fluttered open, but he didn't startle. We smiled at each other, my tears quickly forming.

"You're napping earlier than normal today, daddy." I felt a rush of love in the word "daddy".

"You caught me, baby girl." He sat up, yawning while adjusting his tie.

"Can't wait to get to those good dreams, I bet." I muttered, and my father's eyes narrowed.

Not waiting for his response, I moved to the couch and hugged him with all my might. My emotions quickly flooded forward. I struggled to hold them back.

"Well, this is nice. What did I do to deserve this visit?" He chuckled.

"Can't I just show up at church like all good daughters of pastors should?"

"Sure, if you're not my Samantha." My father joked, and drew me further in his arms.

"Well, starting today, your little girl is changing her ways,"

"You are?" Daddy gently pushed me out of his arms so that he could examine my face.

I smiled, careful not to allow him to look me square in the eyes. He had a talent for knowing my secrets. I wanted to tell him at my own pace and on my own terms.

"To whom should I send my thanks?" He gathered my hands with his two.

"God," I said, enjoying the softening of his expression.

"Is that so?"

We both laughed.

"Yes sir." I was chuckling and crying. And once the tears started, I couldn't seem to stop.

My father's face quickly darkened with worry. "What's wrong, baby girl, why the tears?"

I'd had the whole drive to think about what I wanted to say to my father, where I wanted to go from here. Though I'd been taught at an early age to keep God close, I often chose my own path. I could have been the poster child for a life run amuck. It was time to let go of the reigns. I just didn't know where to start.

"I-I've come from the cabin—" I started but daddy didn't let me finish.

"You went to the lake, why?" He sat up straight.

"I needed to think, and so I went—"

"What's wrong, are you sick?" My father's eyes locked on to me in that way parents do when they're trying to read their children's minds.

"I-I don't know." I gave a standard adolescent response, immediately wishing I could take it back.

"What do you mean, you don't know?" he growled.

Lord, help me! I was sinking fast.

"It's probably nothing, but I've had some headaches recently and,"—I purposely left out mood swings and erratic behavior—"and I fear it might be related to my accident."

"When did all this happen?" He scooted back a tad.

"Memphis or a little before, I-I'm not sure. I didn't mention it, because I wasn't sure myself what it was and I didn't want to worry you." I quickly took his hands into mine, and squeezed them tight hoping to calm the fear I could see escalating in his eyes.

"You haven't been going to your check up's, have you?" He pushed back his hair. "I knew I should have taken you. That's what your mother would have done."

"Daddy, please, really I'm ok." I struggled. "I'm sure it's just part of the healing process, but I will go back to the doctor as soon as possible. I promise."

At first he said nothing. He just kept looking at me with that inspecting gaze. I longed to tell him about Steve. I wanted to talk, unload my sorrow. But I didn't have the stomach to share what I knew would hurt him. Instead, my shield went up. And while he watched me closely, I tugged on my shirt sleeves, desperate to hide the bruises I'd seen in the shower that morning.

"What can I do to help?" My father asked softly.

I let out a slow breath.

"Actually, I'd rather help you, if that's ok?" I waited, and his stunned silence suggested I should continue. "I'd like to come here and help."

"You want to help here… at the church?" His eyes widened in a surprise that made me openly laugh.

"Yes, if you don't mind."

"Of course I don't mind, but I have to ask what motivated this sudden decision?"

"Daddy, you know I've been stumbling down a rocky path since mother passed. You're always preaching that God is grooming us for his purpose, and I'd like to try to find out what mine is." I smiled big, remembering what Elvis had told me back in Tupelo.

My father smiled tenderly. "Baby girl, you may not discover that overnight. God has his own timing."

"I know, but I have to start somewhere."

"Alright," he nodded, and then drew me back into his arms, "and if it makes you happy my dear, you can start as early as tomorrow."

He held me tight, and I wanted to stay in his protective embrace forever, content to be his little girl.

"Would you mind, daddy, if I stayed for awhile today… to sit in the sanctuary. I can lock up if you need to leave."

My father's expression lifted with a look that suggested my upbringing might have finally kicked in after all.

"You may." He stood up, straightened his tie and grabbed his coat, "I'll leave you to God. Oh, and use the phone on my desk to call your doctor before you leave. That's top priority now Samantha, ya hear? And call your work."

I smiled at how easily he transitioned back to my commanding father, ordering me around even as he was hugging me goodbye. He was a good father, and an even better example of a God fearing man, a hero to so many in the community. Though I'd heard so many say how special he was over the years, sadly, I'd only recently come to realize the truth.

"I love you, baby girl" He uttered in my hair.

"I love you to daddy. Tell mama hello for me when you see her in your dreams tonight." I couldn't resist teasing him. I enjoyed the sight of him blushing like a school boy.

He shook his head over my silliness as he left. One day I'd tell him my secret, I thought. One day.

The office door shut behind him, and the room went quiet. Maybe it was nothing more than left over jitters, but the silence felt thick like a presence. So much so, I imagined I could hear it breathe. It was time to leave. I needed peace, and I knew where to find it.

* * *

DREAM ANGEL

From the time of my birth to the age of eighteen, I had spent every Sunday in the old sanctuary. Long before the add-ons and additional parking, this church had been as much a part of my childhood as swing sets and ice cream. I grew up here. I'd kissed my first boy at the age of fourteen in the back pews, and later shed a tear over that same boy as we parted ways one summer to long ago to remember the actual date.

As I exited my father's office, I followed a long carpeted hallway and a moment later arrived at the front lobby. The sight of those weathered double doors to the sanctuary made me smile. Another memory flashed. I could still see myself grunting and tugging on the door. Though small for my age, I flat refused to accept any help from passing adults. Once conquering the seemingly impenetrable fortress, I triumphantly raced to my allotted seat down front.

It seemed stubbornness was an issue even then, I thought with a chuckle while straightening the flower arrangements on the podium near the entrance. As I lingered, I noticed last Sunday's leaflets stacked neatly in a pile. I picked one up to consider it.

"Hungering and thirsting for God, reminds us that only devotion to the Lord Jesus Christ satisfies our soul," it said.

Daddy had a way with words, and I leaned back against the tiny welcome desk, eager to read further. I got as far as the Bible verse for the day when a piano from inside the sanctuary began to play. My eyes stalled mid sentence. The natural informal way in which the pianist played evoked a smile. There was no question; God was the only tutor this composer had ever needed.

My heart leapt with anticipation. I grasped those big doors and this time they swung open easily. The music gushed from the room, and rushed over me in a wave that left me tingling from my ears down to my toes. I made no move to enter. I simply lingered at the threshold, overwhelmed by the aroma of cedar and a lingering mix of colognes from past congregations. The unusual scent stirred fond memories of what I considered to be homespun elegance at its best.

When an "off" note echoed from the stage, my focus shifted to the pulpit and to Elvis. He looked comfortable in his rightful spot. Dressed in white with a sky blue tie, he coordinated beautifully with the baby grand he sat behind. Though he would have claimed he was just fooling around, he played wonderfully. The music was gentle. And I took my time to approach the stage, savoring the view. Who could blame me? It had been a whole twelve hours since I'd seen him, and with dark brown locks, he looked just as natural as God had made him. Even more beautiful than before, if that was possible.

Now this was my angel! This was the angelic force I remembered so well, straight from my dreams. Sure, there was something excitedly dangerous about that famous jet-black look, but "this" shy young man from Mississippi was extra special. In fact his features were so radiant, he glowed. And as I walked towards him, purposely taking my time, he was smirking at me. I could only laugh. He knew me so well.

"Decided to go natural, did we?" The music stopped when I stepped up to the stage.

"I figured you were ready for the real me," he said and flashed that lopsided grin.

"Is it me, or have you always had a knack for dramatic entrances'?" I asked, and laughed when he answered back with a note that sounded a bit off key.

"I try my best, honey." He said with a glint in his eye.

I circled around and took a seat on the bench by his side. His attention was fixed on me, but his hands continued to play. He hummed along to a tune that was not familiar. I wasn't surprised. Even alive his knowledge of hymnals was vast, and as an angel I imagined it to be unlimited.

"How's our *friend*?" I laid my head to his shoulder.

"Dealt with," he said in between a whistling breath.

As I leaned against him in quiet reflection, a flood of emotions rushed to the surface. The knowledge that I may not have been alive to see another day, if not for him, inspired a gratefulness that was too much to contain.

"After how I treated you, I'm surprised you came back for me." My words quivered. "I'll be forever grateful."

The music suddenly stopped.

"I'd never leave you in danger, you know that," he said while gathering my hands and lifting them to his lips for a tender kiss.

I nodded, my bottom lip quivering. I tried to hold back my tears, but it was useless.

"I never meant a word of it, I swear. I'm just so jumbled up inside, everything I do turns into a disaster."

He smiled softly. "Yes ma'am I've noticed," he said, still holding my hands, and managing to stroke my cheek with the back of his own.

"I'm sick in the head." I moaned, and it wasn't until Elvis chuckled that I even realized how horrible that sounded.

"You might be a bit *touched*, baby," he laughed harder, "but I think you'll be fine.

As we both chuckled, he went back to playing. His fingers rolled over the ivory keys in a swaying melody.

"I don't suppose you could tell me what God wants me to do now?" I was shaking my head, already guessing his answer.

"It doesn't work that way, honey."

"Then how does it work, please tell me."

"You practice patience and you wait. He'll tell you when he's ready."

I scowled at him.

"Hey, I just work here!" He was laughing again, only this time I didn't laugh a long.

He cleared his throat and quickly turned serious.

"Baby girl, I know you want me to make it easy for you, but really, I don't know everything. And what I do know, I can't share."

"Why? You knew I'd ask you to leave, and you shared that with me." I crossed my arms over my chest. "Course that's not *how* I'd plan to ask you, all hateful and nasty and such, but...well, you knew."

A sensuous smirk crept across his face.

"What's so funny?"

"Exodus: 20-5." Elvis said suddenly.

I squinted at him, normally well versed, but needing a moment to shuffle through years of bible camp memorization.

"Our God is a jealous God?" My mind was working the puzzle even as I heard myself utter the verse.

"Is he ever," Elvis whistled, punctuating the statement.

"Are you saying you wanted me to choose? Why, does God think I love you more than him?"

"No. I'm saying *you* did."

His words stunned me into silence. I just stared at him, the truth inducing new tears. They rolled hot down my cheek. As I began to cry, he let out an exasperated sigh as if to say—here we go again.

"Samantha, you have the heart of a servant, but you've been too distracted with me to see what's being offered right in front of you." He drew me into his arms. "Do you think God would allow you to go through all this for nothing? He wants to use you, honey, but he can't if I'm always in the middle."

I'd never considered that God, the creator of the universe, would want to use someone like me for his good. I was clearly unworthy. But after all that had happened, Elvis' words made sense. I had to consider that had Elvis stayed away, I would have awakened in the hospital on that fateful day and believed it all to be a dream. The fact that he returned suggested a bigger plan had been in place the whole time.

"I-I'm no good, I'm a mess...weak."

"He'll make you strong."

Me, be a servant of God? My father yes, but I've always lacked the obedience and discipline it required.

"I-I don't see how I can help."

"He'll tell you when it's time."

"How?"

"You'll hear him, honey, if you're listening."

Why me? I was not the faithful Abraham whom God had spoken to, requesting the sacrifice of his only son. I would have failed that test, never to have heard God's reprieve, 'Lay not your hand on the boy'!

"Is this what angels do?" I sat up away from his arms, whipping at my tears. "Ya'll come down here and lead hard headed people to their Godly purpose?"

"It's a tough way to make a living, boy, I tell you."

I was laughing at his quick witted humor when he leaned over and kissed me on the forehead.

"So, if all of this was preplanned, what was Steve's part?" His name almost made me retch, but there was still so much to understand.

"Steve's the reason I'm here, honey. He was a loose end the Devil himself was desperate to tie and you were in no condition to handle him yourself."

The irony that we were right back to that timeless battle didn't escape me, and I no more understood it now then a few days ago.

"The battle continues?"

"Every day." He nodded.

My head floated back to rest on his shoulder. As he went back to tinkering lightly on the keys, I let out a relieving sigh. I tilted my chin upward to look at him, examining his profile. I felt my heart stir with love once again. I know God never makes mistakes, but it seemed to me he could have sent anyone to take me down this road. Why send the one person he had to have known I would fall madly and helplessly in love with?

"Go ahead, Samantha, *ask*." He smiled without looking at me.

I groaned, and briefly considered another round of mathematics. Where did I leave off, the nine-sees? I wondered while next to me Elvis scowled. Never mind.

"Why you?"

He ran a hand pensively across his chin. "I believe God counted on a love that I never fully understood, but one that continues to benefit his greater plan even today."

My soul stirred. I had never considered the genius behind the design. It was only in this hindsight that God's full intentions for Elvis' life could be appreciated. He had lived a life full of great blessings, but it was not a life of his own. He was required to share it with the world. He'd suffered to be Elvis Presley. Now over thirty years later, God had himself an angel who was loved the world over. In fact, I'd bet only Jesus himself was more recognizable. He could send Elvis anywhere to preach, as he'd always wanted to do, for God's purpose. Who wouldn't listen?

It was beyond brilliant, it was devout. And I had to admit I wondered what God could do with me, if I was only willing.

"I don't know how I'm going to get on without you," I muttered and fell back into his arms. .

Elvis chuckled, his humor bouncing my head now at rest on his chest. My nose is running, and he's laughing? I didn't see any humor in this "letting go" business. I hate goodbyes!

"Now what's so funny?" I sniveled.

"You, honey, still thinking *you're* in control." He laughed harder to which I playfully slapped his arm in reply.

"Look at me when I say this," He lifted my chin so that I had to look at him, "I'm your angel until God says I'm not, understand?"

Those baby blues were so intense I pulled back, but only an inch.

"Yes sir." I sniffed.

"You stay focused on what's important and don't worry about me. Can you do that for me, Sam?"

"Yes sir, I-I'll try."

"Good girl," he placed a finger to my nose. "I'll be watching so be sure you do."

He was smiling, but I knew he was serious. He had given me an order, spoken with a snicker and a smirk, but an order just the same. He expected me to do as he asked. Now, I just had to keep my word.

CHAPTER TWENTY THREE

Outside the sun's rays warmed the city. Steam rose from every road and sidewalk as if it were the burning of Atlanta all over again. Only in the South could the weather change so drastically. Standing in the church parking lot, my eyes lifted to the heavens and I thanked God for the uplifting sight of the sun. The Lord was close. My day was by far not over, but I could feel him by my side. And that made everything easier.

I considered my next move. Do I go home or to the police? My mind spun. Part of me was waiting for God to speak, to tell me what to do, while the other half doubted I'd even hear him if he did. My track record was admittedly bad. Besides, reporting Steve seemed futile. I trusted what Elvis had told me, he wasn't coming back. And as I considered all my options, only one allowed me any comfort—home. I could always go home.

Once again, I urged my car into the hustle and the bustle of the city. I was headed for small town suburbia. And after yesterday, I didn't know what I'd find upon my arrival. But when I turned that last corner, and saw Heather's car in my drive, my smile couldn't have been any wider. Clearly our friendship had been given a pardon, and that made me even happier. Now more than ever, I needed my friend.

I glided my car into my drive and shut off the engine. My stomach bounced. I glanced up the road to my right. Not a soul stirred. The neighborhood was quiet. Maybe I could just stay here, I thought then laughed. I knew it was silly to be this apprehensive, but I couldn't seem to help it. I wasn't sure what I was waiting for—someone to yell "all clear"? But after a few more counted minutes, it was time to be a big girl. I looked to both sides of the street and then finally exited.

I stepped up the short three steps, bag in hand, and froze at the door. The urge to knock swelled, but I did nothing. Instead, I checked and rechecked my watch. It was 3:00 in the afternoon. I'd been home an hour, and only made it as far as the porch. This was crazy! Disgusted with my lack of courage, I reached out but before I could knock, the door jerked open.

To this day, I like to think that Heather had been watching for my return. I never asked, but when we came face to face that morning only awkwardness greeted me. My heart sank deeper into despair. I couldn't speak, but it didn't matter. Heather broke the spell first.

"He's not with you?" She glanced around.

I shook my head as I passed. I dropped my bag by the phone and headed for the kitchen. Heather followed, watching in silence as I went straight for the cabinet and the few bottles of alcohol I actually owned.

"You're giving up on baking?" Heather's words sounded with disappointment.

"If we're going to do this, one of us might need a drink." I said, while grabbing the martini shaker Heather had given me last Christmas.

When I turned back, Heather's yielding eyes made me paused. I realized I didn't even know how to make a martini. I never did learn because I always had Heather. As I frowned Heather reached out, and with as sly smile she took the shaker from my hand. She gently patted me on the shoulder, while offering me a seat at my own table. I pinned my bangs behind my ears and sat down with a heaving sigh.

"So, are we celebrating or mourning our friendship?" Heather asked while she tended to the ingredients.

"Neither."

"We'll call it a "peace" drink, then?"

"Sounds ok to me," I said, and just like that it was over.

Friendships that last a life time don't need many words to heal. There was no need for a bunch of "why's" or "how comes". While I knew Heather regretted keeping Steve from me, Heather knew I still loved her. These were sentiments, truths, that didn't need to be spoken. In the end, all that's left is the ritual of making up. It's a respected formality. And weather friends want to admit it or not, the trend for how to handle such a delicate matter is set early on.

"What does it say about us, that all our squabbles are settled over booze?" I asked.

Though I rarely drank, I never bucked the system, and in fact it was greatly anticipated.

"It says that we're brilliant, of course. And while everyone else is busy fighting we're moving on…drunk." She said with a firm nod as she sat with drinks in hand.

As always I waited for her customary first taste. And when her eyes narrowed over the potency, I didn't bother to hold back my snicker. I just let it go. Relief was found in the freedom of laughter, and for a brief moment it felt like old times. I wanted life to pause, allow me to fully soak in the moment. But as usual it just moved on. With or without you, I thought as I sipped timidly, bracing myself for the question I knew would come.

"So was prince charming waiting for you at the cabin?" Heather lifted her glass, but she never got another taste.

CHAPTER TWENTY FOUR

Pesky headaches, everybody gets them. Don't they? Whether its stress, a cold or even seasonal allergies. But who thinks to run to the doctor for every little twinge? I didn't. So imagine my surprise when I found myself sitting at the doctor's office three weeks later staring at a cat scan. Sure I see the "damage", I think. Though, at a second glance, it very well could have been an ink blot for all I knew.

Then the big words start. There's no avoiding them, and because I have no idea what they're talking about, my mind wanders. I question my need for a dictionary, and then consider if asking for one now would be rude. Probably, just nod and smile. Something is bound to sink in, and if it doesn't, call the nurses desk later. They're used to lost people like me.

All of this and more was running through my head as I heard the words Post Concussion Syndrome, or PCS. It was a pretty fancy word for a mild case of amnesia, I thought. But then I'm certainly not a doctor. As it was,

I was literally putting the pieces together as they were explaining my condition in detail. Talk about last minute shock!

"Have you experienced erratic or aggressive behavior?" The very young, too young, doctor asked.

I just stared at him.

"Have you found your senses heightened, say your hearing or your sense of smell?"

I grinned. Elvis does smell good at great distances, but I was sure he didn't want to hear about that, I internally chuckled. Focus Sam!

"You may have found yourself easily aroused."

He had my attention.

"Sexual intercourse would have been very optimal at this time, very heightened, scientifically speaking of course."

Blink-blink-blink.

They told me the symptoms can often stay dormant for months, even years after an accident, and that I was lucky. I didn't feel lucky. The mood swings and headaches, all warning signs of PCS, almost alienated me from everyone I cared about. Not to mention I almost lost my life. All that, and I didn't even get to experience the good stuff, scientifically speaking! If that was good fortune, I'll pass on luck.

When I left the hospital that day, I felt like half a person. It was too much information too fast. The only improvement was that I at least understood why I no longer recognized myself. Yet that didn't turn out to be as wonderful as I had imagined it to be. I couldn't work, and flying was an important part of my life. It was not just what I did, but who I was. Without the daily routine of airports and hotels, I was lost. Who was this woman who was home by six every night and asleep in her own bed by ten? Home-body was not in my dictionary.

If that wasn't enough, there were the counseling sessions. Round and round I'd go, chatting about my problems with virtual strangers. The healing process was tedious and often painful. They'd sit across from me, head down and taking notes. Often, I'd wonder if they were listening so I'd talk about something off track. Each time I'd discover my error, too late, and spend the rest of the meeting drowning in embarrassment. I wouldn't have blamed them if "crazy" had been jotted by my name weeks ago.

I never mentioned Elvis, but we spent a lot of time talking about Steve. Apparently, I was an anomaly in the fact that I'd had a singular memory lapse instead of, say, a whole time frame. Everybody was scratching their heads over the mystery, but I wasn't surprised. I never did anything "normal".

At first, I considered the sessions to be a big waste of everyone's time. I mean really, when did anything good come about when I did all the talking? It seemed hopeless. But I never missed an appointment, and before I knew it I found myself discussing raw emotions like the loss of my mother and my relationship with my father. Nobody was more surprised than me to find I was shedding real grief. After every appointment, I would walk out to my car feeling as if another brick had been removed from my shoulders, and wondering how they'd managed it.

"So what did the doctor's have to say today?" Heather's voice blared through the hands-free speakers of my car.

"Oh, you know just more ink blots and a lot of talking, that's all." I said.

"No really, what did they say?"

I smiled, touched by her concern. "If you really must know, I'll tell you all about it when I get home. Will you be there?"

"Yup, just got home from a trip and I have nothing planned."

"Good, I'll see you in a few," I said and ended the call.

A few weeks ago I'd asked Heather to move in, and was never more relieved when she agreed. While my body continued to heal, my dignity remained in shambles. Minus a few bruises, Steve hadn't hurt me physically but psychologically my scars were deep. He shattered my personal sense of safety, and before I knew it I had become that woman who switches on every light before entering a room. At every turn I was scrutinizing dark corners, checking and rechecking closets. And forget about going outside after dark. If I did, I ran not walked to my intended destination. The doctors told me

DREAM ANGEL

this type of paranoia was normal, that it would pass, but I was tired of being afraid.

Daddy still didn't know about Steve. He believed, without any help from me, that I was seeing a grief counselor. My secret was safe, so far. Life wasn't simple, but it was manageable. The mornings started easily enough, a coffee in one hand and the bible in the other. I would read, always wondering if today was the day God would speak to me. Up till now he'd been quiet, but I was only mildly disappointed. My time would come.

I stayed busy. My afternoons were spent at the church with my father. I loved the way his face lit up whenever I walked through those doors. It gave my spirit a jolt every time. My life was peaceful, but my heart was lonely. And while I had found uplifting ways to get through my days, the nights needed work.

It had been months since I'd seen my angel, but his memory was "everywhere". Even strolling through a department store, his voice would suddenly float out in song. There was no escaping him nor did I want to. Deep down, I guess I hoped God had someone for me to love, but if that man was years away, that was ok with me. There was a lot of "me" to work on.

* * *

February turned to March, March to April, and before I knew it Atlanta was in bloom. I loved spring.

And on a warm day in May, I was cruising through my neighborhood unaware life was about to change, again.

Pink rose buds bloomed and potted flowers hung in full glory from every porch. They were awe-inspiring and the spicy scent in the air lifted my spirits. It had been a good day—scratch that—a great day. I'd spent it driving around town with the convertible top down, enjoying the wind in my hair and the warm afternoon sun on my face.

At just an hour before dusk, I turned one last corner and headed for home. I was to meet Heather and my father for diner. It seemed they'd planned a big festivity, a celebration of health they'd said, and dinner at my favorite local restaurant—Dalton's—sounded great to me. Everyone was excited, including my father. He even called Heather and invited her personally, which shocked us both. This wasn't my daddy's normal choice for dining ambiance—a faded brick, weathered old Blues bar—but with the best fried chicken this side of the Mason Dixon Line, I didn't have to press him too hard.

I was ready in a jiff. Thankfully, the restaurant was only five minutes from my house. I rolled into the parking lot right on time, leaving a cloud of dust in my wake. I was already thinking about my order as I parked. The sun was low in an early evening sky, and a hint of humidity lingered, suggesting a storm was on its way. The air felt charged. It was the kind of night where one could easily imagine something exciting might happen.

Wearing a new periwinkle blue sundress, and a recent tan from an afternoon drive without sunscreen, I felt—dare I say it—confident. The feeling had been with me all day and I was steadily growing attached to it. Parked, I was busy straightening the state of my hair when Heather's red mustang pulled in. I cringed as I watched her hop the curb. Her freshly cut, spiky, blonde hair kept perfect form as she hit the brakes and slid to an almost instant stop next to me. Dust blew up over my roadster. I was coughing and swiping at the dirt while Heather was laughing. I considered an unladylike hand gesture, but then thought twice when I noticed my father's car parked close by. I scowled at her instead.

When Heather stepped out, she looked model-perfect in a slimming crimson dress with three inch heels. I had to hand it to her. She was wild, but she was truly beautiful.

"You should be on a New York runway not here in an old dingy Atlanta bar getting ready to eat something devilishly fattening with a friend and her daddy." I said, while we hugged.

"Could you share that with my date later?"

"Oh, I'm sure he's already captivated by your charms." I slipped my arm through Heather's and we walked together to the front door.

"I'm starting to wonder. He hasn't even made a move to kiss me," she said despondently.

This was a new twist. I'd never heard Heather with anything less than a full cup of confidence. She really must care for this man, I mused. Though I hadn't met him, I did recognize something different in her voice while she was on the phone last week. I didn't mean to eavesdrop, but it was hard not to miss those three special words that ended the call.

"Love looks good on you, friend." I stopped and turned to her, enjoying the flash of surprise in her deep brown eyes.

"Thank you." She gave my hand a gentle squeeze. "I'm sorry I haven't brought him around, but it never felt like the right time."

"I understand. I'm happy for you."

Her face blushed and then we hugged once more.

"I'd like to be happy for *you* one day." She pulled back to look me square in the eyes.

"I'm just now comfortable with *me* again. I'm not sure I'm ready for men yet." I muttered.

"Well, in time maybe that'll change."

"Maybe."

We started walking again, and I could hear the commotion from inside as we approached Dalton's entrance. As I opened the solid door, the mayhem of a business at full tilt overpowered the gentle spring evening. Dishes clanked and patrons hummed. I moved aside and allowed Heather to enter first.

"I love this place," she immediately pointed to the oversized slab of mahogany that made up the bar. It stretched the entire south wall of the room.

I chuckled, pulling my friend along.

"There he is." I spotted my father right off.

He was sitting at a table with an ice tea in front of him and a bible by his side. He looked like a saint sitting amongst the damned. At first I made a bee-line for him, but my gate slowed when I noticed the stranger next to him. Nobody had mentioned someone "new" would be joining us for diner, I frowned, understandably leery. But as Heather passed me, and approached the table with ease, I felt my worries fade.

I watched with growing curiosity as my father, and the man with the sun bleached hair, stood and greeted her warmly. In turn, she hugged my father and then shook the stranger's hand. It was odd. And I don't like odd. But unless I was going to strap on an apron and get to work, I couldn't stand in the middle of the room forever. And when people began to shout out their drink orders around me, I decided I'd better get a move on.

As I approached the table, daddy looked to me and his face sparked with happiness. I quickly returned a wave and a smile.

"Hello baby girl," he said, and practically jumped up to hug me. His embrace was firm as if we hadn't seen each other all week rather than just that afternoon.

When he leaned back to take a look at his daughter, his eyes fell disapprovingly to my neck line.

"You look lovely tonight, Samantha." He said with a fatherly tone I recognized.

"Daddy stop, this is the fashion of today." I grumbled.

"So you keep telling me," he shook his head. "Samantha, do you remember Jim Anderson?"

At just the mere mention of his name, the athletically built man all but leapt my way. His enthusiastic demeanor made me flinch, but I held my ground. He wasn't very tall, and even in a pair of diminutive heeled sandals, we stood eye to eye. That made him, 5'8"? Maybe, but I guessed shorter.

I was sizing him up when our eyes finally met, and a spark of familiarity flashed. His light hair mixed well with his tan face. But it was the glimmer, like that of a secret, in those green-brown eyes that captivated me. Right away, I felt my cheeks blush.

"It's been a long time Sammy, high school in fact." He extended me his hand.

Sammy? My eyebrows drew together. I studied him. Jim. The name reached out, tantalizing me before it suddenly hit me.

"Jimmy!"

His smile widened. This time he held out his arms and I eased in. We hugged like distant friends should, firm but quick.

"Hello, Sammy girl." He chuckled lightly.

Jimmy and I went way back, so far back it was no wonder I couldn't remember. We had been best pals all through high school, a time that felt so far removed from where I stood it could have been someone else's life. We were also an item for awhile, but to say it didn't work out was an understatement. Jimmy was a wannabe musician with a wild side, and my father was another adult trying to hold him down. Needless to say, they clashed and Daddy won.

"I can't believe this." I examined a face that I hadn't seen in more than ten years.

He was as handsome as I remembered, only with a few more years of maturity added in for good measure. The man standing before me was far more sophisticated then the teen I remembered that rarely stepped out of his shorts and flip-flops, even in the winter. Tonight Jimmy, or Jim as he called himself now, wore a lovely soft pinstriped blue suit, stark white shirt and pink tie. He was a welcomed sight. And I loved a man confident enough to wear pink.

"What's up with the suit?" I kidded and enjoyed the sight of him blushing. "I remember you best in a pair of wave breaker's."

We laughed.

"I still surf, but shorts aren't approved daily attire in the church where I'm employed."

Church? I turned to my father, who was standing close by with a smirk on his face. As was Heather, who I suddenly realized didn't look all too surprised either.

"You work in the ministry?" I asked of Jimmy but my focus was on my father.

Daddy held up his hands. "I just discovered this myself on a visit to our sister church across town a few days ago."

I laughed and then turned to Heather, who looked like the cat who ate the canary.

"You were in on this, weren't you?" I comically frowned and she merely shrugged.

I had mentioned Jimmy only once to Heather. It was after I'd arrived home from the hospital. I had spent an afternoon ranting on and on about how I'd dreamt an old boyfriend and Elvis were vying for my attention on a stage—Jimmy on guitar and Elvis on lead vocals. I didn't think she was listening, but tonight her funny little grin told me otherwise.

"Your father said the surprise was a secret, and I can't go against a man who has a direct line to God." Heather grimaced jokingly then took a seat.

My father rolled his eyes at Heather's antics and everybody laughed. Taking my seat, I unfolded my napkin in my lap. I paused in my fidgeting when I heard my name being called by my favorite waitress, Tammy. She was headed our way.

"Well, hello there youngins," she hollered as she approached.

Well into her fifties, Tammy wore a blonde wig piled high on top of her head and a pencil that balanced on the edge of her ear. She virtually bounced as she walked.

"Hello Tammy," I said in an excited voice that surprised even me.

"Well, who do you have with you tonight, Sam?" She grinned as she stood over my father.

I covered up my smile. Tammy imagined herself my surrogate mother. She saw me as a lamb surrounded by lions, and always kept a watchful eye on me.

"Tammy, this is my father, Pastor Richard Bennett."

Her eyes widened as my father stood and extended her his hand.

"It's a pleasure to meet you, ma'am." My father said as he tenderly took her hand for a light shake.

"Nice to meet you Sir," Tammy's eyes clouded over for a brief second, and then she snapped back to the business at hand. "What can I get y'all to drink?"

Heather requested a martini, shaken not stirred. I stuck with water and lemon, which pleased my father and horrified my friend. I was driving, I reminded her. Jimmy ordered tea, which pleased me. Though, I wasn't sure why.

"I have a gift for you to take home later that will help you celebrate in style." Heather muttered close to my ear, but father had uncanny hearing. His disapproval was evident in his frown.

I couldn't help but snicker. The differences between my Daddy and Heather were vast, but the fact that he was not already lecturing her about the dangers of drinking suggested she was growing on him.

"Jimmy, what do you do at our sister church?" I veered back to a safer topic.

"I'm the youth pastor," he said with a brilliant smile that made my heart flutter.

Bemused by my reaction, I averted my gaze and my attention fell to a woman just behind Jimmy. She sat alone at a table near the window. Her long blonde stringy hair laid flat against her porcelain features, and she was gazing at life outside her window with a blank expression that tugged at my heart.

"I'm sorry, when did you say you joined the ministry?" I glanced back to Jimmy, but only briefly.

I noticed that when the food arrived, the lost woman ate eagerly and without pause. I was enthralled by her obvious desperation. Her fork barely paused as she scoped up each bite. It was only when I heard Jimmy say something pointedly and rather loudly that I refocused. I turned to him, about to ask him to repeat his telling when a tiny voice whispered in my ear.

Go to her. My heartbeat jumped up into my throat.

"Jimmy joined God's fight about seven years ago, *Samantha*," Daddy said my name with a firm tone meant to remind me of my manners. "He's been with the church now, for what son, two years?"

I cleared my throat, and sat up straighter. I was trying to pay attention to Jimmy as he spoke, but my eyes kept drifting away as if on their own power. My mind was racing wondering if this was the sign I'd been waiting for all these months. That voice, mine but not mine. The hungry lady sitting there with nothing but a plastic grocery sack between her feet, all suggested "something" special was about to happen.

DREAM ANGEL

Go to her, and give her what you have. The voice rang again, and this time I choked on my water.

"Are you, ok?" Heather touched my arm.

I forced a broad smile. "Absolutely!"

What was this, I wanted to scream out as my hands instantly began to shake. Was this my condition, getting worse, or was it God? It didn't sound God-like, I thought. But then, what did he sound like anyway? My father had once told me that the Holy Spirit speaks to him, or was it that it speaks "in" him? I couldn't remember. Was there a different?

"So, it must be very fulfilling to help with the youth." I was nodding, squinting at Jimmy as if paying close attention.

I could feel the weight of Heather's gaze, and even my father was now scanning the room. Mean while Jimmy chatted away happily, and was none the wiser.

"Yes it's very rewarding. I even manage to catch a few waves in between stirring young minds for God." He lightly chuckled. "Did you ever give surfing a try, Sammy? I remember you said you wanted to one day."

I continued to nod, completely oblivious to Jimmy's reproachful look that I hadn't responded to his inquiry. I was still grinning when Heather kicked me under the table. I scowled at her and then kicked her back. "What is going on?" My father suddenly growled.

Instantly, I was twelve.

"Nothing," I dusted off that princess expression that served me well in my youth. "I need to excuse myself to the ladies room for a moment, father," I said, and batted my eyes giving a respectful nod as I stood.

I was a grown woman, I didn't need permission to go the bathroom but he was still my father.

"Me too," Heather added too quickly, and shot up from her chair.

I cringed. Even Jimmy seemed to remember my father's fondness to manners as he picked up a menu and considered it.

"Girls!" Daddy barked.

Heather and I were both standing, me inspecting the floor and Heather staring at my father. She was clearly unaware of the dangers of making eye contact.

"I don't know what is going on right now, but you sit," he pointed to Heather, "and, you go take care of what you have to and hurry back to your dinner guest."

I didn't wait for Heather's reaction. She was on her own. I grabbed my purse, and all but ran to the restroom. I craned my neck, trying to get a closer look at the woman as I passed her table, my heels clamoring against the aged wood floor and the patrons at the surrounding tables frowning over the disturbance. Everyone that is, except the woman with an empty plate and a look of despair on her face.

Entering the powder room, I slapped my purse on to the vinyl counter top. What did I have that she needed? I stared at myself in the mirror. Looking down to my quaking hands, I wore nothing of value. I had on a pair of dime store bangle earrings and a sterling silver thumb ring. That was the extent of my bobbles. Think, think! I opened my purse and took inventory. Lip gloss, a cell phone, and a small change purse. No help there, I considered, and my hand froze over my wallet. The memory of an empty plate, and the woman's face filled with dread flooded back. I counted my money. $30. My spirit sank. That wasn't enough to pay for her and my meal.

Give as I have given to you! The voice suddenly blared and I let out a loud shriek.

My voice echoed off the walls, and I quickly slapped my hand over my mouth. This better be God or I've officially gone crazy! Closing my eyes, I laid a hand over my racing heart. Deep breath in, deep breath out, I coached.

Relax and don't let the, I paused. Don't let the miracles rattle you? My eyes flashed open.

A moment later, I was out the door. I briefly glanced to my table, taking note that only Heather was watching. Good. I only wanted to explain this once, if at all. With the money clutched in my clammy hand, I headed straight for my destiny. When I got close, the troubled woman looked up to me. Her sad-filled eyes seemed to beg me to sit, and hear her story, but that's not what I'd been asked to do. And I was afraid to veer from my instructions. I kept it simple. I smiled, hoping to convey friendship and kindness while also picking up the black leather case on the table and slipping the money inside.

"God wants you to have this," I spoke close to her ear, and gave a soft touch to her shoulder. Then I left and never looked back.

Heather watched me as I crossed the room, but when I arrived back at the table, she said nothing. The evening continued on smoothly, and my whole body exhaled with relief. I'd passed my first test.

"Sammy, remember that summer when you told Danny Mcknolty that if he climbed that big willow tree behind your church he'd reach heaven?" Jimmy turned to the past.

"I remember Danny fell and broke his arm!" I said right in beat, as if I'd never left the conversation.

"Yup, and then you told him God doesn't like unexpected visitors!" Jimmy roared. Even my father laughed, though he was shaking his head.

All through diner, we reminisced. It seemed I had forgotten so many wonderful childhood memories. Long summer days, spent in blissful innocence and purposeful mischief, had been over shadowed with the dark realities of life. I was happy Jimmy had brought them back into the light so that I could enjoy them. They were worth remembering.

With every story our laughter grew, and by diner's end I had the sore stomach muscles to prove that I'd had a good time. The best in a long while

"All this remembering has tuckered me out," my father said with a satisfying sigh over his empty plate. "I think I'll head home."

"Already?" I whined.

"Yes, already, baby girl. Six in the morning comes early for these old bones." He sighed exaggeratedly, while placing money to the table and grabbing his coat to leave.

"Let me get that Mr. Bennett," Jimmy fumbled for his wallet.

"Put your money away, boy. The man who marries my Sam can pay for her, until then that's my job." He winked and leaned over to kiss me lightly on the cheek.

"My sweet daddy, I love you." I stood up and wrapped my slight arms as far around him as I could.

"I love you too." He whispered in my hair.

My father shook Jimmy's hand one more time, gave Heather a friendly hug, and departed with his bible firm under his arm. We all watched him as he walked away. He was so much wiser than I'd ever given him credit for. I thanked God that I still had him.

"That man has carried a bible everywhere since I can remember," Jimmy murmured.

"He's something," Heather agreed.

"That's my daddy." My tears swelled.

There was a time, after momma went away, when Daddy and I were at such odds, I would have avoided a night like tonight. But those days were long gone.

Turning, I discovered that Heather and Jimmy were gathering their coats to leave.

"Is everybody leaving me?"

"I have a date, Sam. I'm sorry." Heather said.

"Oh, that's right." I sighed, and began to collect my things as well.

"I wish I could stay longer, but I have a date with Bunco. I play every Friday night with the senior ladies of the church. " Jimmy said.

"You play Bunco *every* Friday night?" Heather paused in putting on her coat. She had one arm in and one arm out.

While I internally thanked her for changing the subject, Jimmy laughed at the horror-stricken look on her face.

"Ignore her. She cuts liquor vouchers from the Sunday paper." I joked.

Heather's attention shifted. "There's alcohol coupon's in the paper?"

Everyone paused. Then Jimmy and I exploded into a fit of laughter and Heather rolled her eyes.

"I can see you and Ms Betty Crocker here are going to have loads to talk about," she groaned and did what I'd wanted to do earlier—flipped me off—then headed for the door.

"She's a colorful sort," Jimmy said.

"You have no idea!"

The three of us walked out into a mild Atlanta evening. The sun had dipped below the horizon more than an hour earlier and a chill was in the air. Off in the distance, I could see the storm I had predicted looming, dark and vast. I wrapped my arms tight around my chest, wishing I had thought to bring a sweater.

"I have a jacket in the car if you'd like to borrow it for your drive home?" Jimmy spoke at my side.

"Thanks, but it's not far."

"Oh!" Heather suddenly hollered and I jumped. "I have something to give you. I almost forgot, hold on."

She raced to her car leaving Jimmy and I alone.

While I was watching her, Jimmy's eyes were on me.

"How are you, really?" He reached out and tenderly took my hand.

It had been months since a man had touched me in such a personal way, and I couldn't help but tense from the contact.

"I'm ok." I said softly, slipping my hand free.

He studied me closely. "Good."

"Wait till you see this!" Heather interrupted excitedly, carrying a light green plastic container with a make-shift foil top.

She was two steps away, but I could already smell the scent of chocolate in the breeze.

"You got me an edible gift?" I was as excited as Heather would be over a well made drink.

"It's not often that one *keeps* a friend by cheating death, twice," she said and handed me the goodies. "I'm so glad to have you around my friend."

Smiling, I closed my eyes and drew in a deep breath of the overly sweet substance. I guessed double fudge brownies, and in looking, with nuts. Devilish!

"You always said I should bake more and drink less." Her voice trailed off. "I-I think it's time we start doing all those things we said we would."

I reached out and grabbed her to me. We held each other, both of us shedding a few silent tears.

"Let's go home and have a taste." I said, and then remembered her plans. "Oh, I forgot, wonder boy is waiting."

"I think he can wait." She wiped a tear from her eye.

"Of course he will," I smiled happily.

Heather gave me one more hug, and then surprisingly hugged Jimmy too before leaving. We watched in horror as she bounced back into traffic, giving little pause, and inspiring a collective blare of disapproval from drivers in both directions. As the ruckus roared, her tires grabbed pavement and with a screech, she was gone. I could only shake my head.

"May I ask you something?" Jimmy asked smoothly by my side.

I kept my gaze low and turned to unlock my car. "Would you like a slice? I can share, but only a small piece." I kidded, knowing it wasn't cake on his mind.

"No Sam, but thank you." He chuckled, and the gentle sound of his laughter stirred the butterflies in my stomach.

I hadn't felt that since? Never mind.

"Bunco wins over treats, huh?" I turned back and those hazel eyes of his, so concentrating and warming, made me feel all cozy inside despite my lack of a jacket.

"Did he break your heart?" He's eyes searched mine for the truth.

Though I had no idea why his question stunned me, it did. And while my wide eyed expression gave me away, it was Jimmy who lost his nerve first.

"I'm intruding."

"No." I quickly gathered his hands into mine. "He didn't hurt me, he loved me."

The word "love" felt good on my lips. It rolled off my tongue so naturally, even I paused. I had never spoken so honestly with one man about loving another. And while I was busy feeling exposed from such openness, Jimmy's eyes remained soft with empathy. I wondered if he had a love story of his own to share. The sympathy I saw in his eyes told me he did, but I couldn't bring myself to ask. I couldn't bare another love story with a sad ending.

When he drew me in for a hug good bye, I instantly resisted—a reflex I was working to overcome.

"Maybe you'll share your story with me one day?" He eased me out of his arms, and looked down to me with eyes as misty as my own.

I smiled lightly. "Maybe, if you share yours first." I watched closely as he struggled to restrain a knowing smile of his own.

"Someday," he said with a wave of his index finger and a shake of his head.

* * *

When I walked through my front door, I heard Heather rummaging around in the kitchen. What was she up to now? Surely her domesticated self was worn out after the trying task of brownies? I snickered and headed to join her. I was just about to cross the threshold when a loud crash sounded like glass to tile, and an "I'll replace that" followed. I openly laughed.

"Did you invite him to join us?" She asked with her back to me, hands deep inside my cabinets.

"In so many words, yes, but he declined."

She shot me a grimacing look over my shoulder.

"I did!"

I was aware Heather feared I'd forever be alone, but such things weren't ours to worry about. Everything in God's own time—I'd learned that the hard way.

"That's it then?" She dropped a plate in front of me with a clamor and a frown.

It rattled around than settled face up, thankfully unbroken. And I could only assume she accepted my thoughts on the matter because she turned without a word, and went back to busying herself with the business at hand, whatever that was.

"Well," she finally sighed, "I suppose when it's time you'll step back into life."

"I suppose." As far as I was concerned, the game of life had all but rejected me. The next move wasn't mine, but I held back any further retort.

Leaning a little to the right, I watched as she opened the fridge and began a whole new quest. When she quickly spun around, a bottle in one hand and what looked like chilled wine glasses in the other, I quickly sat up straighter. She headed straight for me, wielding the bottle while balancing glasses and simultaneously tugging on the corked top. She looked like an uncoordinated juggler. I cautiously scooted back to give her more room, and a second later a pop echoed.

"We can't have brownies without champagne." She smiled triumphantly.

"Of course not!"

Not an aficionado, I had never tasted champagne. Alcohol wasn't offered in my family circle, not even at weddings, so I'd never had a reason to have any. It seemed fitting that Heather should pour me my first glass. I was fascinated as the sparkling beverage hit the side of the glass and bounced in festive spirits. Terrific! Though the fizz raced to the top, not a drop foamed over. She was talented.

"Here's to a new start." I lifted my chilled glass, and tilted it towards Heather.

I was eager to experience my first champagne toast, but she wasn't budging.

"What?"

She frowned. "You're really going to toast to a new start and not tell me what happened tonight at Dalton's? Why you raced to aid a stranger?"

"I paid her bill, so what." I tried to keep it simple.

I didn't want to talk about my new gift. I was tired of being "that" weird friend, but her gaze was penetrating.

And while she sat there with her flute up, but not moving, I kept my eyes steady and my smile big. I inched my glass closer.

"Liar," she finally said, and then we toasted with stemware that not only chimed but hummed.

Excellent!

CHAPTER TWENTY FIVE

"Are you alright with me leaving?" Heather paused on the front porch, hesitant to say goodbye.

"P-h-e-s-t," I waved a hand at her.

"I always said you should drink more but two glasses Samantha, that's all you've had." She shook her head and then leaned in closer. "Are you sure you're ok?"

"I'm fine, really. Go have fun."

"Don't get in your car and drive, Ok?"

"Check." I said with a wink.

Unconvinced, she made no move to leave.

"Where's your key's?" She let out a conflicting sigh.

I scrunched up my nose in an effort to think, but she only grunted and stomped passed me. As she headed for the phone station, and I assumed my purse, I looked up into a sky now blackened by the storm that had finally arrived.

When I'm right, I'm right, I nodded to nobody in particular.

"Now you *can't* go anywhere," Heather shook the car keys at me as she passed through the open door.

"Check." I said again.

"Stop saying that!" She turned back to me with a scowl. I flashed a silly grin.

"Call me if you need something," she hollered over her shoulder as she exited into the wet night.

I considered throwing out another "check", just to get under her skin, but I decided to cut her some slack. She was already two hours late for her date because of me. And as it was, she ran not walked for her car. I could tell by the sporadic bounce in her gate that she was excited. If she was happy, I was happy, she was happy. I paused, and then hiccupped. Whatever. I closed the door and locked it. Then I rechecked it, but only once.

That's an improvement, I smirked, and if I don't recheck it all night, it'll be a record. Course the night was young.

All and all, it had been the best day I'd had in months. I'd spent it driving aimlessly in the sun—going nowhere important—eating with great company, and now with a glass of newly discovered bubbly warming my belling, the evening held promise. It promised a good night's sleep, that's what it promised, I snickered. I was already feeling sleepy, loose as a goose, and if I thought about it long enough, drunk. Turns out, I liked wine. Who knew!

I toddled down the hallway. I'd say I staggered, but a lady never staggers. At least that's what I told myself as I stepped through the threshold of my bedroom, took a steady step, and then tripped over my own two feet, stumbling to the bed.

"S-shush." I placed a finger to my lips, and stereotypically inspected the floor. "I-I gotta fix that."

Except for the soft hum of the ceiling fan over my head, the room was quiet. I looked up and followed the spin of the blades. Oh! My stomach flipped. I quickly averted my eyes, and set the champagne flute to the night table.

"Stay!" I pointed at it.

Unzipping my dress, I gave a wiggle of my hips and the fabric fell to ground. I twitched my foot and flung the garment across the room.

"I'll call the maid tomorrow." I looked at the clock by my bed and my chuckle slowly died. It is tomorrow!

Where did the time go? My stomach answered back, and it sounded angry. On second thought, I'm not sure I like wine. Not so much. With a wobbly hand, I snatched my nightgown from under my secret hiding spot—my pillow—and slipped it on, backwards. I didn't care. I crawled into bed, banished my down comforter to the foot of the mattress, and pulled the sheets up to my face. I was finally settled.

Outside, the storm brewed. I could hear the faint sound of thunder rumbling far off in the distance. Since my attack, I had found it hard to sleep during a storm but tonight was different. I suppose the alcohol helped. And as the wind began to rattle the windows of my tiny house, my eyes became heavy. A veil of darkness fell.

As I sank deeper and deeper, a surge of remembering rushed in. Maybe it was the wine, or possibly plain human weakness that led me to my true hearts desires, but I was powerless to stop it. Memories flashed through my head at the speed of light. That laugh, those sapphire blue eyes, and that voice. All of it stirred me closer to what I longed for, desired.

The time travel was instant. One moment I was in my warm bed and the next I was standing upright and looking down at a set of delicate feet. The toes, painted to match the vibrant red shag carpet that enveloped them, looked familiar. I cocked my head and then wiggled them. Yup, they're mine.

The carpet was so—dare I think it—*1970*.

As I stood there an understanding raced. I had stood in this exact spot before. Though when I'd visited it looked different, I told myself, unwilling to look up and confirm what I already knew. Why was I bent on torturing myself?

With my vision kept low, I used only my peripheral to peek at my surroundings. In front of me was a door, a white colonial style door to be exact. My pulse skipped. To my left, and at the farthest parameter, I could see that the red carpet under my feet wove through the foyer and into the living room. The vibrant red was a perfect match to the white and red velvet furniture it accented. There was no need to look further. I knew that beyond the formal living quarters was an entrance, decorated with two stain glass peacocks. And once across that threshold, I'd find a grand piano—the music room.

I was at Graceland! Not Graceland of present, but worse—Graceland of the past. The question was when? What year?

"77." I heard myself say, and then I squeezed my eyes closed.

A tiny seed of worry festered. It started in the darkest corners of my subconscious, and quickly reached the forefront of my psyche. There was no ignoring what I "had" to do now. I had to go upstairs, and yet what was the point? I had come so far accepting my fate—plus or minus—why put myself through the misery? He wasn't here.

I lifted my eyes and my attention fell to the "P" over the doorway. Presley. I covered my face, and let out a painful moan. I was once again sabotaging myself, inhibiting my recovery. It was always the same, one steps forward two steps back. And while I was busy ranting about that very fact, a ruckus rumbled from upstairs like that of a book case falling to the floor. I looked up, and the chandelier swung from the vibration.

I closed my eyes. I strained to hear the smallest sound from "the room", I knew, was over me. *This is just a dream*, I heard myself say. That clamor didn't mean my loving compassionate friend was taking his last breath as I stood by doing nothing. No, that's not what that meant, because this was not August 16th. This wasn't even 1977!

"This is a dream!" I stomped.

This nightmare was the booze talking, that's all. I nodded to myself as if it was just that easily explained, simple. Course I'm never drinking as long as I live, I thought, and crossed my arms defiantly across my chest. My imagination raced, conjuring up a fear as real as any I'd ever felt before. My heartbeat mixed with the rhythm of my inhaled breath, now clattering like an out of tune symphony in my ear. The more I did nothing, the louder it became.

"Uh-h-h," I I groaned.

A moment later, I blasted up the white plush staircase. I took the steps two at time, racing my reflection in the mirror at my side. On my next inhale, I reached the landing. I grabbed a hold of the spindles, and flung myself through the turn. On my exhale, I arrived breathless and shaky at the top. Panting, I reached out for the door that led to Elvis' private sanctuary.

The door creaked when it opened. I made no move to enter. My gaze floated down the shadowy hall, but my feet wouldn't budge. The passage was deep, narrow, and with a low ceiling it reminded me of a closed up attic. The slight space inspired a familiar panic, and the phobia's I'd worked months to overcome—such as dark spaces with no way out—crept back. My hands shook at my side.

In an attempt to control my escalating emotion, I focused on what I knew to be true. Like the fact that there were three bedrooms, not counting Elvis', on this floor. Which meant the hall only appeared to end in blackness. In reality it turned to the right and went back further to more rooms. That meant the main room—

Elvis' room—was off to my left. I could see it from where I stood. All I had to do was take that first step!

As my anxiety rose, my surroundings blurred. The floor under my feet went soft. I felt divided. It was as if I existed in two realms, and I clearly felt my body lying in my bed back in Atlanta while I stood at Graceland. Part of me just wanted it all to end, but my reckless nature—dare I say my dysfunctional half—clung on to the vision. I had to know if he was here.

Determined, I swung my arms and jumped through the threshold like an Olympian in the standing long jump. I landed flat footed, and without hesitation took off at a dead run. I hit the first set of double doors at full speed and pushed through. Glancing around me, I noticed one small piano, a good size desk, and a gun collection in a case over the white couch. I cannot say what else, as a second later I stood in front of a second set of double doors, padded leather and unlike anything I'd ever seen before. And just like the previous room, I didn't stop to admire them. I laid my shoulder into the door like a line backer and exploded into the main room—Elvis' bedroom.

The first thing I saw was a nine foot by nine foot bed decorated with a dark rose velvet comforter. I admit it made me pause. I'd never seen a bed that size before. It practically swallowed up the room, I briefly considered before continuing through to what looked like a small dressing room. Upon entering, I made an immediate turn and stumbled to a stop in the middle of what appeared to be the bathroom. Immediately my gaze casted downward, and he wasn't there.

He isn't here.

I drifted further into the room. My heart was still racing as I leaned heavily onto a two person black marble vanity, my head hanging low and gasping for a breath. Tears streamed. I knew it was silly to cry, but a mix of overwhelming happiness and desolate sadness filled me. *He wasn't here.* The words kept repeating. And had I not been clutching the sink basin, I would have melted to my knees in a sobbing heap.

After a few moments, my breathing settled and my trembling hands stilled. My mind cleared—as much as one can expect for a dream—and my curiosity raged. The details around me beckoned. Everything, from the wide mirror framed with large cosmetic lights, to the everyday items such as tooth paste and antacid, strewn about the counter in a disorganized mess, captured my interest. They sparkled like treasured gems rather than ordinary condiments.

This moment was so surreal, and only one thought reigned—"I" was standing in Elvis' private quarters. A new excitement swelled.

I eyeballed a dark green bottle of Brut, pushed off to the side but with the lid cracked as if someone had just used it, like an illegal substance. Do I dare? I pondered the ramifications, allowing the time span of a heartbeat to pass before picking it up and lifting it to my nose. Inhaling deeply, I relished in a scent that was familiar but not "quite" right. In fact, it was downright wrong. The aroma without the man was not at all as exquisite as I remembered. I could only rationalize that it was the chemical makeup of the man mixed with the fragrance that created this love potion I seemed to crave. And after taking in another sample, I could only shake my head. It was perplexing but true. Deflated, I returned the bottle back to its rightful place.

Now at ease, I looked up and caught my likeness in the mirror. I laughed out in horror. Beads of perspiration glistened on my face, which only slightly distracted me from the matted mess my hair was in. Gathering my locks with both hands, I wound until my long strains served as its own make shift pony tail. Crafty, I thought. And when I stepped back to get the full picture, my chuckle died in my throat.

What was I wearing? I squinted and leaned forward to inspect a blue satin shirt that was so long it reached my thighs. Puzzled, I lifted my arms and my wrists disappeared inside the cuffs. I shook the sleeves and grimaced. I looked like a clown. And to make matters worse, at further inspection, I had on no pants. Great! Where were my pants? I was pondering the mystery when I noticed two embroidered initials on my breast pocket. My eyes widened. The letter's "E.P" told me all I needed to know. Great Lord above! I have on Elvis' pajamas!

"You looking for me?" His familiar voice made me freeze.

Still facing the mirror, I glanced up to my reflection and then behind—to Elvis. He was leaning casually against the door frame, arms crossed over his bare chest and a grin fixed on his face.

"You have my top," he said with a glimmer in his eyes and a measure of attitude in his tone.

Though it was only his reflection, I struggled to hold his gaze.

"You have my pants," I returned coolly.

I turned and mimicked his stance, crossing my arms over my chest in much the same manner. Face to face with the actual man, I'd hoped to display a measure of confidence, but with circus clown cuffs drooping over my elbows like a wet dish cloth it was a stretch. And when I caught him smirking at me, I knew I'd lost what little edge I'd had.

"I rushed up here to—" I tried, but the sight of him nodding along so eagerly made me pause. Why's he looking at me like I'm lunch? I thought and then cringed.

Smiling, he stepped in closer, and I shifted to the right.

"I-I wouldn't have barged in like this, but I was worried that you were," I hesitated, momentarily distracted by the design of my own trickery, "I-I was worried that you needed help. I-I'm trained, you know, in life saving skills like…mouth-to-mouth."

That animated lifted a brow of his rose, and I smiled weakly.

"I-it's what I do." I'm so lame!

"Lucky me," his smile curled upward.

Why am I so nervous? Sure there was "something" different in his mannerism, something nagging at me that I couldn't put my finger on. Worse, he wasn't giving me time to work it out. He just kept strolling, moving confidently to my side, barefoot and gorgeous, and ignoring my personal space. I needed room to think!

I moved to the right. He followed. Then I tried the left and he followed again. And when the only move left was backwards, I found myself pinned between his gorgeously bare chest and the vanity. For a moment, I became submerged in those blue pools of his. I was drowning, and two seconds away from admitting defeat, when I suddenly snapped back. No you don't! I spun around and found myself staring into a beige and black checkered walk-in shower. Room for two!

"You first." His eyes danced.

I swallowed hard, spun again, and this time exited the room. I headed for the first available place to sit— the bed. I plopped down and pulled the edges of my circus tent down around my knees. As I was just about to smartly comment on the iceberg status of the room, a chilly draft blew across my bare legs. It drifted upward, alerting me to what else was missing, and I quickly crossed one leg over the other. I was whimpering while a rush of heat flushed me.

My attention flickered downward to the expansive divan I was seated on. "I can't believe this is happening," I muttered, while also noticing the large statue of Jesus next to the bed. *Great he's here too!*

My gaze floated about. Having never been on this side of Graceland before, I was quickly absorbed by the view. Red lush curtains with white tassels were draped elegantly around the room, covering walls and windows alike. I felt like the fair maiden who had accidentally stepped into the King's boudoir, unprepared and awestruck. She'd no doubt pay for the misdeed of trespassing. *Death by pleasure*, I let out a timid laugh. I glanced behind me to the biggest mirror I'd ever seen seconding as a headboard and swallowed hard. If this room could speak, I thought, while tilting my gaze further upward to the leather padded ceiling— sound proof— and complete with three televisions sets.

"I'm in big trouble."

"Relax, honey, this is your show." His voice sounded from an all together different direction.

I looked behind me and found him sprawled out in bed, comfy-like, and resting on a mound of pillows. His arms were folded behind his head and he had a sly smirk on his face. There it was, I realized, that cocky demeanor. This wasn't my angel. This was some vamped up figment of my imagination. A young man full of tactics, I considered and then paused. Tactics, indeed!

I set my jaw. "So, if I'm running the *show*, how come I don't get to choose the scene?" I asked and then it hit me—I did.

Admittedly, "Jail House Rock" was a favorite movie of mine. However, Elvis' character was egotistical, arrogant, and in taking another look, very sexy. He was 1957 perfection.

Intrigue set in.

"This is your fantasy, baby, not mine," he said in perfect Vince Evert style.

"You look like you," I contemplated while nibbling on my thumb nail, "course you would wouldn't you?"

He wasn't listening; he was busy adjusting something under the covers, arms reaching and legs twitching. What was he doing? It was like some kind of stage move, yet not. I watched curiously as he gave a little hip wiggle and out came his pants. My mouth dropped. He wadded them into a ball, and tossed them to the white furry love-seat in the corner. I followed their flight pattern.

My processing was slow, and it went something like: If A leads to B, and B to C and his pants where over there then he was—gulp. I sucked in a startled breath and looked back at him, wide eyed and mouth still hung open.

"Your move," His tone was so quid pro quo; I was instantly initiating my escape.

I began to inch off the bed, but he was too quick for me. He sat up, grabbed my arm, and moved in for the kill. Suddenly, we were nose to nose, and those long eyelashes of his were practically touching my own. I trembled with anticipation.

"Check mate?" I laughed pathetically, and his lips fluttered into a sultry smile.

The air between us quickly heated. He drew in a deep even breath through his nose and leaned forward, his lips skimming my cheek on his way to my ear. His breathing sounded rough and rattled. My own breath skipped, and when he kissed the nap of my neck, my pulse went to hammering in my throat.

Help! He was playing a game without rules.

"I-I've heard chess is a sport for aristocrats, have you ever heard that?" I stumbled idiotically. "I-I really don't know how to play this...that game."

"Woman," he said huskily while nuzzling my ear, "I don't know what the hell you're talking about."

I pulled back to look at him. Those eyes, that face, and that flawless hair. I was dying to mess it up. He was maddening and intoxicating, a perfect temptation. Every feminine cell in my body screamed to have him. But it wasn't that simple. If I indulged, where would I be come morning, heartbroken and alone? I could do alone, but a girl only had one heart. And I had just found mine.

When I refocused he was unbuttoning my shirt.

"Whoa, let's not get ahead of ourselves." I pulled back my top. "M-my experience with men as of late has been—"

"Limited," he grinned.

He was so close, and his scent was so delicious, my mouth started to water.

"I-I was going to say disagreeable."

"I'll take it *real* slow." The word "real" pursed his lips forward, and "slow" rolled his tongue.

My mouth parted ever so slightly.

"This is unreal." I closed my eyes.

"M-m-m...come have some unreal, baby," was the last thing I heard before bursting to the moon.

He used one hand to tilt my chin, and the other to cradle my head as he descended deep into my mouth. The sound of him moaning aroused a series of delicious shivers through my body. I slipped my hands deep in to his hair and we melted to the bed.

There was no slow seduction. No gentle persuasion. He was everywhere at once. His hand cupped my breast while he used his tongue and the edges of his teeth to sample the delicate place below my ear. He was demanding and I was eager, pressing myself into him. I drew my thigh upward alongside his bare leg, delight found in his gentle shudder. His enthusiasm was intoxicating. And I was quickly lost in my desire to be closer than we had ever been before. For one beautiful moment, I was free to enjoy what had been denied me all these months, and then my continence sparked.

"Wait." I turned my head, gasping for a breath, but he wasn't listening.

Overcome by his own passion, he reached for me and my whole body stiffened, and then melted under his skilled hands. His touch was measured, unhurried. I could feel the hard line of his body over me; hear his own breath rasping in my ear. As he stirred me closer to the edge of ecstasy, my body willingly followed yet my mind continued to object. A tiny voice of reason tried, but was soon lost like a whisper in a raging wind. I was weak with desire. I wanted him. And God forgive me, but part of me hoped to take him, devour him, and be done with the bone aching need for him.

A tear streamed down my moist cheek, and his caresses suddenly stopped. My eyes were closed, but I could hear him panting over me. Baffled by this sudden reprieve, I opened my eyes to find a new soul piercing gaze looking down to me. Where self-assurance and supremacy once blazed, now sensitivity and compassion ruled. This was not the same man. Gentleness filled the depths of these eyes, evidence that the man I truly loved had finally arrived. More tears flowed.

"S-h-h, I'm here."

Not a word more was spoken. None were needed. The magnitude of the moment pulsated in both of our eyes. And when I placed a light touch to his cheek, I felt his jaw line flexing with impatience. I watched as his mouth parted ever so slightly, and when he moistened his lips, I pulled him in.

We met half way, dissolving as one. The feel of his measured lips, patiently tasting instead of devouring, instantly melted me back to the disheveled sheets. When his tongue skimmed over mine, sinking deeper for a fuller taste, a quiver coiled down my spine. I moaned and he softly answered back. We eagerly explored each other, lips never parting. Our bodies molded together like a perfect puzzle, the softness of mine a perfect contrast to his lean hard frame. We were like two hearts sharing the same beat. When I breathed out, he inhaled in. We were almost one.

He stirred me gently, seizing complete possession of my body. I curved into his touch, trembling from the intensity. The musky masculine scent of him made me feel alive. The feel of his hands in intimate places few had ever been felt natural and shameless. I was a woman responding to the man she loved just as nature had intended.

Off in the distance, a tidal wave of ecstasy swelled.

"Samantha." He sounded breathless.

My name spoken so blithe and airy on his lips evoked a rush like that of a drug to my veins. I audibly purred in response, stirring closer to what I wanted. My body all but begged for what only he could give, but still he waited.

"Are you sure, honey?" His face was flushed and his lips were wet from my kisses.

His smile was variant, both bashful and certain, and my consent reflected back to me in his eyes. There was no going back. And when he gently repositioned himself, there was no denying his power, and nothing halfhearted about his passion. I quivered in anticipation.

I kissed him deeply while he moaned something husky, something growly, and then we were one. The sudden pressure, weight, and length of him blasted my body to somewhere between pleasure and pain. I clung to him, and felt his body quiver, just once.

"Like one," he gasped into my mouth.

Stillness enveloped us. If there was to be shame, I felt none. I had wanted him, suffered to be in his arms. I loved him as I feared I'd love no another.

Passion churned. His heartbeat pounded against my chest. Fingers entwined, I could feel his life's blood throbbing inside my damp palms. He was the master of tempo and grace, easily followed. And while an Ocean's tide rolled around us, his body was taut. While I was clutching the sheets, grasping at my wilting self-control, his restraint was firm. Like one-one-one, the rhythm pulsated.

The pressure swelled, and a mighty force of nature rammed my walls of resistance. I let out a tiny whimper of release, and the tempo slowed.

"From your lips, honey," his voice was rough yet soft as velvet, "let me hear you say it."

He merely shifted, and a wave of pleasure washed over me. Ecstasy ignited from every corner of my body in bursts of shimmering ripples. Overwhelmed by a moment I'd never live again, I lifted my mouth to his ear.

"Elvis! Elvis! Elvis!" I cried out, and he groaned back his happiness in response.

CHAPTER TWENTY SIX

My body jolted. Passion shot through me like an electrical shock. My eyes flashed open, and I sucked in a breath so deep my chest lifted upward. With my head where my feet should have been, I was laying flat on my back twisted up in a damp sheet. A ceiling fan turned slowly over my head. There was no need to assess what had just happened, I could feel it. My skin was on fire, his touch like finger prints still fresh on my body. All was clear, too clear. And as the details flooded back in living color, only one thought swelled—I'm going to hell!

Slowly I sat up, and my lack of clothing was evident in the cold air that rushed over me, abrasive and unwelcomed. I pulled the sheet closer to my skin. Where were my clothes? I scanned the room. My nightgown hung on the night lamp next to my bed, and the empty bottle of Champagne lied next to it like the seducer of all that was evil. I frowned. Yup, hell!

I cried. An odd combination of shame and a rush of a thrill seeped from my bones. My dark hair was stuck to my face in a mix of tears and sweat. I'm doomed to love him forever, I sniveled. I'm never going to be a functioning human being. I won't be able to work because I'll be too busy standing in a tourist line at Graceland—I sobbed harder—just to visit my dead boyfriend! I'll have to get a job there to cut the cost—no, I'll move to Memphis! It was official; I was bent on a crying jag.

I was letting it all out when my cell phone beeped with a message. Snorting back one last snivel, I froze. Next to the bottle of spirits responsible for this mess—it sounded good at the time—sat my cell phone, face up and flashing. I stared at it, wondering if I really wanted the outside world to know the state of hysterics I was in. What if it's Heather, or my father, I worried and hit the "view now" button without screening the call.

My boy, my boy, my boy! The words jumped out at me.

Back to the bed I fell, gurgling with tears. What did I think would happen? Of course Elvis was watching, just as he said he would. Mortified, was the first word that came to mind. My private dreams viewed by all of heaven? It was idiotic, unfair.

My anger swelled. I grabbed the phone and hit reply. The return phone number was blank.

"Oh course!" I growled. "You say *I'm* a control freak, well you're a..." I couldn't think of anything bad to call him.

Try as I might, words like skillful and gifted kept popping into my mind which only made me angrier. I stomped my feet like a spoiled child. I want to be mad at him!

"Someone should slap your face for spying on a lady!" I hollered out, hoping I still qualified to be called such a thing.

A second later my cell beeped again, causing me to jump, hand over my heart. Hesitantly, I opened it.

You do realize I'm listening?

"A-h-h-h," I threw the phone across the room. It hit the wall and landed face up.

For a moment my pulse surged with a worry that I'd just broken my only way of communicating with him then I snarled. Someone should slap "me" for being this dysfunctional, I sighed. And as if someone had been listening, my home phone rang. I glared at it.

"Hello, Grand Central Station," I huffed.

"Sammy?" Jimmy hesitated. "I-I hope I haven't caught you at a bad time."

I pushed back my hair. "Jim. Oh I-I'm sorry, I didn't meant to snap in your ear." I pulled the sheet tighter and swung my legs over the side of the bed.

"Are you ok?" He sounded with gentle concern.

"No," I thought twice, "I-I mean yes. It's just been one of those mornings. I have them once in awhile."

"Oh, I see. Can I help?"

Emotion rose, constricting my throat and making it difficult to speak.

"I wish you could, but it seems only I-I can let go of what haunts me. I *am* trying." I was surprised to hear myself speak such confessions.

Silence returned to me. Uncomfortable, I was just about to make an excuse for my blunt honesty when Jim finally spoke.

"Maybe, you're trying too hard." He suddenly said. "Have you prayed about this?"

If only he knew the direct line to God I really had.

"Yes, I have."

"And the gentleman, does he feel the same?"

Was I that obvious?

"Yes, we both agree." In a flash I could see Elvis' face stirred by passion, and hear his words of love uttered breathlessly in my ear.

"Well then, you're over thinking this my friend. At your weakest moments, confess it and let it go. In time God will heal you, but don't guilt yourself Sammy. Guilt is the Devil's strongest weapon."

My tense posture loosened. I sniffed into the phone, whipping a tear from my face.

"Are you there? I hope I haven't upset you further? I'm sure you've heard that old saying, 'Let go and let God', that's all I meant."

"Yes, I-I have heard that." I pressed my lips firmly together, choking back more tears. "Thank you."

"You're welcome." He breathed out a sigh.

It's funny how one can hear similar words spoken over and over, and never have them move you. Then the right person utters them in just the right way and it's suddenly so clear. At the time, and for reasons I still don't understand, Jimmy was that person for me. I'd heard focus on God, from Elvis from my father. I'd heard, move on from Heather. But it wasn't until I heard confess it and release it that anything made sense. I just sat there stunned and with a silly smirk on my face.

"I'm sorry for calling at this hour, but your father said you'd be awake." He nervously shifted back to the purpose of his call.

I glanced at the clock. It was 7:00 A.M.

"Normally, I would be, yes. What can I do for you? Are *you* Ok?"

He laughed. "I am, yes."

"There's no woman haunting your dreams, is there?" I chuckled and then cringed.

Silence, again.

"No, not last night anyway," he said.

I blushed, kicking myself for being so stupid.

"Listen, I'm having an early afternoon youth group event today, and your father said you might want to come down and help?"

"Oh, he did?" My daddy the match maker, I smiled.

"You do like children, don't you?"

"Yes, oh yes!"

"Oh good, well I've got a young boy here that is giving me some trouble. But I've noticed he softens up when around women. See his mother died last year, and now it's just him and his father, who's grieving alone I'm afraid. I thought because you have experienced this type of lost yourself you may be able to help."

"Oh, I see."

"He has no friends, except for this one little boy that comes here as well. He's been trying to befriend him with little success, but other than that he's pretty much a loner."

"Really? That's very sweet of that little boy to want to be his friend so badly."

"Yeah, it's the oddest thing really. This little guy is normally so shy. Yet he will talk with Anthony, that's the troubled boy's name, and really seems drawn to him."

My curiosity perked.

"How old are these boys?"

"Well, Anthony is ten, and Garon, he's maybe twelve."

"Garon?" I squinted.

"He's a handsome kid, dark blonde hair and I think he's got a twin brother."

"You don't say?" Don't say!

"Yeah, his family is struggling right now with his father in prison and all."

"Prison?"

"He's in for identify theft, I think it was or forgery, something like that."

I rubbed my temple.

"It was a crime of survival not of greed. His poor mama looks heart broken by it too. She brings Garon every other week. His little brother rides along, but he never stays, though I'm not sure why. His name is Aaron, I believe."

"Aaron?" I was chewing on my finger nails.

"Their mama is a real pretty young lady, but she has these haunting eyes. My heart aches whenever I see her."

I said nothing more. I simply got up, walked to my closet and pulled out my hiking boots.

"I'm sorry, Sammy, I'm rambling now, but if you could come today maybe you can reach Anthony."

Let go, let God, I internally repeated. Then another thought, not entirely of my own, but similar to the voice I'd heard the night before: *Have a readiness to revenge all disobedience.* Was that Corinthians? I shook my head. Why God needed someone as weak as me on his team, I didn't know. But if he had faith in me, it was time to "show" I had faith in him.

"What time and how do I get there?"

***

An angel once told me, love is the key. It's the most powerful feeling the Almighty ever created. A convoluted emotion that has sparked as many wars as it has peace. And as human beings we have the capacity to love deeper than any living organism. So why is it, so much often goes wrong? Is it because we hold on too tightly? Or possibly we rely too much on ourselves when choosing "what" or "who" we should love so greatly?

Love is a mystery, yet no human life can live fully without it. Find me a miserable person, and I'll show you someone who has no love. No matter how much we may try to deny it, we're made to love. Love our fellow man; love our Lord, love life itself. Love something! We need it as badly as we need air. I was no different.

My path to love was uncertain. God's way required patience with a lot of waiting, but I didn't mind. I had nothing but time. To stay uplifted, I tried to focus more on the love I had then the love I'd lost. It helped and each day was infinity better than the last. Sure, maybe the kind of love I wanted wouldn't arrive today, maybe not even tomorrow. But when I crawled into bed at night it was the "hope" of love that kept me warm.

Will there be a day when I can utter the words 'I love you' to another? For the moment, the idea seemed far-fetched but I knew better. All I had to do was look in the mirror to see exactly how much God loved a challenge.

ABOUT THE AUTHOR

Patricia Garber lives in Washington State with her husband of twenty two years, Marc, their new baby puppy, Brinkley, and the soulful spirit of their Labrador retrievers Sebastian and Winston.